Not Quite Mr. Knightley

A NOVEL

NOT QUITE SERIES

KIM GRIFFIN

Dedication

To the one who believes her sin is unforgiveable.

Isaiah 53:5 ESV - But he was pierced for our transgressions; he was crushed for our iniquities; upon him was the chastisement that brought us peace, and with his wounds we are healed.

1 Peter 2:24 ESV - He himself bore our sins in his body on the tree, that we might die to sin and live to righteousness. By his wounds you have been healed.

Contents

Content Warning

This book contains characters who consider abortion and who have an abortion in their past. Abortion is discussed several times from a Christian perspective, emphasizing forgiveness and healing in Christ. If you have an abortion in your past, please read the resources section at the end of the book and visit DeeperStill.org for free Christ centered retreats.

Chapter One

 ancy Wilson had lived nearly twenty-three years in the world with very little to distress or vex her . . . until now.

Journal of Nancy Wilson
October 2, 1970

Help me, God. I feel like I'm drowning. It's been eleven hours since I saw Henry. In a few minutes, I'll board the plane that will take me an ocean away from the man I love. Have I made the right decision? Should I turn back before it's too late? This burden is too much to bear. I love him . . .

Isn't love supposed to be selfless? I'm trying. Just yesterday, I was sure I would spend forever with Henry, but after reading that letter from his dad, I couldn't follow through with it. I can't be the one to rip a family apart and destroy a family business that has existed for hundreds of years. There's also the fact that my parents don't know my plans. They would be brokenhearted upon finding out I married without them present.

My parents didn't believe me when I told them I was trying to work out a way to marry Henry and that it might be soon. They asked me to hold off so I could be sure, but I ignored them, and here I am. Mourning a marriage that almost was.

We're boarding now. Can I do this? Part of me hopes Henry will come after me. I left my contact information with my landlord, Beatrice, and of course, the embassy has it. Maybe he will . . . They're calling for passengers on my flight to board. This is for the best—right?

Standing and gathering her things, Nancy looked around for the first time since checking in at the gate. An older woman met her gaze with concern. Nancy touched her cheek and imagined how swollen and red her eyes were.

Minutes later, the same woman sat next to Nancy on the plane. "Now, now, dear. God will be with you every step of the way. I don't know what you are going through, but he does."

Nancy smiled at the woman. She had followed God for years, but where was God right now? Had he abandoned her in her time of need? Rubbing her temple, she leaned against the window and scanned the night sky. It would soon envelop her and carry her far from all she had imagined would be her future.

"I have some paracetamol for your head." The older woman reached into her bag and produced a small bottle.

Nancy looked at the bottle and recalled that it was a common pain reliever. She nodded. "Thanks." After swallowing the medication, she closed her eyes. The plane began its trek across the runway, and as it accelerated, she sank deeper into the seat cushion, letting the gravitational force pull her into a fitful sleep.

Tugging her carryon over her shoulder, Nancy exited the jet bridge and said goodbye to the woman she'd sat beside on the plane.

She fought back the tension in her chest as she imagined the looks on her parents' faces. They'd sounded so worried when she made the collect call to tell them she was flying home, but they asked no questions. Her mom said they could talk once she was home. They would have an hour and a half to grill her while driving from Charlotte, North Carolina, to their home in Greenville, South Carolina.

She had no idea how best to explain that she'd quit her internship early because she'd foolishly chased after someone she never should have gotten involved with.

Doubts lingered. Should she have stayed? What had she done? She would be a married woman by now if she hadn't fled. She looked back at the jet bridge, wishing she could reverse time. Shaking her head and turning once more to the terminal, she trudged forward, wondering if a good night's sleep in her own bed would bring more clarity.

"Nancy. Welcome home."

She followed the sound of the familiar voice. "Walt? What are you doing here?"

Swiping her hair back from her face, she suddenly felt self-conscious. After an eight-hour flight, little sleep, and intermittent crying, she could only imagine what she looked like.

Walt was the older neighbor boy she'd had a crush on for ages—the epitome of tall, dark, and handsome. He was seven years older, and she'd always held him up as the ideal when deciding what type of man she should date.

A pang of guilt filled her. Henry was the last man she'd ever planned to date. Closing her eyes, Nancy refused to expose her pain to Walt. When she opened them, she found him watching with concern.

"Are you okay?" He reached out and pulled her carryon over his shoulder.

She forced a smile. "I-I will be." Her eyes darted around, looking for her parents. "Why are you here?" Before he could answer, she changed her question. "What I meant to say is, where are my parents?"

"Your dad had to prep his client for a court hearing this afternoon, and your mom was committed to speaking at a local elementary school. They didn't want to worry you when you called. Your mom would have canceled if I couldn't get away."

"You took off work to come all the way to Charlotte and pick me up?"

"Bankers' hours." Walt shrugged. "We close at noon on Fridays, so it wasn't a big deal to take a half day off. I work so much overtime that my manager was more than accommodating."

"Thank you for going to so much trouble for me."

The corner of his mouth turned up. "No trouble. I'm happy I could help." He scanned her face before his eyes locked on hers.

Heat rose to her cheeks, and she was again self-conscious about her appearance. She'd seen the beautiful women he'd dated through the years, and even at her best, she didn't compare.

When he lifted a bag and pulled out a bouquet of beautiful peach flowers, she gasped. "They're lovely! What kind are they?" She took the offered bouquet and glanced up at him.

"Zinnias. My mom found them at the local nursery and started growing them. She pulled this together for you."

"They're lovely. Please tell your mom thanks."

He wrapped an arm around her shoulders and squeezed. "And this hug is from your parents."

The sheltering warmth of his arm grounded her, and she inhaled deeply. His familiar smell reminded her of her father's woodworking shop.

When Walt was a teen, her father had taken him under his wing and taught him how to make furniture and other items out of wood. That was when her crush first began. She closed her eyes and wished the comfort of his arms could vanquish the memories of the last six months.

"I bet you're tired. Let's get your bags, and you can sleep on the ride home." He guided her toward the baggage claim.

Nancy was thankful her bags were some of the first ones off and she wouldn't have to be on her feet much longer.

Pushing the cart bearing her three large suitcases and carryon, Walt directed her to the short term lot.

The warmth of the air hit her. For the beginning of October, it felt balmy compared to what she had just left. She tugged off her cardigan while scanning the area for his car, and spotted his familiar blue sedan.

Nancy blinked. The sky appeared dim and hazy, but maybe her own gloom filtered through and gave it that look. Ironically, before she went to London, people had told her it was often overcast and gloomy. She never felt that way, especially once Henry entered her life.

After loading her suitcases into the trunk, Walt returned the luggage cart and joined her in the car. "Are you hungry? There's a 7-Eleven just outside of the airport grounds."

"No thanks. They served us breakfast not long before our arrival." The truth was, she'd not had an appetite since leaving Henry.

He nodded. "Let me know if you need to stop for anything. I'm happy to talk if you want, or I can keep quiet so you can sleep."

"I think I'll sleep, thanks." It would be best to feign sleep. Then she wouldn't have to talk about her time in London . . . or Henry.

Why couldn't she catch up with Henry? He was only a few feet ahead of her on the street. He didn't even respond when she called out. It was time for their wedding, but he seemed to be in his own world.

"Henry! Look at me!" Even her own words sounded garbled. "Henry!"

Someone shoved her from behind, and she tried to tell them to stop.

"Nancy. It's okay. You're safe. Wake up."

"I . . ." Nancy opened her eyes and looked around. She was in a car. "Walt?"

"You were having a nightmare. Do I need to pull over?"

"No." She shifted to a more upright position. "Sorry."

"There's nothing to be sorry for. You've had a long flight, and I can imagine how tired you are."

She nodded, and her mind drifted to her dream, trying to piece it together. It had Henry in it, and he was ignoring her. Her heart sank when she realized that must be exactly what he was feeling at this very moment. Rejected.

Nancy blinked and looked at the buildings passing outside. "Walt, why are we at Furman University?"

"Your sister is done with her classes for the day and wanted to come home for the weekend to see you."

Nancy forced a smile. As much as she loved her sister, she wasn't ready to talk. Hopefully, her parents hadn't told Kathy about Henry. "Thanks, Walt. You're always so thoughtful. I hope my dad gave you gas money for all this running around."

"He offered, but I didn't take it. Your family means too much to me to take money for something like this."

"If a random fifty-dollar bill turns up inside your car, you can guess where it came from."

They both laughed. "It wouldn't be the first time he tried that with me."

They pulled up outside of Kathy's dorm, where she was standing on the sidewalk holding her bag while waving them down. Except for her green eyes, she looked like a younger version of Nancy with her brown hair. The car had barely stopped when Kathy ran to Nancy's door.

"Nance!" Kathy pulled Nancy's door open, and as Nancy stood, she leaned in for a hug. "I can't believe it, you're finally home. It seems like you've been gone forever." She pulled back and looked her sister in the eyes. "I want to hear everything. A few three-minute phone calls, telegrams, and the occasional letter were not enough."

"I know, I know. I'll tell you all about it once I get some rest."

"Nancy, you're killing me. I've been waiting months to hear all about it. I was so excited when I heard you were coming home early that I decided to skip our fall social tonight."

"Kathy, I'm sorry. Right now, I can hardly think, and a headache is coming on." Nancy pressed her fingers against her temple and dropped to her seat in the car.

"Your sister is pretty tired. Remember, she's flown all night in a cramped airplane." Walt tossed Kathy's bag into the trunk and went around to the driver's seat. "Nancy, I'll stop by the drugstore and get you some aspirin."

"I've got something in my purse." Kathy rummaged around until she pulled out a small pill bottle. "Here." She passed it to Nancy. "Sorry, no pressure to talk. I'm just glad to have you back. Last week, Mom mentioned you might be staying longer in London, so this is a nice surprise."

Nancy closed her eyes and relaxed in her seat. It seemed Kathy was still in the dark about Henry.

Chapter Two

The house looked just as she remembered it, yet . . . different. It was still the stately two-story red brick colonial with white columns on the front porch, yet after living around buildings that were no less than a hundred years old, her nearly fifty-year-old home looked new.

At the sight of Lucille standing by her home's front door, some of Nancy's tension melted away.

"Oh, honey, you're a sight for sore eyes. Let me get a good look at you. Yes, ma'am, you're as beautiful as ever. When your mama called and said you were coming home today, I told her I was coming in on my day off to bake your favorite cookies and make sure everything was perfect."

Lucille wrapped Nancy in a tight hug. Their part-time maid had helped raise Nancy and Kathy and make their house a home. She was more than just hired help—she was family.

After Walt placed the last of Nancy's suitcases in her bedroom, he stopped in the kitchen, where the ladies sat around the table. "I'm going to head home. Nancy, I'm so glad you're back. I want to hear all about it, but I'll wait until you're rested."

"Oh no, sir." Lucille stood and grabbed another glass. "You're going to sit down with us and enjoy a glass of milk and my famous chocolate chip cookies."

Nancy and Kathy shared a smile.

"You might as well give in and eat some cookies, Walt." Kathy shoved the plate of cookies towards him.

Thirty minutes later, Nancy had touched on every subject from the past seven months in London—except Henry. "I'm overjoyed to see all of you, but I can barely keep my eyes open. I could use a couple of hours to sleep." She looked at her watch and then Kathy. "If Mom and Dad get here before five, could you ask them not to wake me?"

Kathy nodded, and Nancy hugged her, Walt, and Lucille one last time before dragging herself upstairs to her bedroom. It was just as she'd left it and as it had been since she graduated from high school—pale pink walls, white painted furniture, and hot pink checked bedding. The Beatles poster above her desk caught her eye, and she examined it. Only a month after she arrived in London, Paul McCartney had announced he was leaving the band. It seemed that her life wasn't the only one in turmoil.

Dropping to the bed, she gave the room another once-over. She could barely keep her eyes open as she leaned back on her pillows. Home.

A flash of light pulled Nancy from her sleep, and a woman's shadowy figure met her gaze.

"Mom? Is that you?"

"It is, honey. I didn't mean to wake you, but I had to lay eyes on you." Her mother approached her bed and ran a hand over Nancy's hair. "My precious daughter. I've been praying for you. Whenever you're ready to talk, I want to hear what happened with Henry."

Nancy nodded but couldn't bring herself to speak.

"Your dad's home too. He'd like to see you."

At that, Nancy smiled and nodded again. "I'd like that."

"If you're hungry, you can join us for dinner, or I can bring up a tray if you'd prefer."

After rubbing her eyes, she glanced at the clock on her nightstand that said five thirty. It was ten thirty p.m. in London. "I'll get up. If I don't, I'll have trouble sleeping tonight and then be wide awake in the middle of the night. And can we not talk about Henry at dinner?"

"Your father knows not to say anything about Henry in front of Kathy, but in private, I'm sure he will have questions. He's not very patient when it comes to worrying about his daughters."

Nancy nodded. At least she didn't have to worry about that conversation during the meal. She still wasn't sure what she wanted to say. She felt like a failure. Her parents would think she'd rushed headfirst into almost marrying him. In a way, she did, and she would have followed through if not for his father's issues. Again doubts crept in.

It was pitch-black outside when Nancy woke up. She rolled over and could tell from the glow-in-the-dark hands on her clock that it was almost three thirty. She calculated how long she'd slept. Six hours. That was not enough to catch up from her travel and worry over Henry. She squeezed her eyes shut, willing herself back to sleep, but her heart raced, and the urge to return to England overwhelmed her.

"God, help me. I feel so lost," she whispered.

When she left London, it seemed like the right decision, but since landing in the U.S., she couldn't shake the feeling that she'd made the biggest mistake of her life. Sitting up in bed, Nancy grabbed her journal and started writing.

October 3, 1970

Today I'll speak with Mom about how I want to go back to London and why I came home. Maybe she'll talk some sense into me.

Nancy tapped her pen on her chin and recalled the looks her parents gave her at dinner. She could tell they were sympathetic towards her, and she was thankful they didn't push things when she went to bed without talking to them privately. She'd been too exhausted to think clearly. Not that things seemed any clearer now.

After writing a few more lines in her diary, Nancy closed it and ran her hands over her face. Her skin was dry from the hand soap she'd used the night before when she was too tired to dig out her facial products. She slid out of bed, grabbed her carryon bag, and headed down the hall to the bathroom.

Digging through the bag for her cleanser and moisturizer, she found a box wrapped with white paper and tied with a pale blue satin bow. Her heart pounded as she removed it and opened the card. It could only be from one person.

Dearest Nancy,

Please accept this token of my love and devotion for our wedding. There is a story behind it, and I can't wait to share it with you. I would be honored if you would wear it for our wedding. I love you and can't wait to call you my wife!

Love, Robert (Tomorrow I'll start signing your notes "Henry" so there will be no mistaking who the man in your life is)

Tears trickled down Nancy's cheeks as she examined the card. "Henry," she whispered. "What have I done?" Her body shook uncontrollably, and she dropped to the cushioned toilet lid.

As the tears subsided, she reached for the box lying on the counter. Opening it, she found a square royal blue velvet jewelry box sized for a necklace. Her hand shook as she lifted the lid.

A beautiful pendant with a large red jewel reflected the bathroom light, and her hand flew to her chest. The jewel was surrounded by gold scrollwork and hanging from a gold chain. "Oh, Henry, surely not." She stared at the pendant before lifting it and examining it closer. When she flipped it over, she noticed a small marking with three chevrons.

She closed her eyes before affixing it around her neck. Looking into the mirror, she imagined her nightgown replaced with her wedding gown. The pendant was stunning.

Why did life have to be so hard? She'd played out both scenarios multiple times, and each one ended in heartbreak. Surely if she made Henry choose her over his family, he would end up resenting her.

Snapping out of her trance, Nancy removed the necklace and washed her face. She needed to stay busy and stop regretting the choice she'd made. The piles of clothes in her suitcases would keep her distracted.

Back in her room, she removed the wedding gown from her suitcase. Clasping the pendant on her neck and pulling on the gown, she promised herself that she would look at it once before hiding it in the back of the closet forever. She gazed at her reflection in the full-length mirror and allowed her tears to flow freely, silently sobbing and hoping her sister didn't hear in the next room.

"Goodbye, Henry," she whispered before removing the dress and hanging it up.

Nancy tugged her nightgown back on, dumped the contents of the first suitcase on her bed, and threw herself into the task of sorting out the last seven months of her life.

"Nancy, what's going on?"

Her mother's appearance startled her, and she glanced at the clock to see that it was five thirty already. Her mom settled on the edge of the bed and touched her face. "Honey, you're crying. Tell me what really happened."

Nancy slid over and fell into her mom. "Oh, Mom, I love him, I really do."

Her mom brushed back her hair. "Then why are you here?"

"Mom, we were going to get married two nights ago."

"The night before you came back?" Her brow furrowed.

"Yeah." Nancy's voice shook. "I'm sorry—it seemed like the only way. He quit the job with his father and had a week and a half before he was expected at his new job. He only had that small window of time." She bit her lip. "I'm sorry for not including you two."

"This whole situation with Henry is hard for me to understand.

You've never been the type to make rash decisions." She leaned in and reached for Nancy's necklace. "Nancy . . . what is this? Did he give this to you?"

Nancy laid a hand over the pendant she had forgotten to remove. "I . . . I just found it. He left the box in my bag . . ." Her throat constricted. "He intended for me to wear it at the wedding."

"It's stunning. Is it a family heirloom?"

"He didn't say." Nancy pulled out the note and pressed it into her mom's hand.

After scanning it, her mom looked up. "A story? It must be a family heirloom. You said their family owns a jewelry store. Surely it's valuable. If you don't plan on continuing a relationship with him, we need to get it back to him."

Nancy's shoulders tensed. "I'd have to take it in person. I wouldn't trust a shipping service with a family heirloom." Her stomach flipped. "But Mom . . . I need to tell you what made me leave."

"Of course, honey, the necklace distracted me." She frowned. "Did he hurt you?" Her mom grabbed her arms and scanned them.

"No." She shook her head. "He was perfect. It was his dad. While Henry was gone picking up food for us, I found a letter his father sent him. His dad threatened to disown him and said I was after their family money."

She bit her lip. She wasn't going to mention the awful names he'd called her.

"The thing is, they needed money for their jewelry store and were insisting he marry the daughter of a family who promised to put money into their business if they married. Henry didn't want to, but his dad was determined and claimed the woman had loved him for years. According to his father, I led Henry astray." Pain shot through her hands, and she looked down to see impressions on her palms from squeezing them so tightly.

"What do you think you should do? It sounds like you want to go back."

Nancy gulped down the lump forming in her throat and nodded. "I do. I'm sorry. I know it cost you so much money to fly me home, but I might have made the wrong decision. Is it possible . . . can I buy a return ticket?"

"Part of me wants to say yes, but I think you need to call him first. The second thing you need to do is talk it over with your father. He's not going to approve of you flying all over without knowing what's going on. At this point, he thinks there was a problem with your internship at the U.S. Embassy, and he's ready to chew someone out."

"You're right." She didn't like the idea of telling her father, but she could start with the phone call. "So can I go ahead and call Henry?" She checked the clock. "It would be about eleven fifteen in the morning his time. Hopefully, he's home." Her throat tightened. "We would be in Scotland on our honeymoon by now. I wonder if he went without me."

"There's only one way to find out. Go ahead." Her mom motioned to the stairs. "Use the kitchen phone so you don't wake anyone. I'll be praying for you."

Nodding, Nancy leaned forward and hugged her mom before walking down the stairs. A heaviness made every step difficult as she thought about what she would say.

Chapter Three

After dialing all of the numbers, Nancy stretched the cord so she could sit at the kitchen table. She stared at the little daisies in the wallpaper while waiting for the call to connect. With each ring, the knot in her stomach tightened.

"Stafford residence." The sound of Henry's butler was comforting. He had always been kind to her.

"Geoffrey, it's Nancy. Nancy Wilson."

"Of course, Miss Wilson. How may I help you?"

Some of the tension in her neck eased when he recognized her. "May I speak with Henry?"

"I'm very sorry, Miss Wilson, but he is not available. May I take a message?"

She slumped over the table and gathered her thoughts. "Yes. Could you tell him . . . tell him that I'm sorry, but I was trying to help. I realize—"

"Just a moment. Can you speak more slowly?"

"Of course. I . . . realize now that I made a mistake, and I want to come back and try again. Please call me." She stopped and remembered he didn't have her home number, so she added it.

"Is that all, ma'am?"

"Not really, but I won't ask you to write more. Thank you." She pulled the phone away from her ear, then drew it back. "Actually, tell him I miss him and love him."

"I have added it."

"Thank you so much, Geoffrey. I hope you have a wonderful day. Goodbye."

She barely heard him repeat "Goodbye" as she hung up so she wouldn't go past the three-minute mark, which would add quite a bit to their phone bill. She already dreaded asking her father to buy a return ticket to London.

Once she'd hung the phone on the wall and settled back into the chair, doubts and questions raced through her mind. What would Henry think about her message? How long would it take him to call back? Would he call back?

"So you want to go back to London and try to repair a relationship with a man who doesn't have the support of his family?" Mr. Wilson questioned as he shifted in the leather desk chair in his study.

Nancy nodded and glanced at her mom, who smiled and nodded back.

"I love him, and I will always have my doubts if I don't go."

Mr. Wilson shook his head. "I've never known you to act rashly, but this . . ."

"I know. I'm sorry. I'll work to pay you back for the tickets for Mom and me."

"It's not just the money, Nancy, though it is wasteful." He tapped his foot and glanced at his wife. "Let me make some calls tomorrow and see what I can move around. I want to go with you."

"Oh, thank you, Daddy!" She jumped up from her chair and raced around her father's desk to wrap him in a hug.

"What a busy place. This is where you'll be living if you get married?" Her mom spun around to look at the row of shops lining Oxford Street in London. "It doesn't look like an area with homes."

Nancy glanced at a passing couple chatting away and smiled. The familiar sound of British accents was music to her ears. She nodded at her mom. "There are apartments above the stores. See, there's the jewelry store up ahead. They're putting the finishing touches on the store before it opens in a couple of weeks. Our apartment—I guess I should say 'his apartment' until I figure out where I stand with him—is above the store." Nancy pointed out a building halfway down the block. "We planned to stay there until we could save enough to get our own place."

Mr. Wilson nodded. "That looks like a nice place to live. At least it has more character than most of the shopping centers going up nowadays back home. You said Henry has a butler who can help us if he's out?"

Nancy nodded.

"I would feel better about this if we had been able to speak to him before traveling halfway across the world." When Nancy frowned at him, he added, "But I know you, and you will never be happy until you face him and discuss things."

Minutes later, Nancy pushed the buzzer by the street side door that opened to stairs leading to the apartment. As they waited for the butler to get the door, Nancy thought about all of the plans she had discussed with Henry to make the apartment into a home. Even if temporary, it would have been theirs together. Several minutes later, no one had answered, so Nancy peeked into the jewelry store. Movement inside caught her eye.

"I'll just hop in and ask if they know where Henry is." Nancy hurried through the door, followed by her parents. "Hi there," Nancy called out. She didn't recognize the short older man standing in the store. "I'm . . ." She froze, unsure of how to explain herself. "I'm a friend of Henry Stafford's and have come by to see him. His butler isn't answering. May I leave a message for him?"

The man's brow furrowed, and his eyes moved to her parents before settling again on her. "I guess he hasn't told you yet. He moved out last night."

"Moved out?"

He nodded. "He said his situation had changed and he was needed back at De Clare's Jewelers."

Nancy swallowed hard. She'd never imagined he would go back to work for his father. Truthfully, she hadn't thought over his job situation at all. She'd assumed he would move forward as planned except without her and the honeymoon.

"He went back?" She didn't know what else to say.

"Yes, sorry I don't know more details." The man held his hand out to shake hers before shaking her father's and mother's. "I'm Arnold Hornsby, Thomas's silent partner. He called me in to help when Henry quit."

"Oh, I'm so sorry. Do you know if he has moved back to his previous home?"

"It's not your fault. These young men have visions of grandeur, and I guess he decided he couldn't handle being responsible for a startup jewelry shop. Thomas was really counting on him to bring the De Clare's knowledge and the Stafford name, but it wasn't meant to be." He shrugged. "It seemed like a long shot anyway when we got him. Pardon. I shouldn't be ranting like that. You asked where he moved, and I'm not sure about that either. If you give me your number, I can leave a note here in case he shows back up."

Nancy's face heated. It *was* likely her fault Henry changed his mind. She glanced at her father as he pulled out a card. "I've got this with our hotel information."

"Thank you." Turning back to Mr. Hornsby, she handed him the card. "We're staying at this hotel for a few days. If you have a pen, I'll add my name."

One side of Mr. Hornsby's mouth turned up. "I guessed you aren't from here. You must be from what they call the South in the U.S."

They all chuckled, and Mrs. Wilson spoke up. "You've guessed it."

Mr. Hornsby gave them a dinner suggestion and another apology for his lack of answers before they headed on their way.

"I can only imagine he's gone back to live in his parents' mews house," Nancy said as she led the way.

"Mews house? Why is it called that?" Mr. Wilson questioned.

"It's a lot like a gatehouse for an estate in the U.S., but the estates in London are all side by side like these stores and buildings here." She waved around at the road ahead. "They look somewhat like row houses, except the ground floor has a garage. I have no idea how they got their name, though."

"I'm having trouble imagining it from your description, but I guess I'll see it soon enough."

Nancy nodded at her dad. "His parents live in the large estate home, and they share a backyard. It was a blessing that this new job came with a place to live since we wanted to avoid seeing his parents regularly after they rejected me. It's hard to find a house in London, and it could have taken weeks or months to find something decent at a good price." She stopped in the middle of the sidewalk.

"What's wrong?" Her father led her and her mom to the side.

"If he's already gone back to work for his father . . ." She shook her head. "This can't be good." Henry's father was a Royal Jeweler and regularly made jewelry for the queen. He had trained Henry in the craft, and Henry hoped to become a Royal Jeweler as well. From what she'd seen of Henry's work and the way Thomas raved about it, he would one day surpass his father.

After his father mismanaged the shop's finances, Henry wanted to distance himself and start something new. Thomas promised him part ownership of the shop after two years if they worked well together. It was going to be his big break.

By the time they'd arrived at the mews home, Nancy felt her palms sweating. The thought of facing Henry hit her full force.

Her father knocked on the door, and the sound of it being unlocked pulled her from her musings. There stood Geoffrey. The white-haired man's eyes went wide at the sight of her.

Nancy forced a smile. "Geoffrey, so good to see you."

"I'm quite surprised to see you, Miss Wilson."

"Yes, well, I . . . I couldn't stay away any longer." She glanced to her side. "These are my parents, by the way."

After she made introductions, the wetness on her palms returned. It was time to face Henry. "I didn't want to leave speaking to Henry up to chance, so I've come to speak to him in person. And of course, to apologize to him."

"I'm so sorry that you've come all this way. He is unavailable."

Nancy bit her lip and forged ahead. "I understand. I can visit him after he gets done with work."

"That is not a possibility. I have been told he does not want to see you."

Nancy sucked in a breath and felt her mother's arm wrap around her waist. "But as you've said, we've come all this way. Surely he will at least hear me out."

Geoffrey frowned. "Wait right here." He turned and left them on the doorstep.

With a racing heart, Nancy leaned into her mother's arms. Her father squeezed her shoulder. Hope rose as they waited.

When Geoffrey returned alone, Nancy glanced over his shoulder, hoping to see Henry following.

"You can leave a message for Mr. Stafford." Geoffrey thrust a notepad and pen towards Nancy.

"Oh. I . . ." When she looked up and saw Geoffrey's furrowed brow, she closed her mouth and started writing.

"Here's our contact information." Mr. Wilson handed her another card from the hotel. "That's my last one, so just copy it down."

She scribbled the information as quickly as she could before handing Geoffrey the paper and pen back and saying a quick goodbye.

Once they were a block away from the home, she sighed. "I'm sorry for dragging you two all the way across the ocean. Our trip was pointless." She brought her hand up to swipe her hair from her face and realized she was shaking.

"Let's sit down for a minute." Her mother pointed to a nearby bench.

"We need to pray. I've been praying constantly for you, but I'd like to pray over you right now," her father said.

Nancy nodded, and tears slid down her cheeks.

"Father, we lay this situation at your feet. We don't know your plans in this, but we know that you love Nancy and have a good plan for her. If she is not meant to be with Henry, keep that door shut. If she is, help us to be patient and make the right choices as we wait for things to move forward. Comfort Nancy as she waits. In Jesus's name, Amen."

"Thank you, Daddy," Nancy whispered between sniffling.

As the afternoon dragged on, Nancy tried keeping her mind off Henry, but she insisted they stop by the hotel every couple of hours to see if he had left a message. She showed her parents some of her favorite sites, such as Buckingham Palace Gardens, Kensington Palace Gardens, and the Victoria and Albert Museum.

After an early dinner, the jet lag caught up with them and they returned to find the same answer from the hotel front desk—no messages for Nancy. Her father tipped the staff generously for their patience with their constant inquiries.

When Big Ben chimed four in the afternoon the following day and Henry had still not responded, Nancy's father decided it was time to step in. He went alone to Henry's home.

An hour later, Mr. Wilson returned and didn't look happy.

"What happened?" Nancy had hoped for a miracle, but the look on his face told her none was forthcoming.

He shook his head, and a look passed between him and her mom. His jaw clenched. "There will be no reconciliation, and he refused to take back the necklace. He said it would only be an unwanted reminder of you."

"That's it? Are you sure?" Nancy trusted her father's judgment but couldn't imagine coming all this way and giving up. Her father was known as one of the best lawyers in South Carolina because he could convince people of almost anything.

"I am, and I don't think Henry is all that you thought he was."

"You spoke with him?"

"No, but the butler said the reason Henry doesn't want to see you is because it will upset his fiancée. I saw with my own eyes an invitation to their engagement party set for a week from Friday."

"What?"

"The invitation listed his fiancée as Linda."

Nancy's heart sank. The future with Henry that she thought might be possible again vanished with that one sentence.

"He said that after you left, Henry realized he'd rushed into things and it was time for him to do what he should have done months ago. Henry said thank you for helping him see that it was the right thing to do."

Nancy swallowed hard and shook her head. "He's giving in to his father and marrying to save the family business." She shrugged. "I guess I did push him into it." Nancy buried her face in her hands and wept. Both her parents surrounded her in an embrace, and she let out the stress from the past week. "I'm so sorry for pulling you both into this." She shook between words. "I left because I thought that was best for him, but now I wish I hadn't."

"I'm so sorry you're going through this, Nancy. Please don't feel guilty for bringing us into this. We love you and want to be here for you. We wouldn't have felt right if we hadn't brought you and made our best effort. I prayed that God would make things clear, and it seems he has."

All her father said was true, but it pained her nonetheless.

"If you're okay with things, we'll leave tomorrow."

She reluctantly nodded. "I'll be ready."

Chapter Four

Nancy stared at the black spot on the ceiling above her bed. She still remembered standing on her bed and smashing a spider on the ceiling with her high school chemistry textbook years before. Seeing the old spot somehow brought her comfort.

After leaving London three days earlier, she'd finally begun feeling settled. She'd hoped to at least see Henry again for resolution but couldn't blame him for refusing, after the way she left him the night before their wedding. Her hurt was likely only a fraction of the rejection he had felt.

With her father's connections, she had a paralegal job lined up to start the next day and was counting on it to help ease her sadness through distraction. She planned to throw herself into the work like she did with any challenge that came her way.

The familiar sound of the tailgate of Walt's truck creaking open drew her attention to the window. Walt had had the truck since he was fifteen and his dad, a police officer, was killed on the job. That's when her father began mentoring him.

Countless times growing up, she'd hid behind her curtains and peeked at Walt coming and going from the house next door. Sometimes when her high school best friend visited, they swooned over him together.

For old time's sake, she crawled out of bed and peered through the slit between the two white curtain panels. There was Walt, sitting on the tailgate, leaning over with his face in his hands.

She recalled a day when he was in a similar position, except he was about sixteen and leaning into a girl he was dating. It was the first time she'd ever seen two people kissing passionately. Her parents' pecks on the lips were tame compared to what she saw. At only nine years old, it was both eye-opening and disturbing—not to mention it left her jealous, even though she was just a kid compared to him.

A year later, Walt became a Christian, and she never saw him make out with another girl—not that he didn't still date. His faith appeared to have changed not only how he treated the girls he dated but also lots of other things in his life.

Walt often came over for dinner, and her father had Bible studies with him before they went to the detached garage for woodworking projects. In the months before Walt started meeting with her dad, there were days his mom came over to talk with Nancy's mom and spent most of the time crying about how Walt was spinning out of control—his grades had dropped, he was hanging out with a bad crowd, and she was worried about what was happening with the girls he dated. At nine years old, Nancy wasn't sure what that last worry was about but guessed it had something to do with the kissing she saw.

He'd always been a good friend to her when she was younger. He acted like he was her older brother looking out for her and giving her advice. When he was in college at Clemson, he told her that he came home so often because she needed his guidance. After he moved back home after graduation, her crush escalated to dreaming of marrying him. Even as she dated the high school quarterback, she knew she would dump him in a heartbeat if Walt treated her as anything other than a sister. She softly chuckled to herself at how far from that dream she'd come.

As she focused on Walt, it looked like he was praying. That wouldn't be unusual for him. He had grown into a godly man—a handsome one, too, if she was being honest. Not that he wasn't good-looking when he was younger. He was no longer a tall and lanky basketball player but had filled out with defined muscles. How was he still single at twenty-nine?

Ironically, starting tomorrow, she would ride every day to work with the man she used to spend most of her waking moments dreaming about.

"Knock knock," her sister said as she barged in, causing Nancy to jump back from the window. Kathy had never been very good with boundaries. "Spying on Walt as usual, I see."

Nancy shook her head as her sister plopped down on her bed and leaned back. "You're not fooling me. I've always known about your crush on him. I don't blame you. He's a fox."

Nancy rolled her eyes. "It's true I used to have a crush on him, but not now. I heard him sitting on the back of his dad's old truck and it brought back memories, so I had to look."

"Mm-hmm, whatever you say." Kathy swung her legs off the side of the bed. "I can't believe he still keeps that ancient truck. He has a nice car."

"It's sentimental for him."

Kathy bit back a smirk and walked to the door. "Right. Anyway . . . are you coming down for dinner?"

"I told Donna I'd go out with her tonight." She looked down at her watch. "She'll be here in about forty-five minutes. I think we're meeting up with some other girls we graduated from high school with."

"Okay, I'll let Mom know. Come give me a hug before you leave. Dad is taking me back to school after dinner . . . unless I convince Walt to when he comes to dinner." She winked at Nancy and walked out without closing the door.

Nancy shook her head and shut the door so she could change and get ready for her girls' night.

Leaning back in the peach-colored leather booth, Nancy savored a bite of warm Peach of Art cobbler. It was sweet with just the right amount of tang, and the creamy home-churned vanilla ice cream complemented it perfectly.

"Mmm, I've missed this," Nancy said to the other three girls at the table. "I had some good food in London and some not-so-good food." Haggis came to mind. She'd nearly tossed up her meal after eating several bites and finding out it contained chopped sheep heart, liver, and lungs, mixed with other ingredients. She needed to erase that from her memory. "But there was nothing like The Screaming Peach's Peach of Art cobbler."

"What was your favorite thing about London? I can just imagine it was so dreamy." Elaine sighed and leaned onto her elbows.

Henry was the first thing Nancy thought of, but she had no plans to tell her friends about him—not even Donna, her best friend. Nancy glanced around the café as she tried to recall what else she liked about London. There were lots of things, but at the moment, everything about London seemed hazy compared to Henry. She focused on the black and white checkerboard tile floor. "There was a café I liked to go to. It had wonderful tea called Earl Grey with added cream. I also loved their scones that they served with clotted cream and jam." Those memories were tied to Henry, but her friends didn't have to know that.

"Earl Grey tea with cream? Scones and clotted cream? Sounds divine! What are those?" questioned Gail.

Nancy described them, then told about the gardens she enjoyed visiting while there. They wanted to know what the Changing of the Guard was like at Buckingham Palace and if she had ever seen any of the musicians from the Beatles. She had not but shared news that Paul McCartney had left the band.

"Nancy," came a familiar male voice while the girls were still questioning her about Paul McCartney.

She looked up to see her high school sweetheart approaching their table. "Brian."

"I heard you were back home." He flashed the flirty smile that had made her swoon years earlier, then reached up to push back his brown hair. It was longer than he wore it when they dated. Styles had changed from the shorter cuts of the mid-sixties. Her thoughts went to Henry.

Despite the longer styles most men now wore, his hair was fairly short, which she liked.

"I'm back home now too," he continued. "After graduating from Clemson, I returned to help Mom manage the store. You should come and see the changes I've made. We expanded and now carry major appliances like washers, dryers, and kitchen ranges."

Brian's family's department store, McClintock's, was the place to go in Greenville for all the important things—special occasion clothes, wedding gifts like china and silver, and every girl wanted an engagement ring from there. Nancy bit back a smile, and her thoughts drifted to the beautiful engagement rings Henry and his father designed. One night, Henry snuck her in after hours to show her De Clare's. Their artistry and skill were impressive. Because he'd left his family's jewelry shop, he didn't have the chance to finish her engagement ring but promised he would once he started at the new shop. They had just bought each other simple gold bands for their ceremony. Her thumb rubbed over her bare left ring finger.

"I'll come by your parents' place Thursday after work to catch up." He looked back at the checkout counter. "I've got a pickup order, or I'd hang out with you and your friends." Brian winked at Nancy before tapping the table and turning to pick up his food.

As soon as he left, the girls began to chatter, but Nancy's mind drifted to Henry.

"Would you give him another chance?"

"He's so handsome."

"It's obvious he still has feelings for you."

She blinked and looked at her friends. She needed to leave London behind, but it wasn't going to be easy.

Donna squeezed Nancy's leg, and they exchanged a look. Nancy had shared with Donna how midway through their freshman year of college, Brian said they needed to be free to date other people and see where God led, since they were at different schools. He made it sound logical, but their schools were only forty-five minutes apart, so it didn't hold water.

"What will you do?" asked Elaine.

"Nothing. I'm not interested in Brian." She wanted to say she needed a break from dating, but that would lead to more questions.

Gail leaned in conspiratorially. "He won't be on the market long. Someone's sure to scoop him up fast. I'd go out with him in a hot minute if he asked."

The bell over the door dinged, and in walked Rebecca. The redhead had graduated with them, but she hung out in different circles. Rebecca glanced their way, but before Nancy could wave, she turned away.

"Don't look," Elaine whispered. "It's Rebecca. You've been gone, Nancy, and missed it, but she's pregnant. No one knows who the father is."

"She's become such a sleaze. It's really no surprise." Gail scoffed. "She probably doesn't even know whose it is."

Nancy found herself watching Rebecca. When she turned, the baby bump was noticeable under her dress. She'd always felt bad for Rebecca. Her mother died when she was little, and her father was a drunk. If she didn't know who the father was, Nancy could only imagine how hard it would be to provide and care for the child.

Rebecca grabbed a bag of food and turned to leave. This time when she looked their way, Nancy was quick to smile at her.

"Seriously, Nancy, you do not want to get mixed up with her," Gail chimed in.

Nancy couldn't keep quiet. "You guys shouldn't be so hard on her. She probably needs a friend."

Donna looked at Nancy before nodding in agreement.

Gail leaned back and crossed her arms. "Whatever. So what are the guys like in England? I would have a hard time not wanting to date every guy there who gave me attention, just so I could hear them speak."

"I agree, the accent does add to a guy's attractiveness." Donna bumped Nancy's shoulder.

Nancy forced a laugh that she hoped didn't sound too fake. "Yeah, it was nice hearing everyone's British accents."

"Soooo give us the details. Did you go out with some of those 'blokes'?" Elaine gestured with her fingers. "With that nice accent?"

"I . . ." This was what Nancy had been dreading, and she hadn't decided what to say. "I did, but nothing came of it."

"Oh, that's too bad. You could be living in England, or maybe have dual citizenship or something and go back and forth." Elaine clapped her hands and grinned.

Donna waved her fork in the air. "Even better, she could introduce us all to Englishmen."

"Well, I'm back now for good and don't imagine I'll have a reason to return for a long time." As she spoke, tension filled her chest. "So, tell me what's been going on here while I was gone, other than Rebecca's situation." She needed to talk about something else.

Donna perked up and told her about the two guys who had asked her out recently. She was trying to decide if she preferred one over the other. Both Gail and Elaine had opinions about the two.

At some point, Nancy's mind wandered back to England. There were so many things she'd left behind—not just Henry, though he was the most important. Despite his rejection, her pain eased a little more each day. She hoped it wouldn't last forever, but sometimes it seemed a never-ending hole would always remain in her heart.

A yawn escaped, and Nancy tried to cover it. "Sorry, I'm still not completely adjusted to the time difference. I should probably head back."

"It's been great, girls." Donna stood up and slid out of the booth.

"You don't have to go, Donna. There's a payphone just outside. I'll go call my parents or maybe Walt. I'm sure any of them will come pick me up."

"No way. I'm your ride. Tonight was all about you, and if you're ready to go, I'm ready."

"Thanks." Nancy scooted out and waved to the other two. "Girls, I loved catching up. We should do this again soon."

"Yes!" Elaine and Gail both agreed.

"Say hello to Walt for me," Elaine called out just as Nancy turned to walk away.

Nancy nodded at Elaine before waving again and following Donna out the door. Outside, she turned to Donna. "Does Elaine have something going on with Walt?"

"At the church picnic a couple of weeks ago, he spoke to her in the food line and followed her to our table. The week after, he began hanging out at her house and playing basketball with her little brother, who's in high school. She's hopeful he'll ask her out."

"Oh. I. Okay then."

"You can say it."

"What?"

"That Elaine is fickle. You're protective over Walt. I get it. Or are you still interested in Walt yourself?"

"No, it's not that." It couldn't be.

"Well, I think Elaine's ready to start thinking about settling down. It's obvious *he* is. He's worked his way up to assistant manager at the bank, and he won't be around Greenville much longer."

"What do you mean?"

"At the picnic, he mentioned that the bank's headquarters wants him to manage one of their branches, but they haven't decided which one yet. He said they promised him something within a three-hour driving radius of Greenville. So that's some consolation. If Elaine marries him, she'll still be able to visit regularly."

At this new revelation, Nancy felt her insides twist. She nodded and zoned out to most of what Donna said as she drove her home.

Was Elaine truly ready to settle down? Walt hadn't given her any indication he was interested in Elaine. She'd try some low-key interrogations when he drove her to and from work the next day.

Chapter Five

A slow whistle greeted Nancy as she walked out the front door
Monday morning. She grinned up at Walt and did a quick
turn. "You think I look like I belong in a law firm?"

"Dupre, Garrison, and Haynsworth won't know what hit them."

"Thanks. I had to dress professionally at the embassy in London,
but I was always in the office and my desk was in the back, so I rarely saw
anyone important. Dad says for this job, I'll be with the lawyers when
they're meeting with clients and going to court. That feels more serious." She ran a hand over the navy pinstriped A-line skirt that her
parents had given her along with the white blouse for her first day.

"You'll have them taking you seriously. They'll be begging you to get
your law degree so you can become a partner."

They both chuckled. It hit her that she'd never thought about
getting a law degree. Nor did she know any female lawyers.

"I loved studying law in school, but one day . . . one day, I hope to
be home with little ones. Law school would be a waste." The reality of
her recent loss and what could have been hit her once more.

She hurried to Walt's car as if she could outrun her thoughts. "I
appreciate you driving me to work every day."

"It's no trouble." He opened her door before she could get to it.
"Your new office is only two blocks away from my bank."

"That is convenient. This office is in the opposite direction from my dad's, so I don't know what I would have done without you."

"I'm always happy to help you and your family, Nancy."

By the time he sat down in the car, Nancy had other things on her mind. "I heard your bank wants you to be the manager of another location."

He glanced at her before looking behind the car and backing out of his driveway. "Elaine told you? Yeah, that's the plan. Don't worry, I think it's still a few months away. Maybe by then you'll have a car or you'll find someone at your office from this area."

"I'm not worried about that. I'll figure something out. But that's great news for you. Congratulations."

"Don't congratulate me yet. A lot can happen between now and then."

"Elaine said to tell you hi."

One side of his mouth tilted up. "She did?"

"Mm-hmm."

"I should probably stop by her house tonight after dinner."

"You should?" Nancy's chest tightened.

"I've been working with Elaine's brother on his basketball technique. He's a junior this year and on the high school team but not getting the playing time he'd like. He's hoping to get offered a basketball scholarship next year."

"Wow. You're a good man, Walter Moore."

He turned, and she was gifted his full smile. It had always made her weak in the knees. Good thing she was sitting, but why was she feeling these things when she still wasn't over Henry?

Walt pointed up ahead as he slowed the car. "Door-to-door service, Miss Wilson. It's been a pleasure. I'll be here to pick you up at five ten." He pulled out a business card and handed it to her. "If you need anything, I'm just a call away. The address is there too. If you want some company for lunch, I'd be happy to join you."

"Thank you for everything, Walt." She reached for the card, and he grabbed her hand. "One more thing." She raised a brow. "I'd like to pray for you."

"That would be nice." She bowed her head.

"Father, I lift up Nancy and pray you would give her peace as she begins something new. Give her favor with those over her, and help her to think clearly as she learns new things. Most of all, let her be a light."

Nancy's insides warmed as he prayed over her, and moisture welled up in her eyes. Today felt like something big. When she opened her eyes, Walt's gaze met hers, and a smile graced his face.

"Thanks again." As she exited the car, the tall building loomed in front of her, but she felt a renewed peace.

When Nancy exited the elevator on the tenth floor, she glanced around Dupre, Garrison, and Haynsworth's simple but stylish waiting room. It contained four plush chairs covered in burnt orange chenille, arranged around a mahogany coffee table. Light spilled into the space from the floor-to-ceiling windows.

A woman with dark hair graying around the temples and pulled into a bun waited by the elevator. "Welcome, Nancy. It's so good to have you here. I'm Florence Nelson, Mr. Haynsworth's legal assistant. You'll be working alongside me for a couple of days to help you get acquainted with how we do things."

"I'm excited to be here. My father speaks highly of this firm."

Florence guided her to the reception desk. "I'd like you to meet Alice, our receptionist."

Behind the mahogany wood and black marble-topped reception desk, a petite blonde woman stood to shake Nancy's hand. "Pleased to meet you, Nancy."

"Let me show you to your desk and introduce you to the partners." The no-nonsense Florence moved her past the desk to a corridor lined with doors. "Here is the large conference room." She pointed to the open door on the right before pointing to another next to it. "And this is one of our small conference rooms. The other is accessed from the opposite side of the hall."

Nancy peered into the smaller room.

Florence continued walking her through the U-shaped hallway and pointing out the location of the lawyer's offices as well as their assistants and secretaries.

Nancy nodded and tried to take it all in as they walked past the offices and desks.

"As was discussed before you came, you will be working with Mr. Dupre. It's my understanding that you studied to be a paralegal, which is a first in this office, so there may be some things you do that are different from my job. But rest assured, I will help you in any way I can."

"I really appreciate that."

"You may even be able to teach me a thing or two. I'd love to know what they're teaching in those paralegal programs. That wasn't an option in my day."

Nancy smiled, remembering one of her professors telling her what an honor it was to have a groundbreaking role in a new profession. Though her embassy job in London looked good on her resume, she wasn't able to use much of her training and was eager for more challenging work assignments. It sounded like she would get her wish.

"One minute, Mr. Dupre was dictating court rulings to look up before his meeting with a client tomorrow, and the next, he was laughing at himself over a joke he made." Nancy twisted in the seat as she told Walt about her day.

"Mr. Dupre sounds like jolly old Saint Nicholas."

They both chuckled as Walt approached a stoplight a few blocks from their neighborhood.

"Minus the white beard. He takes his work seriously, but it's clear he likes to enjoy life too. I think he'll be great to work with."

"I'm happy for you. It appears to be the perfect place for you."

Nancy grinned as she thought about her new job, but couldn't stifle a yawn. "Sorry, long day. What about you? Are you going to miss your bank here? Are you looking forward to a change in scenery?"

He turned to Nancy. "There's a lot to miss here. And I can't imagine living without the wonderful Wilson family next door."

"We'll miss you too." She'd gotten used to having him next door whenever she was home.

"Don't worry, I'll come back regularly." He winked as he pulled into his driveway.

Just as he moved around the car to open Nancy's door, her mom came out on the front porch. "Walt, your mom is here, and we're about to leave to play bridge with the girls, so she won't be home for dinner tonight."

"You ladies enjoy," he called as he reached down to help Nancy out.

"Oh, and you and your mom are invited to dinner tomorrow night."

"Thanks, Mrs. Wilson. I'm sure it will be delicious. Just let my mom know if there is anything I can pick up to bring."

"Will do."

Nancy hesitated before crossing to her own driveway. "I know you have plans after dinner, but you're welcome to join me and Dad tonight. It won't be anything fancy, just Sunday dinner leftovers. But the roast yesterday was delicious."

"Sounds nice, but Elaine's brother called the bank and invited me to dinner tonight before we practice."

"Okay then. Enjoy dinner. Thanks so much for driving me."

"See you in the morning, Nancy. Get some rest."

"Will do." This time when another yawn came on, she covered her mouth. "It's taking me forever to get over this jet lag." She waved before stepping onto her front porch.

"That rocking chair sure does look comfortable."

Nancy opened her eyes to find Walt leaning against one of the white columns on her porch. "I didn't hear you come up."

"Sorry. I didn't mean to startle you." He approached and pointed to the rocker next to her. "Mind if I join?"

"Of course not. But watch out—they're so comfortable, we just might miss dinner."

"I'm so hungry, I don't think my stomach will let me forget."

With a few blinks and a yawn, Nancy tried to snap out of her sleepy state. "I needed some fresh air after being in the office all day. Lucille already had the table set and dinner almost done, so I thought I'd take a few minutes to relax. These past two days at work have been great, but it's a lot of new information at once. It may not be physically taxing, but it's leaving me feeling worn out at the end of the day."

"There's nothing wrong with having some time to yourself. In fact, I'll leave you to it and check to see if there's anything I can do in the kitchen." Walt leaned forward in his seat.

"No, wait!" She reached out and grabbed his sleeve. He looked down at where she held him, and she pulled her hand back. "Sorry. You're not imposing."

He dipped his head, and a smile crept up on one side.

"I enjoy your company. It's nice to talk about something other than work."

"How can I say no to that invitation?" He settled back in the chair and began rocking.

Nancy pulled her cardigan sleeves down. "There's a chill in the air tonight."

"I think fall weather is here to stay." Walt slipped off his jacket and laid it over Nancy's legs.

"Now you'll get cold." She handed it back to him, but he pushed it towards her.

"I can handle a little chill."

"Thanks."

"I hear our moms had a good time at bridge last night."

"Yeah, Mom said they had the most points for the night."

"They did. They make good partners. Speaking of partnerships, did you get roped into making pies for the baked goods table the church has at the Greenville Fall Fest next weekend?"

"My mom signed us up for ten pies. Maybe if we get Kathy home to help and convince Lucille to make the crust for us, it won't be too bad."

"Mm-mmm. Lucille makes a good pie crust. I don't think I've eaten a pie with a crust as flaky as hers. Has she taught you her secret?"

"She's tried, but I can never get mine quite like hers. She has the magic touch."

"Her lemon meringue is my favorite." He licked his lips.

"You're in luck then, because I think that's what she made for tonight."

"Sounds like a perfect night. My favorite food and my favorite people."

Nancy looked up, and he held her gaze.

Feet pounding on the sidewalk broke into the moment. "Walt! You're just the man I need!" Elaine ran up the walkway, breathing heavily.

"Did you run all this way?" Nancy couldn't think of a time she'd seen Elaine run other than P.E. in high school, and she lived five blocks away.

Elaine nodded and stopped at the top of the steps. "Walt, Dan is going crazy. The girl he's been seeing said she's going to the high school dance with another guy, and he lost it. He punched a hole in his bedroom wall, and he's throwing things around. I'm afraid he might have damaged his hand, and that's going to make it hard on him with basketball. Dad will be home any minute, and Mom and I can't get him calmed down."

Walt jumped up and placed a hand on Elaine's shoulder to comfort her. He turned back to Nancy. "I'm going to have to take a raincheck on that lemon meringue and the rest. Give my regrets and explain to everyone where I've gone."

"Of course. Elaine, I'm so sorry." Nancy stood and hugged her friend.

"Thanks." Elaine turned to follow Walt to his car.

As they drove off, Nancy felt guilty for the jealousy she had towards Elaine for turning Walt's head. How could she have those thoughts so soon after her relationship with Henry ended?

<h1 style="text-align:center">Chapter Six</h1>

A knock on Nancy's door woke her. "What is it?"

"Nancy, sorry to bother you." Her mom entered the dark bedroom. "Are you feeling okay?"

"Just tired from work." She sat up and switched on her bedside lamp. "Is it dinnertime? I'll come help set the table. I didn't mean to fall asleep."

"You're fine, dear. I know it's been a long day. Dinner still has a few minutes. I came up because Brian McClintock is at the door. He says you're expecting him."

"What?" Nancy rubbed her eyes. "I'm not . . . Oh wait, at The Screaming Peach last weekend, he said he was coming by on Thursday after work."

"It is Thursday, dear."

"Ugh." She threw her hands over her face.

"If you want, I'll tell him you're not feeling so great."

"Thanks." Nancy sat up. "I should go downstairs and get this over with."

"True. If you have no interest in starting things back up with him, it's better to squash it now. You've had enough emotional turmoil recently." Her mom leaned over and hugged her.

"Will you tell him I'll be a few minutes?"

"Sure." Her mom slipped out and closed the door, leaving Nancy with her thoughts.

Just when she thought she had all her emotions tucked away, they surfaced again. She'd been crying before she fell asleep.

When she stood up and saw her reflection in the mirror, her eyes were swollen and red. Thankfully, she'd taken her makeup off, or she'd look like a raccoon. She grabbed some concealer and dabbed it beneath her eyes. It would have to be good enough. Her goal wasn't to impress him.

As she walked down the stairs, she imagined different ways she could explain she wasn't interested, but nothing sounded right.

Opening the front door, she found Brian looking out over the front yard with his back to her. He'd always been handsome and well built, but his muscles had filled out more since his high school days. Her friends were right—most women would be happy for the opportunity to date him. He had always been good to her and made God a priority in his life, but after he broke up with her so he could date other people, the thought of dating him again made her insides twist.

Nancy cleared her throat, and Brian turned around with a grin that quickly dropped. "Are you okay?"

"I'm not feeling the best and fell asleep after work."

He rubbed the back of his neck and came closer. "Sorry to wake you. Are you up for chatting a bit?"

"Sure." She moved to one of the rocking chairs, and he sat in the one next to hers.

"It's been a long time since we sat together out here."

Her eyes moved from the yard to his, but she said nothing.

"Nancy, I regret ending things with you. You were the best thing that ever happened to me. I was just a stupid freshman back then and so caught up in being the Clemson Tigers' quarterback that I got side-tracked."

"I'll say." Donna had dated a guy from Clemson that year, and he'd filled them in on all the news of Brian's women after he broke up with her. He was the big man on campus there.

"I'm sorry. I wish I could undo the hurt I caused you. Is there any way you could give me another chance? I know I don't deserve it, but

I've always held you in such high esteem. And to tell the truth, in some ways, I didn't think I was good enough for you. I imagined you would find some doctor or lawyer and Greenville would be in your review mirror by now."

"Hmph." He hit closer to home than he imagined, though Henry wasn't a doctor or lawyer.

"So . . . do I have a chance?"

"Brian, I . . ." She was glad he apologized. It was long overdue. "As much as I appreciate your apology, I have to say no. My heart is not free."

His brow furrowed. "You're in a relationship? I should have guessed. I just assumed, since there was no ring."

Both of their eyes fell to her ring finger, and the familiar ache in her chest surfaced.

"It's not something I want to talk about."

"I guess I missed my chance." He found her eyes again. "Just know that I'm around if you need someone to talk to. I realize I don't deserve you."

"Brian, it's not that you don't deserve me, but you did lose my trust when you broke up with me to date other people. If your feelings weren't strong enough for me then, I have a hard time believing they would be strong enough now."

He nodded. "I understand. The offer still stands to hang out or whatever. Maybe over time, I could show you I've matured."

Nancy stood and held out a hand. "Thanks for coming."

Brian grasped her hand and held it longer than necessary before turning to go. With a wave, he ducked into his car and left.

The sound of the wood saw in the backyard drew her attention from the conversation with Brian. For years, her dad's woodworking shop in the backyard was a place to let go of her burdens. She could usually find her dad or Walt inside to chat with. Sometimes both of them greeted her, ready for her to tell them whatever was on her mind.

When she peeked in through the window, Walt was working inside.

She waited until he stepped away from the saw before entering. Her father had always made it clear not to startle them when they had the saw on.

"Nancy." Walt raised an eyebrow and spoke before she could. "What brings you here?"

"I heard the saw going and thought I would check things out."

He nodded and leaned forward. "Are you okay? Did Brian upset you? You look like you've been crying, and I saw him drive up a while ago."

She touched her face. "He . . ." She didn't want to lie to him. "He didn't make me cry. There's not much to say about him." She looked down at the piece of wood he was sanding.

"Is he hoping you'll give him another chance?"

Her eyes found his. "How did you know?"

"Just a guess. He was stupid to give you up in the first place." Laying down the wood, he held her gaze. "If you were mine, I wouldn't need to break things off and test the waters elsewhere."

Nancy felt her face heat. Was he flirting with her? Walt had never spoken to her that way. She broke their connection and reached out for the wood he'd been sanding. "It made me feel like I wasn't enough. He apologized, but I don't think I would ever be able to trust him again." She looked up, and Walt nodded.

"Trust is important in a relationship."

"That's what I've always felt too." She froze, recognizing she'd lost Henry's trust by running away the night before their wedding. No wonder he didn't want her back. "One day, maybe I'll find that."

"I think you will." He smiled softly. "You're a beautiful woman inside and out."

"Thanks." Her heart fluttered. "What about you?" Something inside urged her on. "I'm surprised you're still single." Would he tell her about his intentions with Elaine?

He shrugged and leaned on the workbench, causing his muscular forearms to flex. "Until now, the timing has never been right with the woman who held my interest."

She raised her brows and envied Elaine. It wasn't the first time she'd felt that way since hearing about his visits to her home. She pushed those thoughts down. Elaine deserved a good man like Walt, and she wasn't in any shape for a relationship herself. "Someone I know?"

He shrugged again.

She swallowed and tried another tactic. "Someone whose brother plays basketball?"

His brow furrowed. "No, there's nothing going on with me and Elaine. Do you think I've given her the impression I'm interested because I spent time with her brother?"

Surprisingly, relief filled her. "I . . ." She didn't want to embarrass her friend. "Yes, I think it does appear that way."

He rubbed a hand over his face and frowned. "What should I do? I told her brother I would help him with basketball."

Nancy shook her head. "Maybe you could have him start coming to your house, or even meet at the school's outdoor courts. Somewhere other than their home."

"That's a good idea. She's a sweet person, but I'm not interested in dating her." He held up the piece of wood he'd sanded earlier. "What do you think of my kitchen table leg?"

She chuckled at how quickly he changed the subject.

"Oh, that's what it is. I wondered. I like the cut. It looks somewhat modern."

"That's what I was aiming for. It's also why I chose walnut. It will look good with more modern-colored wood stains. You'll have to help me pick one when I get to that point."

"I'd love to. Is the table to take with you when you get transferred?"

"It is." He grinned. "Mom wouldn't be too pleased if I took all of her furniture." His smile faded. "In some ways, I know she's ready for me to be out of her way, but in others, she might not be. You remember a few years back, I moved away for about a year, and she felt so lonely."

"I do remember. It was my sophomore and half of my junior year in high school. Mom and some of their other friends tried to help her through. Mom said she was depressed." Nancy also recalled Walt choosing to take the out-of-town job in the first place because his college sweetheart had ended things and started dating someone else. She had tried to be a shoulder for him to lean on, but at fourteen, doubted she'd been much help.

"Yeah. Well, this time, she's practically kicking me out, so it should be different. She's also been spending some time with Mr. Duncan at church. I think that may have something to do with the change of heart. He's a widower and seems like a good man."

"She deserves to find someone. I hope this works out for them."

"Me too."

"What shape will your tabletop be?"

"I've already cut it." He walked over to the back wall. "It will be these four pieces here." He slid out two large rectangles and two smaller narrow ones. "These two make a square for four people to sit around," he said as he gestured to the large ones. "And these smaller pieces can be added to expand it for six or eight."

"Wow! Seating for eight. Do you plan to entertain a lot?"

"I hope to have room for Bible studies and dinner parties, but mostly I'm planning ahead for marriage and children."

"Oh. That's a good idea since you're putting so much time and effort into it." She tried to imagine what kind of woman he would end up with. Even if the woman who held his interest turned him down, likely wherever he moved, women would vie for his attention. He was good-looking and had a job that paid well. That was enough to entice most women, but once they got to know him, they would see how wonderful he was. No doubt he would have a steady train of welcome meals brought over by every single woman he met. Again she felt a possessiveness over him, and he hadn't even left yet or met those imaginary women.

"I want to build things that last. I'll make the chairs next." He held out the wooden table leg to her and ran a hand over it. "What do you think? Is it smooth enough?"

She felt the wood and nodded up at him. When their fingers touched, her breath caught.

Walt covered her hand with his. "Have I mentioned how happy I am you came back?"

Beginning in her hand, warmth filled Nancy, and she shook her head. His words pleased her more than they should. "I—I should get back to the house. I'm sure my mom is wondering what happened with Brian."

The smile on his face faded, and she hated to think she put it there. "It's good to be back, Walt. See you in the morning."

At the door, she glanced back and found him watching her with a faint smile.

"Goodnight," she called.

"Nancy, if you ever want to talk about the things that have made you sad, I'm here. Goodnight."

After all this time apart, how did he manage to read her so well?

In the dark, she made her way to the back door of her house. The feeling of his hand on hers echoed through her body and left her heart racing. "Stop it," she whispered to herself. *As if Walt would be interested in me. I'm a mess and have no business thinking this way about any man.*

The sight of her mom snapped her out of the Walt haze.

"What's going on with Brian?" Her mom frowned. She knew how hurt he had left Nancy years earlier.

"Can we sit down in the living room? I'm spent."

She'd heard emotional turmoil could be as exhausting as physical exertion. She needed to find peace in her heart somehow, because this constant exhaustion was wearing her out.

Chapter Seven

Walt held the car door open for Nancy as she pulled her jacket tighter against the cold morning breeze. He leaned close and offered her a hand.

"Walt. I warned you I was sick this weekend and still feel a bit off. You might not want to get so close."

She'd awakened Saturday morning with nausea and almost didn't make it to the bathroom in time. It had eased as the day went on, and she was able to keep down toast, bananas, and ginger ale. Then Sunday, she woke a little queasy, but the saltines still next to her bed settled her stomach. This morning, she felt more like herself, but she didn't want to get Walt sick when he was being so kind to offer her rides to work every day.

He hopped into the car. "I told you not to worry. I have a stomach of steel. And worst-case scenario, I have lots of sick days."

"If you say so. I hate that I was sick this weekend. I really wanted to help you put the stain on the table and chairs. How did they turn out?"

"I finished the table and four of the chairs."

"So you still have four chairs left? Great, I can help you."

"I'd love your help, Nancy. The color you chose is beautiful, by the way."

"Thanks." Her eyes followed the power lines strung along the roadside. "Good thing I'm feeling better. Mr. Dupre will be in court this morning, and I get to be with him. I can't wait."

He glanced at her and grinned. "You've been waiting to do that since you started."

⌒◟◍◍◟⌒

The lunch line at Morrison's Cafeteria was the longest she'd seen it since she started working at Dupre, Garrison, and Haynsworth. After a busy morning in court, she was famished. Florence was saying something about the new D.A., but Nancy concentrated on the filled trays of the restaurant patrons as they exited the line.

As one woman passed, Nancy caught a whiff of something that smelled off. She covered her mouth and motioned to Florence before darting to the bathroom and praying a stall was open. Seconds later, she flushed down what little was left of her breakfast. She exited the stall just as Florence entered.

"Are you okay, dear? You must not be over your illness from this weekend."

"I guess not. I thought I was doing better, but it hit me all of a sudden."

"I have a great doctor right across the street from the office. It makes it easy to go for checkups on workdays. The receptionist and I are good friends, and she always makes sure to get me in the same day if needed. I'm sure she'd help you out."

Nancy nodded. "I had thought it was a twenty-four-hour thing and I was recovering, but at this point, I might need to be checked out."

"Here, take this peppermint candy. It always works to settle my stomach."

While the peppermint worked its magic, Florence led her to the doctor's building. She had an appointment within minutes and sent Florence back to the office with a message for Mr. Dupre that she might be a few minutes late.

The nurse took her vitals, and the doctor soon joined them. He first questioned her about pregnancy, and she insisted that was not possible. With the erratic nature of her nausea, he ruled out anything contagious. His questioning turned to possible urinary tract infection symptoms, migraines, stress, and low blood sugar. She'd not had migraines, though she'd had numerous headaches since breaking things off with Henry. The whole situation with Henry caused stress.

"Low blood sugar seems like a possibility. I've been so hungry. Just before I got sick today, I felt like I was starving."

"I'd like to have my nurse take some blood we can use to check your blood sugar. We should also get a urine sample to test for a UTI just so we can rule that out. I can give you a prescription for promethazine. You probably know it as phenergan. You can keep it on hand and use one half to one tablet every six hours as needed for nausea, but be careful—it will likely make you drowsy."

After the doctor wrote the prescription, he left the nurse to take blood.

The more Nancy thought about his first question, the more she started to wonder. She looked up at the nurse once she'd completed drawing her blood. "With the medicine he prescribed . . . could there be any . . ." She didn't want to say the words out loud. "Would it be a problem if I *am* pregnant?"

The nurse placed a seal over the vial of blood and turned to her. "There can be. He doesn't recommend it with pregnancy unless the woman has extreme problems with nausea." She touched Nancy's shoulder. "When did your last period start?"

Nancy frowned. She'd been so stressed with Henry, coming back home, and her new job, that she'd forgotten about her period. She slipped a small calendar from her purse and found the red dot. "September the eighteenth."

"And you had intercourse a couple of weeks after that, I'm guessing?"

Nancy swallowed and nodded. The nurse pulled out a small round multilayered flat dial. She turned the top circle and angled it towards Nancy. "With that as your last period, your likely date of conception was October 2nd, and your due date would be June 26th."

The sick feeling came back, and Nancy rubbed her stomach.

October 2nd was the night she'd spent with Henry. The evening before their wedding. It had been the one and only time they'd been together that way, and she'd had every intention to follow through with the wedding until she'd found his father's letter.

She silently asked God to let it be low blood sugar or something else causing her nausea. If it wasn't, she had no idea what would come next. How could she tell her parents? How would she tell Henry when he wasn't taking her calls?

"I can tell this is distressing you." The nurse slipped a card from her pocket and held it out. "This clinic offers free pregnancy tests. They are discreet, and the results come back in only two hours. They can also put you in touch with a clinician who can get rid of unwanted pregnancies."

Nancy's chest tightened. "Are you saying what I think you are?"

The nurse nodded. "Don't worry. It's a very simple procedure, and this early, it will be quick and painless. No one will have to know, and the recovery is nothing more than minor discomfort and what seems like a heavy period. They can tell you more about it there."

The idea mortified her, but Nancy was too curious and distraught not to take the card. She looked down to read it. *Planned Parenthood of Greenville.*

"They offer other services as well, such as birth control. You might want to consider that if you are trying to avoid pregnancy."

Nancy fought to focus on what the nurse said after that. She left with her prescription and the card buried in the bottom of her purse. Her purse had never felt so heavy.

It was all she could do to get through the rest of her day. Every few minutes, her mind drifted to the card in her purse. When the doctor's office called and said her blood glucose was fine and so was her urine test, it became even harder to stay on task.

By the time Nancy went to bed, she'd decided she had to take the chance and stop by the clinic over lunch the following day.

After taking the pregnancy test at lunch, the day dragged on forever. She'd never looked at her watch so much.

Just before leaving the office to meet Walt for her ride home, Nancy called Planned Parenthood to request the result of her test. The office worker found her file and read the results.

Her worst fear became a reality. How did she get to this place? The image of Rebecca walking into The Screaming Peach and being shunned by her friends came to mind. Nancy grabbed her things, rushed to the bathroom, and locked herself in a stall. Tears slid down her face as she silently released her pain. "What now?" she whispered. Silence answered.

After allowing herself to grieve for a moment, she wiped her face and went to find Walt's car. He was leaning against it with his legs crossed, and grinned when she first opened the door. His face dropped as she approached.

He ran up to her. "Nancy, what's going on?"

She shook her head and walked past him to the car. If she spoke, the dam would break. And what would she say? She wasn't prepared to see his face after he knew the truth. She recalled when she'd dated Brian in high school and Walt had made a point to warn her against premarital sex. It had been an embarrassing conversation. The guy she had a crush on talking to her about sex with her then-boyfriend.

"I can see you're too upset to speak." Walt helped her into the car and went around to start it.

Ten minutes into the drive, she found her voice. "Why don't you drop me off at that park down the street from our houses? I can walk home when I'm ready."

He pulled into a convenience store parking lot.

Nancy looked up and scanned the area. "Why are we here?"

"You're not ready to go home. I'm trying to give you some time."

"You're right," Nancy whispered, eyes focused on her hands entangled on her lap. "But why are we here? I asked you to drop me off at the park."

Walt laid a hand on her shoulder. "I can do that, but I'm staying with you. You don't look like you should be alone."

Her eyes darted to his, then back down. Tears burst forth.

"Hey, whatever it is, I'm here for you." He unbuckled and slid over to pull her into a hug.

Pressing her face into his chest, she let the tears flow. Whimpers soon increased to sobs.

Walt's hand tenderly rubbed her back as he murmured comforting words. "Whatever it is, I'll help you. You're not alone. We'll get through it. God, please help Nancy know how loved she is. Give her peace in this storm. Help her look to you as her hope and shield. Show me how I can best help her."

When her heart calmed, she pulled back and wiped her face with a tissue from her purse. As she laid her purse down, it tipped over, spilling some of the contents out. Walt helped her gather the items and froze when his hand landed on a pamphlet. Panic gripped Nancy.

"What's this?"

Nancy stared at the pamphlet, the words in bold echoing in her head —*Abortion Services*. Her body shook as she snatched it from him. The man she'd always looked up to and admired would never look at her the same. She reached for the door handle, not knowing where she would go, just that she had to escape.

Walt's hand squeezed her shoulder. "Please, stay. I meant what I said. I'm here for you. I'll help you."

Her heart raced, and she tightened her grip on the handle. Closing her eyes, she considered his offer and her other options, but nothing came to mind. She relaxed her grip on the handle and nodded, still afraid to look into his eyes. The thought of what she'd see there might leave her feeling worse than she already did.

"Okay. Good. Can I . . . How about I go use that payphone to call your parents and tell them I'm taking you to dinner?"

She nodded again without looking in his direction.

"You promise to stay put?"

"Yes," she whispered.

"I'll be right back."

Once he was out, she looked up to follow his progress to the phone booth. She hoped he didn't tell them there was anything wrong. His face looked calm during the conversation.

When he returned, he didn't look at her and his face was unreadable. "Your parents said it was fine. I told them we might be a while."

He started the car and backed up, never once glancing her way. Was he regretting his offer? Maybe she should let him off the hook. "You can just—"

"I was thinking we could pick up something from Bonnie's Drive-In. We can take it to the park and talk there. Is that okay?"

"Oh . . . sure. Thanks." She *was* hungry after missing lunch. She'd only eaten a pack of crackers she bought from the vending machine in the lobby of her office.

He laid his free hand on hers, and the worry about him having regrets subsided. Her mind shifted to finding ways to explain her situation.

"What would you like to eat?" he questioned as they pulled into a spot at the drive-in restaurant.

"Their burger with everything, fries, and a chocolate milkshake." Normally she'd order their club sandwich. Was this a pregnancy craving?

"That sounds good to me too."

Once their food was delivered, he pulled out and drove to the park. The familiar streets and landmarks didn't hold the comfort they normally did. Tonight they felt more like markers counting down the time she had before her sin was exposed.

He pulled up in front of a picnic table. "Does this work?"

"Sure." She picked up the bag of food and jumped out before he could come around. Taking a seat, she separated the food and couldn't stop herself from grabbing a fry.

"You're hungry. Why don't we eat first, then talk?"

She nodded, and he prayed for their food and for her. They both ate silently, which was a first, as far as she could remember. As the sun began to set, the temperature dropped. The evening chill and milkshake made her shiver. Her light jacket wasn't enough, and she rubbed her arms.

"Why don't we talk in the car? You're already getting cold, and it will just get colder." Walt pulled off his jacket and placed it on Nancy's shoulders before clearing away their empty wrappers.

He held out a hand. She hesitated before taking it and following him to the car.

The moment they were both in the car, he spoke. "So I'm guessing the father's in England and this pregnancy has something to do with why you left again briefly after you came home."

Now would be a great time for her pregnancy nausea to act up. She could pretend to get sick. She glanced outside. Eventually, he would find out—better to get it over with. He might have some advice or talk her out of the terrible temptation that was stuffed into her purse.

"Yes, the father's in England, but I just found out about the pregnancy today." It was easier to call it a pregnancy. To admit there was life living inside her would complicate things and blur her ability to think.

"It was only once . . . I never thought I'd get pregnant the first time. But we weren't worried, because we were eloping the next day."

Walt's quick inhale made her look up. His brows pinched together, and his lips flattened into a straight line. At least he wasn't looking at her.

"When he left to buy us dinner, I went to get something from his bag and found a letter from his dad to him. His dad was against us getting married. That's why we were eloping." She went on to explain the problems with the family jewelry store and his arranged marriage with Linda. She even told him about her trip with her parents back to London, his refusal to see her, and the announcement of his engagement to Linda.

"This is a lot to take in. I understand why you worried about causing a rift in his family, but I can't imagine how he rebuffed you so easily. He should have been a man and at least given you a chance to explain yourself."

"I'd like to think so, too, but after the way I hurt him when he was willing to give up so much for me . . . I guess it was too much for him to get past."

Walt rubbed his face, and they sat there in silence.

"How did you end up with that brochure?" Walt asked several minutes later. "The abortion one." He motioned to her purse.

She stared into the distance as the dark descended. "I went to the Planned Parenthood clinic today, and they gave it to me."

"Is that what you want to do? Get rid of your baby?" Walt's voice sounded strained.

That was the question that plagued her. She'd always thought having an abortion was a horrible thing. Her faith had condemned women who had them, yet now that she was in this situation, it seemed like the only way out. The past few years, there had been much controversy around the country over allowing it, and if she had one, she would be breaking the law. She didn't even recognize herself with the thoughts that swirled in her head.

"I—I don't know." Tears streamed down her face as she admitted it, and she pressed both hands to her face, wishing she could block out the world.

Walt pulled her into a hug and ran his fingers over her hair while she cried.

He leaned back when her shaking slowed. "Nancy, this isn't you. You've always defended the lives of unborn children. I've heard you have this conversation before."

She raised her eyes to his, and what she saw there broke her. "But how can I raise a child by myself? I wouldn't be able to work and take care of a child. I couldn't make enough as a paralegal. The position is such a new thing that most law firms don't pay much more than a secretary's salary for it. It's not fair to my parents to expect them to take us in. I don't see how it could work."

"What about adoption? There's that couple at our church who have tried for years to have a child without success. They recently started the application process for adoption, but that will be a while too."

"I can't imagine giving my child up for adoption and watching someone else raise him."

"Or maybe someone out of town would adopt your child."

"I don't know." She squeezed her hands into fists. "It's too big a thing to decide. And besides figuring out what to do with the child, I don't want anyone to know. I don't want to be like Rebecca."

"Rebecca?"

"She graduated with me. The other night, I was at The Screaming Peach with my friends when she came in. She's pregnant and not married. No one knows who the father is, and none of the girls would have anything to do with her. They wouldn't even make eye contact with her."

"That's harsh. I'm sorry. I wish I could take this away from you." He tapped his fingers on the dash several times. "You should try to contact the father again."

"When I call, his butler answers and I never get through. I'm not giving the butler the message that I'm pregnant, and I can't see flying all the way over there to be turned away again."

"No, that's not practical. If you write him, how long does it take to get there?"

"I got one of my letters from home three weeks after they sent it. The fastest was two weeks."

He shook his head and tapped the dash some more. "Let's send a telegram. He'll get it the next day."

"Okay. I guess I can do that."

"Let's leave early tomorrow, and we'll go by Western Union before I drop you off. Don't forget that I'll be going out of town directly afterward for my interview at the bank in Columbia. It shouldn't be a problem for me to get back in time to pick you up."

Nancy bit the inside of her cheek and nodded.

"Why don't you work on what you want to say in the telegram tonight."

Now her stomach *was* churning. "I have no idea what to say. He's obviously moved on."

"You don't move on that quickly. When you love someone, it sticks with you for a long time." He reached for her hand. "Even when they do something that hurts you, you still want to make it work."

"Then maybe it wasn't love."

"What?"

"If he's moved on so quickly, maybe he never loved me. And I can't love someone who would move on so quickly."

"I don't know what to tell you. Maybe he agreed to the marriage with that other woman out of desperation."

She shrugged. "He didn't seem desperate before. I don't know, my mind is playing tricks on me, and I'm second-guessing everything."

Walt sighed. "I've made a mistake. I should have prayed over you as soon as you told me what happened. Can I pray now?"

She nodded. She'd always loved to hear Walt pray. Some men were too embarrassed or didn't find prayer important. Henry never prayed, that she knew of, which made her wonder if he was only a Christian in name. Maybe she should have talked more about God and faith with him before planning to marry him.

Walt's voice started softly but grew in strength as he prayed. "Father, this is no surprise to you, and you have a good plan for Nancy and this child, even though right now it seems like nothing good is possible. I pray you will give Nancy peace and wisdom in this. I pray for protection for her and this little one. Please soften Henry's heart. I don't know if he belongs to you or not, but if not, please draw him to yourself. Also I pray that he will do what is right for Nancy and this baby. And God, help Nancy to hold back from the temptation to end this child's life. In Jesus' name, Amen."

Tears once again flowed, and Walt gently laid his hands on her cheeks to wipe them away.

"Thank you. I . . . I don't really want to have an abortion."

"Good. Please don't start feeling desperate while I'm gone tomorrow. Tell your parents tonight that I'm taking you to dinner tomorrow again. We'll go out and talk through some options. I have an idea. And maybe Henry isn't supposed to be your husband but will come through and offer financial support for his child."

"Maybe. At least if he marries Linda, his family will be better off financially."

"We'll see. We'll trust God to provide a way. Don't lose hope."

She hesitated. "I want to agree, but right now, I don't have any hope to lose."

The ride back was quiet. Nancy imagined Walt was as lost in his thoughts as she was. He'd handled it a lot better than she imagined, and she was glad to have him on her side.

As soon as they pulled into her driveway, she turned to him. "I'm not telling my parents yet. Please don't tell anyone."

"You have my word. It's not my story to tell."

"Thank you. Do you think thirty minutes early will be enough time for Western Union?"

"I do. It's not far off the route to your work."

"Good. Thank you, Walt." She unbuckled and gave him a hug. "You know," she said as she pulled away, "with all this extra time we're spending together, my parents might think you're the father."

"That doesn't bother me one bit. I'll do whatever I can to help you, Nancy."

Tilting her head, she studied him. He really did seem to mean it.

"Goodnight, Walt."

"Goodnight, Nancy. I'll be praying constantly for you."

She forced a smile. "Well, I'm hoping you'll take a break long enough to get some sleep before you drive to Columbia."

He smiled back and winked. "You know what I mean."

Walt's smile and wink were so familiar and comfortable, she almost forgot she was in the worst storm of her life . . . Almost.

Chapter Eight

October 28, 1970

Once again, I feel like I am drowning. I thought I was at my lowest when Henry wouldn't respond to me. But this is so much worse. Now I have a child and no Henry. My child has no father, I have no money saved, and I'm ashamed. Everyone will shun me. I've worked hard to become a paralegal. Will I have to give that up? I'd planned to eventually, but now I feel like my choices are being ripped away.

God, tell me what to do. Why did I leave England? And why did I sleep with Henry before we were officially married? I wish I could go back in time. Are you even listening? Do you care about these details? You have so many things that are bigger than me to deal with. I'm just a worthless sinner. I can understand why you would turn away from me.

I'll push forward somehow. At least Walt is there for me. I can't believe he didn't brush me off as fast as he could when I told him my situation. I guess I'll work on writing a note to Henry. I'm not even sure what to say other than "I'm pregnant." Here goes nothing.

Nancy laid her journal on her bedside table. This was the first time she'd written in it since the entry where she lamented Henry refusing to see her during her visit to London with her parents. It had become a way to release her feelings. It felt like a cross between talking to God and talking to herself. If anyone else ever read it, they would probably think she was schizophrenic. Lately, she was starting to question that herself.

She rolled off her bed and pulled a piece of paper from her desk drawer. Not wanting to risk her parents walking in and asking what she was working on so late, she crawled back on her bed, folded the paper, and slipped it inside her journal. Now if they saw her, they would assume she was writing in that. She tapped the pen against her lips.

Henry,

She could write that much without thinking it through, but she had no clue how to phrase anything else she needed to tell him. Not to mention that it needed to be concise for a telegram. How do you say something so important in a few brief sentences?

Henry,
I'm sorry I left. Please forgive me. Best wishes

Scratch that last part. She refused to say best wishes for his wedding. Not that she didn't want the best for him. But some part of her hoped he would see this and break things off with Linda to give her another chance.

Henry,
I'm sorry I left. Please forgive me. Even if you don't want to give me another chance, you should know that I'm pregnant. Yes, it's yours.

There. She was planting a seed for him to give her another chance. She battled herself about whether to write 'Love' before signing her name. Would that seem too desperate? At this point, she had nothing to lose.

I miss and love you. Love, Nancy

That was it. She added her return address and phone number so he could contact her. She would send that message with a prayer for the best—that he'd see it and they would live happily ever after. That's what she hoped to dream about as she slept. More likely, her sleep would be broken and filled with nightmares of life as an unwed mother.

She took her letter and slipped it into her purse to copy the next day onto the Western Union form. Crawling back into bed, she pulled the covers up and stared at the sliver of light dancing on her ceiling. *God, I don't even know what to say to you anymore. Goodnight.*

Nancy played with the fabric napkin on her lap and glanced around the restaurant. It was as classy as she'd imagined when she heard about it— white tablecloths, candles, a stage with its elegant multi-arched back-drop overlooking the dance floor.

"This is my first time here. It's beautiful. I've always imagined coming on a date here during the weekend to dance," Nancy said to Walt once they ordered.

"I've never dined here either. I'm glad we can make this memory together."

After the waiter placed her grilled shrimp and Walt's New York strip on the table, she leaned forward. "Walt, this seems a lot like a date. Do you really want people to think we're dating? There's likely someone here we know."

He pulled at his collar and straightened his tie. One corner of his mouth pulled up slightly. "You deserve the best. I don't want your situation to make you feel like you don't."

He reached across the table for her hand. "Can I pray for our meal?"

She nodded, and Walt prayed a sweet prayer over her "situation," his job, and their meal.

"So, you've not said a word about the interview at the Columbia branch. How did it go?"

"They offered me that job. They'd like me to begin as soon as possible. The current manager wants to retire early."

"I thought the bank wanted you for a new bank and not an existing one."

"That was the plan. They weren't expecting him to retire for a few more years. He wasn't planning to either, but his wife was just diagnosed with terminal cancer, and he wants to spend his time with her."

Nancy leaned in. "How sad. That makes what I'm going through seem so unimportant."

"It's not, but his is a sad situation."

"So will you take it?"

"I think so."

"Oh." Nancy fell back against her seat. Her one ally was leaving soon. "When will you start?"

"I've asked them if they can give me two weeks, and they agreed. They plan to let Mr. Woodhouse, the current Columbia manager, go ahead and leave, and they will manage until I arrive. I may have to field some calls for them while I'm still here, but my manager here has agreed to work with me on that."

Two weeks was better than him leaving right away. "I'll miss you. I know it's selfish, but I've become used to our chats and having you around all the time."

He reached for her hand again. "I have too. I enjoy spending time with you. It's a highlight of my days." He looked down at her plate. "Why don't we enjoy our meals while they're hot, then we can talk about more serious things."

"It would be a waste not to enjoy this amazing meal. Thank you for this."

While eating, she tried to imagine she was on a regular date with a handsome man and no difficulties looming in the future—just two people dating, later marrying, and one day having children. That fairytale had always been her dream. It wasn't that she expected her life to be perfect, but she didn't think the dream would fade so quickly.

Once she'd eaten the last bite of cherry-topped cheesecake, she knew it was time to come back to reality. Walt was still her handsome date, but this was no fairytale.

Walt took a shaky breath, drawing her full attention.

"Nancy, I've been praying over this since you told me about your situation yesterday. With hours on the road today, I had extra time to consider the options, and . . ." He rubbed a hand across his forehead. "Like I mentioned, with this new job, I'll be leaving in a couple of weeks. And if Henry doesn't respond to your message, I'm guessing you'll want to leave too. At least for the next eight months or so." He stopped and wiped his forehead again. "I'd like to invite you to come with me to Columbia."

Nancy's eyes went wide. "Like to live with you? That's generous, but Walt, my parents would never let me live with a man I'm not married or related to."

"I know." He shook his head. "I'm not making myself clear. I'm asking you to marry me."

Her heart raced, and she stared into his eyes, searching for sincerity. She'd never known him to tease about something serious before. A year ago, she would have jumped at the chance to marry the man she'd had a crush on for years. But when imagining her fairytale, it didn't look like this. And what if Henry gave her another chance? "Walt, I can't let you give up your freedom to date and marry for love to help me. You're an amazing man and will make some woman feel like she's the luckiest in the world to marry you."

"But not you?"

"I don't want to be someone's burden."

"I promise I don't see it that way."

"Maybe not now, but you will. One day you'll meet someone, and you'll think, 'What if.'"

He slid his chair closer to hers and placed his hand on hers. "You don't have to give me an answer tonight, but I'm serious. I . . . care about you deeply. Besides, you'd be doing me a favor. The Columbia branch would prefer for me to be married but hasn't made it a requirement since they are in a bind and feel like I'd be a good fit otherwise. People will be much more likely to take financial advice from a married man than a single one.

"Please pray about this. Like I said, you don't have to decide about marriage tonight. I know you're waiting to hear from Henry. In the meantime, we could 'date.'" He put the last word in finger quotes. "So that if we do get married, it won't seem like too much of a surprise."

She looked down at their hands. He rubbed circles on her palm, and tingles shot up her arm. How was that possible when she was so distraught and hoping Henry would contact her? Glancing up, she found him still watching her and biting his lip.

Swallowing, she considered her words. But what if . . . what if Henry still refused? She had no other options. Dating Walt wouldn't be a hardship. It was what she'd always dreamed of. He said she didn't have to decide tonight. She looked into his eyes and studied them. What she saw made her stop second-guessing herself.

She gave a slight nod. "Okay, let's 'date.'" She imitated his quotation marks and wondered what quotation mark dating Walt would be like. Strangely, she felt hope spark inside.

Hope turned to doubt when Walt took Nancy home. He prayed about their situation before he helped her out of the car and escorted her to the door. She could barely look at him. She mumbled something to her parents about being tired and managed to make it upstairs without further questioning. In the shelter of her room, she fell to her bed. Pregnant and fake dating. How had she ended up here?

She wanted Henry to contact her and save the day while simultaneously committing to date Walt. Had that been a mistake? Was she risking her friendship with Walt to have security? He'd insisted their dating didn't have to lead to marriage. Yet truthfully, she wanted to see what it was like to date Walt. For so long, she'd imagined it, and now she had the opportunity. Such a jumble of emotions.

It felt like she was being unfaithful to Henry—the man she was ready to commit her life to weeks earlier. But she had tried to repair their relationship, and Henry was the one who got engaged to someone else so quickly. She would hang on to hope until it was clear he had no interest in being part of her life or that of their child.

And what of Walt? He didn't deserve to have to give up his future for someone else's child.

Chapter Nine

For the first couple of days after she sent the telegram to Henry, she held out hope that they could work through everything and be a family. Walt patiently spent time with her—eating with her family and spending the evenings with them. He did ask if he could take her out Saturday if she had still not heard back from Henry.

On Saturday, there was still no word, and she knew it was time to move on. Walt asked her father if he could court her, and he agreed.

There was one more thing Nancy needed to do before their date.

She borrowed the phone in her father's study and called Elaine.

"I'm sorry, Elaine. I hope you know I wasn't looking for a relationship. With Walt, things just evolved naturally."

"No. I understand. I misinterpreted things between us. Now that I think about it, he was probably trying to see if I had information about you when he was hanging out at my place. He's a good guy, and you've had a crush on him forever. I should be the one apologizing to you."

"That's not necessary, but I'm glad there are no hard feelings."

Apology done—she was ready for her first official date with Walt.

He showed up right on time with the beautiful zinnias his mom grew. Both of her parents greeted him, but she was thankful they didn't linger or make a huge fuss over their date. She was making a big enough deal of it herself.

As they drove away, Walt spoke. "Why don't we try to avoid talking about the wedding or pregnancy tonight. We already know so much about each other, but it might give us a chance to go deeper and leave behind some of our worries at the same time."

"I could use a night like that."

"Me too."

Silence filled the car. Nancy couldn't think of a thing to say. Walt's request focused all her thoughts on those two forbidden topics. She glanced sideways at him. He nervously tapped the steering wheel.

Did he feel the same way she did? The past two nights since agreeing to date, they had been together with family, but with this being an official date—possibly leading to marriage—her nerves had taken over, and she'd been edgy all day.

At a stop sign, Walt turned and caught Nancy watching him. His mouth quirked up into a smile. "Are you having as much trouble finding a topic of conversation after I laid down the law for the evening?"

She chuckled and nodded.

"I promise I had a million topics in my head before I said that. Forget I said that. We can talk about whatever. What did you do today?" He pulled through the intersection and focused again on the road.

The sun was setting, and a stream of light came through his window, drawing her attention to his strong jaw and the dusting of a five o'clock shadow. She recalled the time when he was a teen and complained that he couldn't grow a beard. She giggled again.

"What?" His voice broke through her distracted thoughts. "Did something funny happen today?"

Nancy covered her mouth. He'd asked her a question. "I was . . . uh, your face."

He wiped at his face.

"I was remembering when you were younger and wanted to grow a beard but were frustrated that you couldn't."

"You think I should grow one?"

"Nope. I like you clean-shaven." Heat rose to her cheeks. "The sun hit your face, and you've got some stubble. I bet you wouldn't have a problem growing a beard now."

Rubbing over his chin, he glanced her way and grinned. "Were you staring at me, Nancy?"

She shook her head at first. "Okay, I . . . yes."

His hand went to her thigh. "I don't mind. Hopefully, you like what you see."

Now her cheeks were on fire. She always liked what she saw when it came to Walt. And he'd only grown more handsome with time.

What was the question he'd asked before they got sidetracked? "My mom and I baked apple pies and cookies today. We'll share if you're nice."

Walt laughed out loud. "*Now* you answer my question. I'm on to you, little lady. I'm guessing that means you do like what you see. And yes, I would love to sample your baking. I've always enjoyed your cooking."

She smiled until she realized that if they did marry, he'd be eating her food for the rest of their lives. That thought made her nervous again. How would she make it through the whole date?

The burgundy leather booths and tables topped with red and white checked tablecloths beckoned Nancy into her favorite Italian restaurant. It was a cozy spot owned by a couple who had immigrated from Italy in the fifties. Soon after, they opened this restaurant.

Dino and Mama Rosa always had a smile and kind words for their guests to make them feel at home. They recognized Nancy and Walt right away.

"Ahh, my friends, so good to see you! This looks like you are on a date. Did he finally man up and ask you out?" Dino slapped Walt on the back.

Walt grinned and nodded.

"Good for you. You treat this one right. She's something special, like my Rosa." He turned and made eyes at his wife.

Rosa shook her head. "This one . . . always trying to flatter me."

"What can I say? I know what she needs."

Mama Rosa raised her brow and shrugged. "It's true." She pulled over a waitress. "Giana, seat these two in the Mona Lisa booth, and their appetizer is on the house." While the waitress grabbed two menus, she turned back to Nancy and Walt and clapped her hands. "You have a romantic date. Si? Enjoy."

Nancy and Walt slid into the semi-circular booth. It was secluded from the other seats and presided over by a beautifully framed copy of the Mona Lisa. A crystal chandelier with dimmed lights further set it apart from the other tables in the restaurant.

Nancy whispered, "Is it that obvious we aren't just here as friends?"

Walt winked. "I might have mentioned it to Mama Rosa."

Dinner was going smoothly and Nancy had started to relax when Elaine's mom passed their table.

"Nancy? How wonderful to see you! Elaine told me you were back. She has been talking nonstop about your adventures in England." She turned towards Walt, and her brow shot up. "Oh . . . Walt. I . . . so good to see you." Her eyes darted back to Nancy before returning to Walt. "I forgot you two are neighbors." She chuckled, but it sounded forced. "You have been such a help with Ben. When you came over to talk him down after the situation with that girl, it made all the difference in the world."

"I'm so glad. He's a good kid. I know how much it meant to me, having Nancy's father come alongside me and get me through some things."

"Well, you are always welcome in our home. Elaine speaks so highly of you as well."

"Thanks."

"It was good seeing you, Mrs. Little." Once she walked off, Nancy blew out a breath. She was glad she'd spoken with Elaine earlier. "It looks like she might have had designs for you and Elaine."

Walt's brown eyes settled on Nancy's, and one side of his mouth crept up. "That ship has sailed."

The room felt warm. With Walt around, there wasn't much need to wear blush. She reached for her fork and ate the last bite of her manicotti.

Before she'd had time to swallow, the waitress came by with a dessert platter enticing them to buy the tiramisu or cannoli.

Nancy eyed them both, then glanced up at Walt.

"We'll take both."

"You didn't have to order them both."

Walt smirked at her. "Nancy Jane Wilson, you and I both know that you love tiramisu *and* cannoli. You love Italian food in general. That's why I brought you here."

She bit back a smile. "No fair. Most people don't know nearly this much about each other when they have their first date."

He leaned forward in the booth, and his voice grew husky. "I consider it a blessing, and you'd better believe I'm going to use everything at my disposal to make our marriage work too."

She sucked in a breath and studied him. He'd lost the smirk from before and looked entirely serious. How was she going to make it through the rest of their date when this man already had her frazzled?

As Eliza Doolittle's father sang "Get Me to the Church on Time" on stage, Nancy felt Walt's hand clasp hers. He intertwined their fingers and squeezed but didn't look her way. Her heart skipped a beat. She didn't dare move her hand for the rest of the play lest he pull his away.

In the final scene of *My Fair Lady*, the actors danced and sang before them. Nancy glanced down to where Walt's hand still lay intertwined with hers. Without turning her head, she tried to make out the look on his face. It was hard to read. What did all this mean to him? Sometimes she thought he was flirting with her. Did she want him to flirt with her? A few days ago, she would have said absolutely not, but now she wasn't so sure. Was it her need to feel wanted after Henry's rejection? What did these feelings mean for her future with Walt?

Should she share her thoughts with him? As much as they'd shared through the years, this was new territory. The thought of exposing herself intimidated her. In some ways, she still felt like the young infatuated girl who idolized him yet hid it.

The stage lights went out and the house lights came up. Nancy scanned the theater as her eyes adjusted.

"What did you think?"

"It was wonderful." She dropped her voice to a whisper and spoke into his ear. "But I still think Audrey Hepburn is the quintessential Eliza Doolittle. Though their Professor Higgins was much more handsome and just as good."

He raised a brow. "You thought him handsome, did you?"

She nodded.

"I must say that hurts, darling." He spoke in a British accent, held a hand to his chest, and pouted.

"Well, you know what they say about British men."

"No, darling, what do they say?" He continued his dramatic impersonation.

"That their accents make them so much more attractive."

She blushed when she registered the truth of that in her own life—not that Henry wasn't good-looking to start with. He did remind her of Robert Redford, after all. She squeezed her free hand into a fist. Henry shouldn't be on her mind when she was on a date with Walt. She'd done so well at pushing him out of her thoughts lately.

Walt stood and pulled her with him. He motioned with his head. "Little traitor. Are you ready?"

Nancy smiled and followed as he tugged her down the row and into the aisle. The sight of their hands still tangled together sent her heart racing.

On the ride home, Walt tapped the steering wheel to the music on the radio. When "We've Only Just Begun" by the Carpenters came on, she realized it told the story of a couple newly starting out in marriage. She was only beginning to adjust to the newness of dating Walt. The reminder that if things went as planned, they would be married in a few weeks, hit her hard.

Walt stopped in his driveway and reached for her hand. His eyes found hers and uncertainty filled his face. "Nancy, I'd like our relationship to be centered on Christ. We have a lot going against us, but if we let God direct us, we'll have a good chance of making it." He reached back and lifted a Bible from the backseat.

Flipping it open, he found a page he'd marked. "I wanted to read from Colossians 3, verses sixteen and seventeen. 'Let the word of Christ dwell in you richly, teaching and admonishing one another in all wisdom, singing psalms and hymns and spiritual songs, with thankfulness in your hearts to God. And whatever you do, in word or deed, do everything in the name of the Lord Jesus, giving thanks to God the Father through him.' In the second verse, it tells us to do everything in Jesus' name. It also says to give thanks."

He slid his hand into hers. "I want our dates and marriage to glorify God. I hope that despite the unusual circumstance, we can see it is a gift from God and be thankful for it." He inclined his head. Was he asking for a response?

She nodded, and it seemed to suffice.

"The first verse talks about the word of Christ dwelling in us and using it for teaching, admonishing, and singing. Again, I want our relationship to embody that—to be guided by the Word of God."

Moisture filled Nancy's eyes. Everything he said was perfect. How was this real? She could hardly focus as he laid down the Bible and wrapped both of her hands in his as he prayed.

"Wait right there." He hopped out of the car and helped her out.

As they approached her house, she tensed. Once on the porch, he reached for her hands and tugged her close. He slid a hand to her cheek and rubbed his thumb in circles while his eyes roamed her face, hesitating on her lips.

She held her breath and closed her eyes, then felt a gentle kiss on her forehead. As she opened her eyes, he pulled her into a hug.

"Goodnight. Thanks for giving me a chance," he whispered in her ear.

Releasing her, he grinned and winked as he backed away. "I'll drive you to church in the morning."

"Okay. Goodnight, Walt."

Her hands felt like they were shaking as she closed the door and leaned on it with closed eyes. For a moment, she'd thought he was going to kiss her on the lips. She'd dreamed about kissing Walt for years. If she weren't pregnant and recently out of a relationship, she would be shouting for joy. This would be a happy time. Instead, her heart was divided.

She shook her head. Walt took her on a perfect date, and she didn't want to spoil it. She'd rather bask in the good feelings.

Pulling away from the door, she noticed the house was dark. Her parents were likely in bed, since it was after eleven. That was just as well. She wasn't in the mood to talk.

After getting ready for bed, she snuggled under the covers and pulled out her journal to record her thoughts about the date. Again the tug of war over her heart took over. "It shouldn't feel this way," she whispered. Henry made his choice. She had to make the best of things and move on.

An amazing man—the man of her dreams—had offered her his hand. What did it matter if he didn't love her romantically? He was treating her well. Maybe she could help him see her in a different light. Nothing came to mind at the moment. She yawned and switched off her light before sinking back down and tossing the journal on the night-stand. Operation Win Over Walt could start in the morning.

Nancy entered The Screaming Peach and joined her friends in their usual booth. It had been a week since she'd agreed to date Walt, and he was the topic of conversation.

"So what's he like on a date? Did he kiss you?" Gail asked.

"He's the perfect gentleman, and no, we haven't kissed yet." But the thought made her heart race.

"Yet." Elaine wiggled her eyebrows.

Nancy tried to act natural but didn't like fooling her friends. They were truly dating, but it all felt fake because of the reason behind it.

It had been a week and a day with no word from Henry. She'd even sent a second telegram in case he didn't see the first. At this point, she had accepted that he wasn't going to contact her. He was not the man she thought he was, and it was a good thing she hadn't married him.

Walt, however, was everything she'd ever wanted in a man, and he was standing up for her in a way that the father of her child wasn't willing to. The only difficulty was accepting that he wasn't marrying her for love. He was so good-hearted and loyal to her family that he would take on this life-changing burden even though it meant possibly missing out on real love.

She loved him. She always had but was distracted by an accent and the attention Henry gave her. Not that Walt had never given her attention before, but with her being seven years younger, her role in his life was more like a sister.

"Hey there." Elaine waved a hand in front of Nancy's face. "Daydreaming of Walt?"

"I guess so." She didn't hold her full smile this time. Whatever the reason Walt was so good to her, she would take it. She needed a friend and support right now.

"I can't say I didn't see that coming ten years ago," Gail said.

"It's as it should be." Donna hugged Nancy. "I'm happy for you. The last year in high school, I thought he had an interest in you that went beyond seeing you as a little sister."

"You did?" Nancy didn't remember it that way.

"I did. He hung out at your house so much."

"Yeah, but he's our next-door neighbor. Also my dad mentored him, taught him woodworking, and led him to Christ. Not to mention our moms are close."

"True, but he gave you a lot of attention he didn't have to. I didn't see him do the same with your sister. There were also times I thought he looked at you differently than he looked at others."

She doubted that was true, but she would let Donna believe it. It fit the narrative they were working to create around their relationship.

Swallowing the last bite of her peach pie, Nancy checked her watch. "Speaking of Walt, I promised I'd spend a few minutes with him tonight, and it's a work night so I need to get going."

"We see where your priorities are. Give Walt a hug for us." Gail winked at Nancy.

"Enjoy your time," Elaine said.

"Ditto." Donna waved as Nancy slid out of the booth and waved back.

Chapter Ten

Walt gently rocked the hanging porch swing in front of Nancy's home and stared into the darkness. "Not to put any pressure on you, but we need to get married as soon as possible so you aren't showing. It's already more than a month since conception, and you add two weeks to that, which makes you seven weeks along."

"You've been doing your homework. I've thought about that too." She shivered and pulled the blankets tighter around them. "I haven't told my parents about the pregnancy. Do you think we could get by without me ever telling them?"

"Maybe, but I'd rather not. I respect your parents too much to keep this from them. I also think it will help them accept a rushed marriage so soon after Henry." He slipped his hand under the blanket and squeezed her knee. "I know this is going to be hard, but how about you tell your parents tomorrow? You can tell them I know too and still want to be with you. I'll contact your dad and ask him to meet with me Friday night. That's when I'll ask for permission to marry you. Then Saturday is our night. It's not ideal that you know when I'm asking you, so I'd like to at least surprise you with where we go."

"You make it all sound so simple and logical." She turned and examined his face. He was taking this duty seriously.

"I know this isn't a simple situation, and I don't mean to make our engagement and marriage sound logical and boring. But we're working with a time constraint."

"You're right."

"How about we get married the week after Thanksgiving? I think that Saturday is December the fifth. It gives us a month, yet you won't be too far along."

Heat rushed to Nancy's face. She looked up, and his brow was pinched. This was a good option for someone in her situation. She couldn't think of a better man for a husband and father of her child. "Yes, I'll marry you that day."

His face relaxed, and she smiled, thankful he was willing to be her knight in shining armor. Her heart raced as she pondered a life with Walt.

"You've barely eaten, dear. Are you feeling okay? I'm worried about you. You've not snapped back since you were sick last week. We may need to take you back to the doctor."

"I'm okay. I just don't have much of an appetite tonight." She looked at her parents' plates. They were almost done with their meals. Now was as good a time as any to share her news. She'd dreaded it all day and had trouble focusing at work. More than once, she'd had to ask Mr. Dupre to repeat himself. At least her sister wasn't home to hear the discussion. Maybe Kathy wouldn't ask questions when the baby came two months early.

"I have something to discuss with you both." She looked from one parent to the other and caught her mom smiling at her father.

"Does this have something to do with all the time you've been spending with a certain neighbor?" Her father pushed his plate back and tried to hide his smile.

They wouldn't be smiling once she shared her news. "Not directly, though it will have an impact."

Her father raised a brow, and his smile faded. "Go ahead."

Nancy looked down at her plate and took a deep breath. *Please, God, help me get this out.* She looked back up. "I'm pregnant, and it's Henry's."

Her mother gasped and threw a hand over her mouth.

Swallowing hard, Nancy dared to look at her father. His brow was pinched, and his head shook. He stood up and began pacing.

Her eyes filled with moisture, and she closed them. "It was just the once—the night before the wedding. Not that it matters now."

"Oh, Nancy." Her mother moved to the chair next to her and wrapped an arm around her. "How long have you known?"

"Since last Tuesday."

"So that's what caused the nausea?" Her father joined them again at the table.

She nodded.

"But you went to the doctor Monday." The lawyer in him was always looking for discrepancies in a person's testimony.

"Yes, and a nurse there gave me a card for Planned Parenthood in case I was pregnant. I went there Tuesday, and they did a pregnancy test."

"Planned Parenthood," her mother grumbled. "I don't like that organization. Did they try to convince you to have an illegal abortion? I've heard they do that."

Nancy exhaled. She couldn't believe she'd considered an abortion. Thankfully Walt had talked sense into her. "They gave me a brochure. I'll admit it was tempting, but I decided against it."

"Does Walt know?" her father asked.

"He does, and he still wants to date me."

"He's a good man. Is the pregnancy the reason he's dating you and why he contacted me and wants to meet tomorrow night after dinner?"

Nancy nodded.

"I suppose you already know why he wants to talk with me?"

Heat rose to her face, and she nodded again.

"And are you willing to marry him? I'm guessing that's why he's meeting with me?"

"Edward, he hasn't even asked yet," her mother scolded.

"These are serious topics, Betty. There's no use tiptoeing around." Mr. Wilson turned back to Nancy. "Are you? Willing to marry him?"

"I am."

"And you're sure that's what you want to do? Adoption is an option."

Nancy sighed. "I know. I've thought about it, and I can't imagine knowing I have a child and not being the one to raise him or her. And I'd never make it as a single mom. Between being shunned by everyone I know, even people I don't, and raising a child without a father." She shook her head.

"I understand, but if you did decide to raise the child on your own, we would support you."

Her mom nodded in agreement. "He'll be moving away—next week, is it? I guess that will be a good thing, since you'll start showing soon. Have you discussed when you'll get married?"

"We're looking at Saturday, December the fifth."

"One month. At least you're giving yourself some time." Her mom squeezed her hand. "Have you sent a letter to Henry? Even with his engagement, he still deserves to know he's a father."

"I've sent him two telegrams and not heard back."

"Shame on him." Her father hit the table with his fist. He was normally in control of his reactions, even when angry. "I'm glad God spared you from tying yourself to a man like him. And I don't think you could marry a better man than Walter Moore. There is much more to discuss, but right now, we need to pray."

Her father held hands with her mom and Nancy and prayed for wisdom, grace, and the life of the child. He also prayed for Nancy and Walt's relationship.

As Nancy lay in bed, her mind swirled and her heart raced. Her parents responded better than she'd imagined, and now she was left with reality —she was marrying Walter Douglas Moore, her forever crush, but they weren't in love—at least for his part. Had she agreed to marriage too quickly?

No. This felt like the right thing, though it was a big decision to base on feelings. Was it God pushing her towards Walt? Maybe God did care about her situation. Many women didn't have a man who would step in and offer to marry her and raise another man's child.

What would married life be like for them? She'd always been attracted to his appearance, personality, and spiritual maturity. What would he expect from their marriage? Her face heated thinking about having that conversation with Walt. Maybe things would happen organically and they wouldn't have to have *that* conversation. Her heart fluttered. Was it strange that she felt excited despite the circumstance?

She smiled and her eyes drifted closed.

Nancy's father crossed his study and propped a hand on the fireplace mantle. "Your relationship will be built on a foundation of faith, respect, and friendship. Many marriages have been built on less. I think yours can go the distance."

Like an outsider looking in, Nancy watched as her parents interrogated Walt about his intentions. Her father had spoken to Walt for thirty minutes before calling her mother and her in.

Walt reached for Nancy's hand and interlaced their fingers. "I agree. You've been a good example and mentor, and I will do all I can to make a happy home for Nancy and this child."

"It will be hard raising another man's child. Do you think you're up for that challenge?" interjected her mom.

"I will raise it like it's my own." He looked at Mr. Wilson. "It will be up to your daughter if and when we tell the child that he has a different biological father."

"That will be another challenge that you'll need to plan for. And also what to say if people question the timeline. So many young people are into the idea of free love nowadays, but in church and the business world, it's frowned upon."

Walt nodded up at her father.

"You may think I'm rushing things, but we need to talk about the wedding if it's going to be in a month." Mrs. Wilson looked between Nancy and Walt.

Nancy frowned and shook her head. "I don't expect to have anything big because of the circumstances. I definitely don't think I should have a church wedding when pregnant. It feels disrespectful."

"I anticipated something like that, so I went by the Greenville Art Museum and checked. It's available on Friday night or Saturday night that first weekend in December. Since I volunteer there, I can get it for next to nothing." She turned to Walt. "If you haven't been, the museum is in Gassaway Mansion. It's lovely inside and out. What do you think, Nancy?"

"Mom . . ." Her voice was strained, and a tear slipped down her face. "That's . . . I don't feel worthy of such a beautiful place."

Walt slipped his hand from hers to wrap her in a hug. With his free hand, he wiped her tears.

Mr. Wilson spoke up. "Nancy, it's true, you should have waited until you were married, but you need to talk with God about that. Ask for forgiveness and then forgive yourself."

Looking at her father, Nancy was at a loss for words. She understood what he was saying, but her heart didn't believe it was possible.

"So will you let me plan something there? It can be small but still nice."

"Okay. Yes. Thank you, Mom."

"Why don't you look at my dress too? I've saved it all these years. You and I are close to the same size. You could leave off the train, which is cathedral length. The dress itself is fairly simple, but I think it's beautiful. I pulled it out of the storage closet, and it's still in good condition."

"That would be nice. It does look like a beautiful dress in your pictures."

"Wonderful. I have a lady who can alter it if needed. It will look lovely on you." Her mother turned to Walt. "Don't get any ideas about hunting around to find my wedding photos. I want her dress to be a surprise for you."

He chuckled. "Yes, ma'am. I'm sure she will look beautiful, and I will patiently wait to see it at our wedding."

A vision of walking down an aisle in that dress to Walt flitted through Nancy's mind, and her chest tightened. This didn't feel real.

"Well, Betty . . ." Mr. Wilson stood and approached his wife. "I think we should leave these two alone. They have much to discuss." After taking Mrs. Wilson's hand, he turned to Walt and Nancy. "Let us know if there is anything you need from us. Your mother will continue to work on the wedding. Nancy, you'll need to let Mr. Dupre know when your last day will be. If I may, I suggest your last day be the day before Thanksgiving. That will give you almost three more weeks and allow you to have a full week after Thanksgiving to make sure everything is as it should be for your wedding or travel to Columbia if necessary."

"I hadn't even thought about quitting work. You're right. I hate to let him down so soon after starting."

"He'll understand. Goodnight, you two."

After everyone said goodnight, Nancy turned to Walt. "Walt, are you sure about this? I worry about you throwing away your future for me and a child who isn't biologically yours."

"Nancy, I promise you, I do not feel like I'm throwing my life away, and this child will never feel like it is not biologically mine. This child will have my last name and all the same love and provision I will give any child we may have in the future."

Nancy felt her cheeks heat.

He reached for her hand. "Right now, we are good friends, but I hope one day we will be a couple in every sense of the word. I understand it's currently far from your mind because of your feelings for Henry. I won't rush you to get past that. I want to be your friend and partner in every way that you need. It's up to you to decide the pace for the physical side of things."

She looked down at her lap. It was hard enough admitting to him she was pregnant. This conversation was way out of her comfort zone. "Thank you," she whispered.

They sat there quietly until Nancy had the courage to speak again. "You don't have to take me out tomorrow night."

"Oh no, I'm doing this right. We may not have a history of dates for you to look back on, but we can start making memories now."

She looked him in the eye. "You are too good to me."

"Please don't say that. You are worthy."

Nancy forced a smile. When Walt said sweet things like that, it made her feel good, but she didn't agree that she was worthy.

"Something else we need to work on is a house in Columbia. I was hoping you could meet me there next Saturday to go house shopping. I have a realtor who is ready to work with us."

"You want me to help you pick a house?"

"Nancy, it will be our home. I'm sure you have an opinion on what you'd like and what's important to you. I'm thinking at least three bedrooms and two baths. And close to a good elementary school. But as far as the style and amenities, I'm flexible. Will you make a list for me to take to her?"

"I can do that. Thank you for including me."

Walt's brow pinched, and he leaned in but didn't respond right away. He finally spoke. "We're a team. Walt and Nancy against the world."

A soft chuckle bubbled up from her throat. She wouldn't repeat it out loud, but he *was* too good to her.

A soft knock on Nancy's bedroom door drew her from her journal. "Come in." She sat up on her bed just as her mom entered holding her wedding gown. "Oh, Mom!" She hopped off the bed and touched the bodice of the gown. "It's gorgeous. You're really okay with me wearing it?" She looked up to watch her mom's response.

"I really am. I would much rather you use it than for it to continue sitting in the closet. If Kathy wants to use it, too, we can have it worked on to fit her as well. But you and I both know she has a particular style, and I doubt my dress will fit with that. We'll see."

"This is amazing, and it would be an honor to wear it. Thank you." She wrapped her mom in a hug.

"I'll hang this in the closet for you. Saturday we'll try it on and take it to my friend if it needs adjustments. We can make sure it is slightly loose around your belly, though I don't imagine you'll grow much there just yet, with this being your first pregnancy. Speaking of that, I'll call my gynecologist's office tomorrow and see if they have a recommendation for an ob-gyn in Columbia."

"When do you think I'll need to go?"

"I would think it could wait until after the wedding, but you can go ahead and get on their schedule. Or you could set up an appointment there the week before the wedding and do that while moving things into the place you'll be living."

The thought of living with Walt brought that now familiar heat to her cheeks—especially after their earlier conversation. She watched her mom as she placed the dress in the closet, and imagined him carrying her over the threshold in it. Would he do that? Uncertainties lurked in every corner of her mind. She had thrived on a carefully planned life until Henry crossed her path.

"Honey, what's this?" Her mom held up the tea-length white dress she had shoved into the back of the closet.

A flood of memories washed over her—Henry smiling at her as they strolled through Kensington Gardens, tea at their favorite café, a picnic by the Thames. She closed her eyes and let the memories fade like a ripple from one of the pebbles Henry tossed into the Thames.

"It was my wedding dress—the one I would have worn for Henry."

Her mother silently examined it. "Do you want to get rid of it? We could donate it to the church's help center."

"I . . . I don't know." Part of her wanted to toss it in the garbage or burn it, but another part wanted to hang on to every memory. "I'm not quite ready to make that decision." It wasn't that she held out hope of Henry coming back into her life. But her time in London now seemed like someone else's life, and she worried it would be lost forever without reminders.

Her mom sighed and placed the dress back in the closet before joining Nancy on the bed. "I'll say it again—we will support you if you choose not to get married—even if you decide to keep this child and not give it up for adoption. I don't want you to think you don't have options."

Nancy shook her head. "No, there's no way I'm bringing this child into a situation like that. They would be treated differently by both adults and their peers. Even you two would be ostracized. If it were just me, I might consider it."

"I hear what you're saying, and you aren't wrong about what would likely happen. But your father and I will put up with anything if it is beneficial to you and this child. If you insist on following through with this marriage, will you try . . . try to love Walt and create an environment where love can grow?"

"I want to." Was it possible to turn her previous crush into real love —even if he didn't feel the same way right now?

"Did you know that my parents were basically an arranged marriage?"

"What? Grandmother and Papa seemed so in love."

"They did love each other, but when they married, it wasn't that way. They married for convenience. My father was working for my grandfather at the family hardware store when Grandfather became sick. My mom had not dated anyone since her fiancé was killed in action in World War I several years earlier. So my grandfather, practical man that he was, convinced my parents to marry so there would be a man in the family to help take care of the women when he died. It was the 1920s, and things were different back then."

"So they went from being acquaintances to loving each other?" Nancy wanted to add, "And having three children."

"They did. And I'll tell you some things I've learned from being married. Feelings ebb and flow. Love requires work, even in the best of marriages. Your father and I were madly in love when we got married, but when you girls were young, we went through a rocky period. He was busy growing his law practice, and I was exhausted with two busy little ones. Yet even through that rocky time, we were committed to making it work. We had made a promise before the Lord and planned to keep it. As time passed, we learned that love is not always that driving desperate feeling—sometimes it is in the patient day to day caring for one another even when the other doesn't have the energy or time to reciprocate. Love is an action, it's a promise."

"That gives me a lot to think about. I've always held your marriage up as an ideal. My relationship with Henry was passionate and happened so fast but ended just as quickly. It's left me reeling, confused, and fearful of ever finding love again. I jumped into this marriage idea with Walt out of desperation, doubting we would have romance in our marriage."

"Don't give up on that. Put everything you can into it. Make your home a place where romance can flourish."

"That sounds great, but it also scares me. I don't want to be rejected . . . again."

Her mom leaned in and laid her head against Nancy's while caressing her hair. "It's scary in a marriage that starts with all the romantic feelings too. But I can see that it would be even more scary when it doesn't. Walt is a good man. I don't think he'll ever leave you feeling rejected."

"Thanks, Mom, for the encouragement. I've been an emotional wreck."

"Pregnancy hormones will do that to you. Add in all of the other stress in your life, and you have a recipe for depression. I'm here for you anytime you need to talk."

Nancy hugged her mom back before pulling away. "Speaking of Walt being a good man, did you know that tomorrow night he's taking me out to officially ask me to marry him? Who does that in a situation like this?"

"That sounds like something he'd do. You need to get your beauty sleep to be ready. I'll let you get some rest. Goodnight, dear."

"Goodnight, Mom."

Once the door closed, Nancy dissected their conversation. Walt *was* a good man, and she was willing to work for all the things that might be lacking in their relationship. Her mom's words gave her hope, but now that she was alone, the doubts crept back in. *You're not worthy.*

Chapter Eleven

"I want to surprise you." Walt reached across the car's front seat and held out a scarf. "I borrowed this from Mom. Do you mind if I blindfold you?"

A smile broke through, and Nancy shook her head. At work that day, she had struggled to keep from thinking about her date with Walt. Her emotions waffled from excited to worried. What she didn't expect was a blindfold.

She held on to the armrest on the door to brace herself for turns and tried to guess which way they were heading—right turn, right turn, faster for a stretch, left turn . . . Somewhere along the way, she lost track, and when the car pulled to a stop, she had no idea where they'd ended up.

Walt guided her out of the car, and she listened for any noise that might give her a clue. Only the sound of passing cars reached her ears.

"Any guesses?"

"I'm at a loss."

"I'm going to attempt to lead you up a lot of steps." His arms tightened around her.

She smiled at the warmth and strength she felt in his arms. What was she thinking before he held her? Oh yes—she was trying to figure out where they were. They were still outside and walking up steps. "Are we at church?" Heat rose to her face at the thought.

Without answering, Walt continued to lead her up. "That's the end of the steps. Let me get the door."

She heard a door open, then he guided her through. They walked on a hard surface, and it changed to carpet. Her guess was still the church. Tension worked its way from her shoulders to her back. Since finding out about her pregnancy, there had been a strange push and pull in her relationship with God. Her logical side said Jesus died for all of her sins, but something else kept telling her, *you had sex outside of marriage, and you are unworthy.*

They stopped, and the heat of Walt approaching warmed her. Gently he lifted the blindfold. She looked up and saw the cross at the front of the sanctuary before it occurred to her that Walt was kneeling before her. He became blurry, and she blinked back tears.

"Nancy, I know you think you don't deserve to get married here at church, and that's fine. But I will say it again and again—you are worthy and you are forgiven. I know that this is an unusual start for a marriage, but I think we have a chance for something wonderful. I will love you and this child with all that I have. I wanted us to take this first step here in church because I want God to be at the center of our marriage. Will you marry me?"

She thought she was prepared for this question, but all the emotions from the past month converged on her at once. She closed her eyes. Tears streamed down, and she fought to keep from wailing out loud. When she opened her eyes, she recalled his question. She had made her decision, and it wasn't fair to keep him on pins and needles.

"Yes." She bent down to meet him. "Yes, thank you, Walt, for being a good friend and going above and beyond what I could even imagine."

His smile faltered, and he fumbled to open the ring box. It displayed a beautiful emerald-cut diamond ring with a small diamond baguette on either side. The stone was suspended in a simple platinum setting.

Her hand flew to her mouth, and her eyes found his. "Walt. This is too much."

With his free hand, he drew her left hand close. "It's not. Please stop thinking that way. I hope I keep surprising you until it sinks in." He carefully slid the ring onto her finger.

"It's stunning." And huge by her standards. She couldn't stop from wrapping her arms around him and holding on like a lifeline until his strong arms calmed her.

Pulling back, she stared into his eyes, searching for answers. *Will we make it? Will we have romance? Am I enough for you?*

She couldn't read the secrets he held, but what she saw made her want to kiss him. His eyes dropped to her lips, and electricity sparked. A sudden thud drew their attention to the window, and the moment was lost.

"A bird?" Nancy questioned, and Walt shrugged.

"For our dinner, I have another surprise."

"I guess you want me to put on the blindfold again."

"I do, but I won't make you walk down the stairs with it." He winked, grabbed her hand, and pulled her down the church aisle to the exit.

Nancy's eyes darted around the sanctuary as she imagined what it would be like to leave after a wedding in the church. Even if she had married Henry, it would have been in a tiny chapel and they wouldn't have had anyone they knew present. Though her wedding to Walt would be small, she looked forward to having their close friends and family there.

At the bottom of the church steps, she looked back at the tall, imposing columns and steeple. *A marriage with God at the center.* That was something Henry had not offered. She hoped she wouldn't mess this up.

"Can I take off the blindfold now?"

"Patience."

He lifted her out of the car, and she inhaled the savory smell of grilled steak. With a grin, she guessed. "Ye Olde Fireplace Restaurant." He slid off the scarf, and she turned.

"You're good."

"This is where you asked me the first time." When he nodded, it dawned on her. "I mentioned I always wanted to come here and dance, so you brought me on a weekend." She wrapped her arms around him and felt him stiffen. "Thank you." She was determined to follow her mom's advice and make their home a place where love could thrive. It started now.

He patted her on the back before reaching for the door.

The band's music poured out.

"You're going to dance with me?" she questioned.

"Absolutely."

As they arrived at their table, she noticed theirs was the only one with a vase holding a dozen red roses. She looked at Walt, and he winked.

This time when they perused their menus, he urged her to get the lobster.

"But it's so expensive," she whispered.

"I'm twenty-nine and have been saving for years for my engagement and marriage. Most of that time, I lived with my mom. We'll be fine. Plus, I want to make up for our shortened courtship."

"Okay, but do you think lobster will be messy?"

"Look." He pointed to a couple a few tables over. "The waiter is getting the meat out for them. No mess."

"Thank you. I'll get that then." She tapped her fingers on the table with the beat as she watched the band. "Once we place our order, let's dance."

"I'd love to."

"That's Charlie Spivak leading the band. I've heard great things about him. Did you know he was a big band icon in the forties?"

"I did hear that. We're lucky he moved here and plays so often."

She turned back to the band, her attention divided between watching them and the dancers. A memory flashed in her mind, and she looked back at Walt. He was watching her with a lazy smile. Her heart raced. "Do you remember teaching me to dance when I was little?"

A full smile graced his face. "I do. I was learning myself and practicing for prom. You may not remember, but you were my guinea pig."

"You seemed like a giant, and you let me stand on your feet."

"I was sixteen, so that would make you nine."

The memory was vivid. That was likely when her crush for him fully bloomed. He was the perfect gentleman and made her feel special even though she was so small. Her handsome neighbor had always been kind, but as he held her hand and turned her around the living room, she'd imagined what it would be like to one day marry him.

Her heart fluttered at the thought that she was accomplishing the dream of her younger self.

The waiter approached, and they placed their order. Then with a crooked smile, Walt held out his hand and said, "May I have this dance?"

"Why, of course." When he pulled her close, she whispered, "Don't tell my fiancé."

That earned her a chuckle as they joined several other couples on the dance floor. They were quickly caught up in a swing dance to the orchestra's music. He swung her out, and when he pulled her back in and dipped her, she nearly lost her balance. It wasn't the dip, but the look she caught in his eye that made her legs wobbly. The next song was slow, and he held her close. She was happy to have the extra support.

Their waiter brought their food out, and they returned just as he was removing their lobsters from the shells. After he left, Walt prayed over their meal and marriage.

As she took her first bite, he cleared his throat. "There's something I wanted to discuss with you."

Heat rose to Nancy's face. Was this the talk? Here at a restaurant?

He continued. "Despite this not being a conventional marriage, I think we should have a short honeymoon of sorts."

Nancy stared at him without blinking, wondering what he would say next.

"My mom told me about a bed and breakfast in a historical Charleston home she thinks we would love. Don't worry, it has a suite with not only a king-size bed but also a daybed. You can have the king. It might be nice to drive to our home in Columbia to stay Friday night.

We could leave for Charleston the next morning. From what I've gathered, it's only about two hours from Columbia."

She finally blinked. "Honeymoon?" No other words formed in her mind.

"Like I said . . . of sorts. A time for us to get used to one another as husband and wife and make some memories."

"As husband and wife?" Her heart raced, and her face was fully on fire.

Walt rubbed a hand over his face. "I'm making a mess of this. I don't mean in *that* way, I mean . . . well . . . even though we've been friends for years, things will be different. We'll have to learn to do everyday things together. There's a different comfort level that we'll begin developing with one another. Am I making any sense?"

Nancy smiled. She'd never seen Walt so flustered. "I think so. That could be fun. I haven't been to Charleston in several years."

On the ride back home, she stole glances at Walt. This gorgeous man whom she had always admired and crushed on forever was going to be her husband. Her nine-year-old self would never believe this was her reality.

At church Sunday, word of their engagement spread quickly. Her girlfriends were in shock, but Donna was the first to admit she'd always seen it coming. Elaine and Gail weren't far behind in their praises of what a catch he was and how happy they were for her.

The week after the engagement was exhausting, especially with the pregnancy. In addition to work, she had to make decisions for invitations, the cake, flowers, and several other wedding-related things.

Walt spent every spare moment with Nancy—helping her make decisions, eating meals with her, and even taking her on another date before Wednesday, when he started his new job.

The new bank set him up temporarily in a gatehouse apartment belonging to a friend of the previous manager. Wednesday morning, Walt dropped Nancy off at work and gave her a tight hug.

"I'll miss you." He pressed his forehead to hers. "I'll call you tonight and tell you about my first day."

She nodded, and a strange tightness filled her chest.

When he pulled back, he reached down for her hands and squeezed them. "You have my number. Call me if anything comes up . . . or even just to talk."

Nancy forced a smile. "Okay," she squeaked.

Sliding out of the seat and stepping away from the car, she waved and watched him pull away. Emptiness filled her, and she rubbed her chest. She didn't expect this feeling, considering their circumstance.

That night, she went to the church prayer meeting with her mom and still felt hollow. She'd avoided the prayer meetings since returning, but tonight she needed a distraction. It didn't work. Between Walt leaving, pregnancy, and God seemingly so far away, her nerves were shot.

Donna caught up with her as she exited the sanctuary. "I'm meeting Gail and Elaine at The Screaming Peach. Join us?"

She looked over at her mom, who nodded and said, "Why don't you take the car? I'll ride home with Grace."

Nancy reluctantly reached for the keys. Her mom had her driving more and planned to give Nancy her car when she got married. She insisted Nancy needed her own transportation in Columbia, since she didn't know anyone there. Nancy had gotten her license back in high school but avoided driving like the plague. Finding rides or using public transportation had never been a problem, but her mom did have a point.

As they entered the café, Donna questioned her. "What's wrong? You look upset."

Hesitating, Nancy thought about what she could share. She had decided her pregnancy would stay between her parents, Walt, and herself. At this point, his mom did not even know, and she wasn't sure she would ever tell her if it could be avoided. "Walt left today. I'm having a hard time with that."

Donna's face lit up. "You've got it bad. I knew if you two ever got together, it would be explosive. Just think, in a few weeks, you'll have him all to yourself all the time. And don't forget the honeymoon." She wiggled her eyebrows.

That last comment heightened Nancy's anxiety.

"Where are you two going?"

"Charleston."

"Ooh. That's such a romantic place."

Nancy nodded. Thankfully Donna didn't ask how long they would be there. One night might make Walt seem cheap, but it was more than she expected for a marriage of convenience when she was the one getting most of the benefits.

Inside The Screaming Peach, Elaine squealed, "Here comes the bride!"

All eyes were on them, including Brian's. He was sitting two tables down from her friends. His face tightened, and he frowned at her.

"So tell us how all the plans are coming." Gail interrupted her thoughts.

Nancy described the invitations and cake she'd chosen. "Because this wedding is happening so quickly and we're trying to keep things low-key, I'm only having Kathy as a maid of honor and no other brides-maids. But I would like you ladies to help serve the cake if you're willing."

Gail fake pouted. "As much as I would love to be your bridesmaid, you know we would do anything for you."

"Thanks."

"Same for me," Donna said, and Elaine nodded in agreement.

"Wonderful!" Nancy smiled as big as she could and tried to act happy despite the unsettled feelings still lingering.

Half an hour later, she swallowed her last bite of peach cake and checked her watch. "I need to get back home. I'm expecting a call from Walt."

"So romantic." Gail batted her eyes and mimicked swooning.

"Tell Walt hi," Donna called out as Nancy stood up and grabbed her purse.

"Will do. Bye, ladies."

"Nancy." Brian's voice startled her as she stepped towards her car.

She turned and caught the hurt in his eyes. "Hey."

"So . . . um . . . I hear congratulations are in order."

Biting her cheek, Nancy nodded.

"I guess this is why you said your heart wasn't free."

She shrugged and looked at the ground. She'd forgotten she said that. At the time they spoke, Walt wasn't in the picture.

"Walt's a lucky guy. I always wondered if you had feelings for him."

Her eyes darted up.

"The way you looked at him . . . and he was always hanging around, so I wondered if he reciprocated. Though it would have been weird, because back then the age difference seemed much bigger."

"I'm sorry if it seemed that way. I had a crush on him for years, but I did care about you."

"There's nothing to be sorry for. We were just kids, and you certainly don't owe me anything now. Especially after how I left things back then." He kicked the gravel under his foot. "It's my loss. Anyway, congratulations. Maybe I'll see you sometime when you come back to visit."

"Thanks."

Nancy got in the car and pulled away as she thought about Brian and her friends' comments. Memories from the past surfaced—Walt, his older brother, and his mom sharing holiday meals with her family, Walt teaching her to play basketball, Walt showing her how roast a marshmallow to perfection for s'mores. The memories were endless. He had been there for so much of her life, and she had adored every minute of it.

Was it wrong that she longed to hear from Walt about his day? Everything inside still felt topsy-turvy. She *should* want to spend time with her husband-to-be, but something inside kept telling her she shouldn't get over Henry so quickly.

Another part of her said her relationship with Henry wasn't worth dwelling on because she jumped into a relationship with him too quickly in the first place. The way he rejected her when she tried to apologize and was now unresponsive to her pregnancy announcement should have been more than enough to get rid of lingering guilt. Was all this chaos inside a result of pregnancy hormones?

As Nancy entered the house, her mom called out, saying Walt was on the phone.

Nancy followed the sound of her mom's laughter and found her sitting at the kitchen table, holding the phone.

"Here, dear. He's all yours."

As Nancy reached for the phone, her throat tightened and her mind went blank. What had she planned to say? "Hi."

"Nancy. How was your day?"

"It was good." At hearing his soothing voice, her mind began to clear. "But I should be asking you that. I want to hear all about your first day."

"I'm happy with my choice. The other employees made me feel welcome. They brought lunch in for me. Oh, and you'll like this— lunch was from the local Screaming Peach Café."

"Ooh. That's nice to know. I want to check it out when I come in. I wonder if it has the same menu as the one here."

"All the food they brought were items I've seen on the Greenville menu, so maybe it is the same. I also had a chance to speak with the real estate agent, and we have an appointment for Saturday after lunch. I was hoping you would come out and join me. I already checked, and there's a bus from Greenville to Columbia that leaves at nine a.m. and arrives here at about ten forty-five. When we're done here, I can drive you back and we can go to church Sunday in Greenville. Will that work for you?"

Looking at houses made their upcoming marriage seem all too real, but she knew this was what she wanted. "Yes."

Chapter Twelve

The look on Walt's face when she stepped off the bus in Columbia had Nancy second-guessing the trajectory of their relationship. He smiled as he reached out a hand to her, but it didn't quite reach his eyes. Tension flashed across his face. Was he having doubts about marrying her?

Her heart beat hard. Surely he felt it as he hugged her. He slipped his hand into hers and tugged her to the car. His mouth was moving, but she couldn't think past the pounding in her ears.

"Nancy?" He squeezed her arm with his free hand.

"What?"

"I asked how your trip over was?"

"Oh, the bus was fine. I had a seat to myself, so I read."

Walt smirked, and all traces of earlier tension disappeared. "An Austen novel?"

She smiled. He remembered. Biting her lip, she shook her head. It had been weeks since she'd looked at her collection. Her copies of *Emma* and *Pride and Prejudice* were still buried in a pile of things she'd dumped out of her suitcase on her return from England. "It's a book on legal precedents."

"A little light reading?" He laughed, but it sounded stilted. Or was that her imagination?

Over brunch, they discussed what they wanted in a house. Walt had a lot to say, yet his tone was clipped.

"Are you okay?" Nancy finally questioned him.

"Yep. Everything is fine." He didn't elaborate.

Their real estate agent, Mrs. Murphy, was a friendly middle-aged woman with a salt-and-pepper shoulder-length bob. The first house she showed them was an old fixer upper. One step in, and they knew it wasn't for them. It required more work than either of them were prepared to take on in light of her pregnancy. They left before going past the entry.

The second house was only seven years old. It had potential. As they walked through all the rooms, Nancy tried to imagine herself in it with Walt and a baby. It was all one level. Everything was nice. It had a simple front yard and backyard. They agreed to keep it in mind.

Mrs. Murphy told them the third house was Craftsman-style and built in 1922. It had been renovated two years before.

Nancy grinned the moment they pulled into the neighborhood of the third home. There were sidewalks and mature trees in every yard. The homes all had large front porches. It looked family-friendly.

The home itself was two stories, covered in gray stucco, and had a central gable on the upper floor. The painted wood columns and trim, large front porch, and landscaping were picturesque. She could see herself tossing a ball with a little one in the front yard, then hopping onto a porch swing after dinner at the end of the day. When she glanced at Walt, she found him watching her. His smile seemed more relaxed this time.

"I hope the interior is in good condition," she whispered to Walt. "I really like it on the outside."

He wrapped an arm around her waist and squeezed as they followed Mrs. Murphy to the front porch.

Their agent opened the door and waved them in.

The small entry was just as beautiful as she'd hoped. It had honey-colored oak trim details and framing that opened up to a study on the right with built-in wood bookcases on either side of a fireplace. There was no furniture, and it allowed the character of the home to shine. The large study windows looked out onto the front porch.

Beyond the entry, they found a living room with windows overlooking a small tree-filled backyard. Boxy wooden columns above low built-ins supported a framed opening to the dining room. A cozy window reading nook sat off to one side of the living room, and a fireplace on the same side of the room had built-in bookcases on both sides. The dining room had built-in hutches on either side of a fireplace with glass doors accented with stained glass on the upper sections. Walt's table with all of the leaves installed would fit perfectly in the dining room.

The kitchen had a perfect little breakfast nook with built-in seating and a table that seated six. According to Mrs. Murphy, the appliances were only two years old. They were the latest shade of avocado green and blended with the natural wood and cream-colored walls.

Nancy tried to hold back her enthusiasm in front of their agent until she had a chance to talk to Walt, but unless the upstairs was in a shambles, this was her dream house.

Mrs. Marsh told them the upstairs had been reworked so the master had its own bathroom and there was a separate bathroom for three other rooms to share. With the half bath on the first floor, it had enough bathrooms for a whole houseful of kids. Though less detailed with wood trim, the upstairs was perfect for their needs. It had lots of windows in each room and plenty of closet space. When she opened the master bedroom's French doors to the balcony, her mouth dropped. It overlooked a spacious side yard and the adjacent parklike area between several houses. She imagined drinking her tea and reading in the peaceful setting.

"Walt." She pulled him out on the balcony with her. "This is it, don't you think?"

"I can see you love it. Umm . . ." He gave her a tight smile and ran a hand through his hair. "Why don't we tell her you and I will talk about it over dinner and call her tonight with our answer?"

"But I'm sure about it." Nancy studied his face and noticed the tick in his jaw. "You're not?" She continued to analyze him. "Or maybe something else is bothering you." She thought back to his earlier unease. "Okay, we'll talk about it over dinner."

The worry she'd had at the beginning of the day returned threefold. Something was definitely wrong.

The drive to the Columbia Screaming Peach was quiet. Walt didn't look at Nancy, and his entire body was stiff. Nancy felt like someone was squeezing her chest.

The minute they were seated in a back corner booth, she questioned him. "Walt, what's going on? It's not the house situation that's bothering you, is it?" Nancy dreaded hearing the answer to her question. She feared the worst—he'd come to his senses and wanted to break the engagement. She had a baby to plan for if he wasn't going to marry her, so she had to know.

He rubbed a hand over his face. "Why don't we order first, then we can talk."

Ordering food was the last thing she wanted to do in her distraught state. She stared at him, but he stayed focused on the menu. It was obvious he wasn't going to talk until he was ready. She slapped her menu down on the table and flipped it open. When she saw it was nearly the same menu as Greenville's except for a few additions, she closed it and waved at the waitress. She had no plans to drag this out.

"Okay, we've ordered," she said when the waitress walked away. "What's on your mind?"

His face was angled towards the table. "I owe you an apology." He peeked up through his lashes.

Nancy clenched her fists and held her breath. Her mind raced through her options. Maybe she could move to Charlotte with her roommate from Furman—if Loretta's parents would let her. It was just under two hours away, so her parents could reach her pretty quickly if necessary. Or maybe she could stay with—

"Nancy, I've not been forthright with you. I . . . Do you remember the girl I dated in college? Brenda?"

Oh God, help me. He wants to get back together with her. She slowly nodded and wondered if she could make it on the last bus back to Greenville. She remembered Brenda, the beautiful woman he'd dated in college. She'd been jealous every time he brought her home. Brenda was the woman who left him so brokenhearted, he'd left town for a year.

"I . . . We . . ." He rubbed the back of his neck. "I loved her, and we planned to get married when we graduated from Clemson."

The waitress arrived with their food. They silently stared at their food until Walt broke the silence with a short prayer for their meal and wisdom about what to say.

"You can eat if you want, but I need to get this out."

She shook her head. "I'll wait." She'd lost her appetite.

He pressed his lips together before nodding. "So, like I said, we planned to marry and . . . I don't know if you knew, but before becoming a Christian, I struggled with . . ." He closed his eyes and ran a hand through his hair. "Getting too physical with the girls I went steady with. But I never . . ." He dropped his voice. "Had sex with them." He glanced up, and deep creases lined his brow. "After becoming a Christian, I changed the way I treated the girls I went out with."

He stopped and took a huge gulp of his peach sweet tea. "With Brenda, things got so serious . . ." He raked his fingers through his hair again. "What I'm saying is . . . you're not the only one who made a mistake. I actually made that mistake way more than once. Just because we never had a baby doesn't mean that what I did was any better than what you did with Henry."

He took another sip of his drink, then looked right at her. "I'm so sorry for letting you think you were alone in this, and I understand if you're too angry with me to get married. It's been eating at me for weeks, and I felt like God has been throwing it in my face so I would confess to you. That's why I didn't want to get into a house contract right away. In case you want to back out."

Nancy stared at him, unsure of what to say, much less how she felt. Was she mad that he didn't tell her earlier? Or hurt to think that he had been with another woman intimately—apparently a lot. Or was something else lurking behind his sudden confession? Maybe he was hoping she would back out. Did *she* want to back out, or should she? Was she holding onto something that wasn't meant to be?

God, please show me what to do. She'd not spoken to God much lately. Actually —she had done some talking but no listening. She still wasn't convinced God wanted to be involved in her life after her poor judgment. But here was a man who confessed to the same sin yet was very close to God. Was that kind of relationship with God still possible for her too?

She studied the engagement ring on her finger. *God, I want this to work, not just out of desperation.* She squeezed her eyes shut. She listened.

"Do *you* want out of this engagement?" She opened her eyes and found him frowning.

"What?" he asked.

"Do you want to end things?"

"No. Of course not. I just . . ." He rubbed his face. "I know I might not be all you thought, and it wasn't a good start, with me lying. We talked about how important trust is, and I understand if this is too much. I don't want you to feel like you have to marry me."

"I don't want to end things either. I forgive you for not telling me earlier. Maybe you can help me learn to work through my own failures and how to reconcile with God. Ever since I found out I'm pregnant, I've felt guilty and unworthy of forgiveness and a relationship with God. It took pregnancy to make me acknowledge my sin. Before finding out, I pushed it so far back in my mind and planned on never thinking about it."

He reached across the table and grabbed her hand. His face visibly relaxed. "My relationship with God isn't perfect, but I have repented and now I don't let my past keep me away from him. I want to walk through this with you. It will be good for both of us."

"Okay then." The weight bearing down on her lifted a little.

"Can you forgive me for not being forthright with you about this?"

She frowned. "I'm upset that you didn't tell me earlier, but I also remember how hard it was for me to admit to you what I'd done. Yes . . . I forgive you."

"Thank you. Now let's eat before our food gets cold."

"Yeah." She looked down at her chicken noodle soup and dipped in her spoon before tasting it. She was pleasantly surprised to find it still warm.

In between bites of meatloaf, Walt questioned her about the Craftsman house and admitted he thought it was what they needed too.

"The reason I didn't seem very excited about it was because I had this confession looming over me. I'm not better than you, and I'm truly sorry for waiting so long to tell you." His voice lowered. "And Brenda is the only person I've been with—*that* way. Not that it's much of a consolation. I'm so sorry."

Nancy's cheeks heated, and she remembered he wanted them to be married in *every* way.

When they left the café hand in hand, she felt closer than ever to Walt. Before leaving for Greenville, he stopped at a payphone and called their real estate agent to make an offer on the home. She met them at her office, and Walt wrote a check for their earnest money and they signed papers for the offer. Mrs. Murphy said she'd call Walt's mom's house that weekend once the seller responded.

"I can't believe we did it. We signed a contract," Nancy squealed once they were in the car. "I hope they accept our offer. The house is so dreamy."

"Mrs. Murphy said we have a good chance. The seller moved a few months ago and wants out from under the mortgage."

Upon their return to Greenville, Walt invited Nancy to spend some time at his house in case the real estate agent called.

They joined his mom at the round wooden kitchen table and told her about their house tours and the offer.

Mrs. Moore yawned. "I'll leave you two lovebirds alone and wind down in my room with a book. I'm happy for you both." She kissed them each on the cheek and left.

Walt reached across the table for Nancy's hand. "This is really what you want, right?"

She blinked at him, and her shoulders tensed. Was he talking about their marriage again? He'd been so chatty on the ride home that she thought everything was fine.

"To buy the house," he confirmed as if reading her mind.

"It is." She relaxed into her seat. "Every time I think of it, I get a warm feeling. It's beautiful and has so much character. Much more than the new homes going up.""That's a good point. I think that's what I—"

The phone rang, and their eyes darted to it on the wall.

"Maybe this is Mrs. Murphy," Walt said as he stood up. "Hello . . . Hi, Mrs. Murphy." He raised a brow and smiled at Nancy. "Mm-hmm. Okay. Yes, she's here with me . . . That's great!" He reached out to Nancy and moved next to her chair. "Nancy, it's ours."

She jumped up into his arms and squealed. "I can't believe it. It's ours!"

"I can be there for that." He pulled the phone closer. "Yes. That sounds good. I'll talk to you later. Thank you!"

He hung up the phone and wrapped his other arm around her while she bounced up and down. Finally some good news.

His mom came around the corner in her pale pink night robe. "I take it they accepted the contract?"

"They did!" Nancy enthused.

Once Walt's mom left again, they moved to the living room, where Walt settled beside Nancy on the sofa. "We've got to make some plans for our house."

Our. Nancy pondered the word. She still struggled to wrap her mind around this relationship with Walt.

"We won't need a loan, since I've saved enough. So it's just a matter of getting the inspections, appraisal, and title search done. Maybe in a week or two, we can close and start moving our things in," Walt explained.

"We'll have to sort through our things and see what we have and need."

"Why don't we do that tomorrow after church?"

"Okay."

"I mentioned I want our relationship to be built on God, and I was thinking we could do a Bible study together—long distance. We could write each other our thoughts and also call a couple of times a week. What do you think about that?"

"That would be nice. I've been struggling in that area."

"I figured. I went through the same struggle when I was processing my guilt from my time with Brenda. Eventually, I turned to I John and studied it. The verse that drew me there was I John 1:9. 'If we confess our sins, he is faithful and just to forgive us our sins and to cleanse us from all unrighteousness.'"

She let the words swirl around her mind. "I need to remember that. I've confessed my sin, but when I'm down, I forget he is faithful."

"I went through the same thing. Even now, I sometimes have moments when I question his forgiveness, especially since asking you to marry me. But I've learned that the quicker I give it back to God, the faster he can remind me it was fully forgiven and I am free. Tomorrow we can talk more about I John chapter one, and I'll give you some other scriptures we can study and take notes on separately through the week."

Nancy nodded as she twisted her hair, trying to think of a way to ask the question that had been at the back of her mind since their earlier conversation. "Walt, can I ask you a personal question?"

He stretched his arm across the back of the sofa behind her. "I hope so, since we'll be married soon."

"How . . . actually, why did things end with Brenda? When it happened, you were pretty vague with me about the details."

Walt sighed and looked away from her. "The summer after our junior year, she wanted me to move to Charleston and work as an intern for her dad. He was the president of a bank there. He said he wanted to train me to work for him after I graduated. It would have been a great situation, but that was the summer after my brother got transferred to Atlanta with his wife. My mom was still struggling with depression and had a setback when my brother moved, and I was still living on campus. That's why I moved home the last month of school that year and drove the half hour each way to school.

"When I changed my plans about going to Charleston that summer, Brenda worried I would have the same struggle moving away from

Greenville the following summer, and she had her mind set that we would live in Charleston after we married. She said we needed to break up and she would think about getting back together in the fall. By the time school began again, she had started dating someone else and decided not to come back to school. I was devastated."

Nancy knew a little of that feeling with Brian, but they weren't planning to get married. "Do you wish you had made a different decision and gone to Charleston?" He wouldn't be her knight in shining armor now if he'd married Brenda, but she had to know.

He frowned. "No. It was for the best. We weren't good for each other. During our relationship, I pulled away from God. After finding out she was with someone else, I spiraled. Do you remember? You tried so hard to encourage me."

She nodded. It had been difficult seeing the man she admired and secretly loved broken like that.

"I was at my lowest point since my dad's death. That's when God got hold of me the second time and reminded me that he comes first. I had been acting like Brenda came before God."

"I'm so sorry, Walt. I never knew how to help you."

"You were a bright spot at the time, but l was so broken that no one but God himself could shake me up." His mouth pulled into a small smile as he lifted a hand to her cheek.

The way he held her gaze looked different than that of a brother. She almost thought she saw longing. Moments like this gave her hope that they had a chance at a romantic marriage.

She remembered that year when he moved back home. She was over-joyed he was home, and when she heard their moms talking negatively about Brenda, she felt vindicated for her dislike of her.

"You're still a bright spot for me. I look forward to having my bright spot with me every day." His eyes dropped to her lips, and her heart raced.

Yes, please kiss me. She hoped he could sense what her heart was speaking.

Unbidden, a yawn overcame her, and she tried to cover it.

Walt pulled away and grinned. "We've had an emotional day, and I'm sure the little one is taking his share of your energy too." He patted her tummy, and tingles of awareness radiated from the spot. "Do you think we'll start feeling him move soon?"

"My mom said it's not usually until about the fourth month."

"Good. I'm glad we'll be married then. I want to be around when that starts happening. Let's get you home so you and little guy can get a good night's sleep." Walt stood and pulled her up with him.

"It might be a she." She chuckled softly. "Lead the way." *My knight in shining armor.*

Chapter Thirteen

9

April 1970
Dear Nancy,

Since the first time I saw you in the café reading Emma, I've not been able to get you out of my mind.

Nancy ran her fingers across the words as if touching them would take her back to the day she received the letter. It was the first one Henry sent during her time in London. It seemed like she opened it for the first time years ago. So much had happened since.

Her mom had been urging her to sort through the London pile for weeks, but with Walt closing on the house tomorrow, it needed to be done soon so she could decide what to move.

She spread the other letters out and wondered if she would feel worse if she tossed them with or without looking at the rest.

Just one more.

28 August 1970

My Dearest Nancy,

I earnestly beg you to be patient with me while I come up with a plan to get out of this marriage. Even though my father did not respond well during my first meeting with him to discuss it, I have hope that I will be able to get him to come around.

Clutching her heart, she laid it back down. This one was too painful to read. His father never did come around, and it was clearly too much for Henry to deal with. Stacking the letters back together, she stood, walked to her trash can, and dropped them in.

Her heart belonged to Walt. He might not have romantic feelings for her—yet—but she was going to do everything in her power to set their marriage up for success. They weren't even married yet, and he had made her feel like a princess despite her failures.

The jewelry box on the desk caught her eye, and she remembered the necklace Henry had given her. She lifted the lid and touched the pendant. It was beautiful and would one day become a treasure for her child—part of his or her heritage. As she lowered the lid, she noticed some of the fabric lining inside the lid had come loose. She pulled a bottle of glue from her desk drawer, opened it, and held the loose fabric in place. Before she touched the glue to the fabric, an idea came to her.

Nancy leaned down and removed the letters from the trash. Gently, she tugged on the loose fabric of the jewelry box and slid the envelopes inside. They fit. She glued the fabric back to the wooden lid and laid a paperweight along the edge to hold it in place. Now she could keep the letters in case her child ever had an interest in seeing them.

She once again dropped to her spot on the floor, next to the pile of items she'd dumped out of her suitcase. She'd never been so disorganized, but the pile represented pain, sadness, and a life left behind. There was plenty to save, but some items—pressed flowers, a silver hair barrette, a scarf, and a few other things from Henry—those items could be tossed or sold at a secondhand store. The necklace and letters would be enough for her child. She didn't want additional trinkets constantly tempting her to scrape the scabs off old wounds.

Sorting the items, she started several piles—to throw away, to sell, to move to Columbia, and to store in her parents' home. Two of her treasured Jane Austen books surfaced. She would never part with her leather-bound copies of *Emma* and *Pride and Prejudice*.

Smiling, she picked *Emma* up. It may have been the book she was reading when she met Henry, but many other memories were bound between its pages. She flipped to the first page and recalled in high school fancying herself as Emma Woodhouse while wishing Walt was her Mr. Knightley and felt something more than brotherly affection for her.

Nancy may have been the older sister rather than younger, as in Emma's case, but she felt a camaraderie with the lively, opinionated Emma. Nancy's strong opinions were what drove her to become a paralegal. They ignited a desire to do something with the internal fire that was stoked whenever she learned that someone had been wronged.

She pulled the book to her chest, walked to her window, and peeked down at the spot where Walt's dad's old truck remained. That truck brought a smile to her face. In just over two weeks, he finally would be her Mr. Knightley.

A knock on her door made her step away from the window.

"Yes?"

"Walt is on the phone." The sound of her father's voice surprised her.

"I'll be right there." She placed her Austen books in the moving pile, grabbed her Bible and journal, and rushed to the door, thinking of her Mr. Knightley.

"Hi," she said while trying to get her breathing under control from running downstairs.

"Guess what," came Walt's deep voice through the phone.

"What?"

"Sorry, I should have said hi first. I'm a little distracted. We own a home! The paperwork was ready early, and I just finished signing papers. It won't be official until things are filed tomorrow."

"How wonderful! I can't wait to move things in this weekend. I was just sorting through my belongings so I can get them ready to move."

"That's good. We've got so much room to fill. We'll need to do some shopping soon too."

"We know we have a kitchen table with chairs, and beds. Those are the essentials." Nancy threw a hand over her mouth. She didn't mean to bring up the embarrassing subject of a bed.

"We do, and I still insist that you get the master bedroom and the queen bed. I'll sleep on the twin in the extra room."

"But you—"

"I'm not taking no for an answer."

"Okay."

"Good. So how was your day? Is the nausea still bothering you?"

"Mornings, I still feel off, but most days, eating saltines before I get out of bed settles my stomach. Then I make sure to eat some throughout the day between meals. I'm hoping this ends before my second trimester."

"Me too. I've been praying about that for you."

"Thanks. I gave in on the bedroom at the house, but can we renegotiate the honeymoon? You shouldn't have to pay for that and take time off when this isn't even a real marriage."

The line was silent. "Walt?"

"I heard you." He sighed. "This *is* a real marriage. We've spoken about this too. We're having a real wedding, signing real papers, and I am going to be this child's real father. You're not getting cold feet, are you?"

"No." Was she? She didn't mean to hurt his feelings, but the idea of a honeymoon sent her heart into a tailspin. It did make it seem real. She wanted it to be real, but she still worried that after the new wore off, he would have regrets.

"Good. Then we are going on our real honeymoon. Don't worry. Just like I promised before, I won't expect us to share a bed there. I'll stay on the daybed I told you about. You should know, though, that I've spoken with the owner and changed our reservation from one night to two. I was going to surprise you, but since you don't seem very excited about one night, maybe two nights wouldn't be a good surprise for you."

"I'm sorry. That's not it at all. It sounds lovely. You are already doing so much for me. I don't want to be a burden to you." She was making a mess of things with everything she said.

"Nancy, I've always loved spending time with you. None of this is a burden to me."

"You keep saying things like that, and it makes me want to believe it."

"Good. I plan to continue saying things like that."

"Have you told your mom yet?"

"Told her what?"

"You know. That you're marrying me because I'm pregnant."

"No. I have no plans to."

"But it's already been so hard for my parents to not say something to her. It will be especially hard for my mom to keep it up since they're so close."

"I'm sorry, Nancy. I don't want to give her anything to worry about. She's had enough to go through in her life with my father's death. I want her to enjoy this. We can discuss it again in a few months if you still feel this way."

"Hmph. She's your mom, so I guess you know what will be best for her." She twisted the phone cord between her fingers. How did he go from saying sweet things to being so one-sided?

"I'm sorry if it seems like I keep saying no to the things you want. I'm doing everything I can to set us up for a good marriage. One that is all you've hoped for."

Nancy chuckled, thinking about how right now, Walt very much reminded her of Mr. Knightley, who frequently frustrated Emma.

"What's so funny?"

"I was just thinking about how your bossiness is reminding me of Mr. Knightley."

"Mr. Knightley?"

"You know, from my favorite book."

"Right, *Emma*. Nancy, I'm sorry. You're right. And if you want to go ahead and tell my mom, I can do that or we can together. I guess part of me was also trying to give you an out, but I agree, it will be hard for your mom, and before the baby's born, we'll probably want her to know."

"Thanks." Now that he'd said that, it didn't seem so urgent. "I'll let you know what I decide."

"Good." He sighed. "You know what?"

"Is this going to be our new game? Me guessing what you have to say."

"Maybe. This time I'm admitting I made a mistake again. I think we need to pray at the beginning of our conversations. Things are already stacked against us. I'll pray now."

"Thank you for thinking of that."

"Putting God at the center of our relationship is important." He cleared his throat. "Father God, you are all-knowing and all-powerful. You have laid this plan on our hearts. Help us trust you. Help us trust one another and protect us from things that might tear us apart. Help our love grow into everything that a godly marriage should be. God, I lay everything I am before you. Help me to be in this marriage fully and to be the leader who consistently loves Nancy the way you love your church. I pray that Nancy would know she is worthy of your love and mine. In Jesus' name, Amen."

Tears began streaming down her face somewhere around 'help our love grow.' This man had her heart in every way. *God, thank you. Help me have the courage to accept all that Walt offers and trust him when he says one day we will have a marriage that is all I've hoped for.*

"Do you have your Bible? I'd love to talk to you about what we've learned this week in Psalm 103."

"I do." She was excited to hear his thoughts. He'd made some comments on the Bible passages he was studying in the two letters she'd received from him this week.

"Are there any verses that stood out to you? Ones that seemed particularly meaningful or left you with more questions."

"Verses eleven and twelve are the two that helped me this week with my guilt and shame."

The sound of rustling pages echoed through the phone, then Walt said, "'For as high as the heavens are above the earth, so great is his steadfast love toward those who fear him; as far as the east is from the west, so far does he remove our transgressions from us.' Keep reminding yourself of that. Any other thoughts?"

"David knows what he's talking about after going through the situation where he committed adultery with Bathsheba and basically had her husband set up to be killed. I can't imagine the shame and anger he would have had towards himself when he came to his senses." Nancy had read the story many times, but this time, she had looked at it more closely.

"You're right. It makes a lot of his psalms that much more meaningful. Verse fourteen says, 'For he knows our frame; he remembers that we are dust.' He knows that we struggle with sin and still has compassion for us. Verse thirteen, before it, talks about that very thing—his compassion for his children. In my situation with Brenda, I struggled repeatedly with the same sin. God had to totally remove her from my life. At the time it was hard, but now I'm thankful he spared me from continuing down that path. Psalm 51 is another good one where David processes his sin. Can you find time to read over it tomorrow on your own, and we can talk about it this weekend?"

"I can read it before work in the morning."

"Nancy?"

"Yes?"

"I'm looking forward to seeing you this weekend."

Her insides felt warm. "Me too."

Once back in her room, Nancy headed straight for the hope chest at the foot of her bed. She opened it and found her letters from Walt. He'd been writing to her since he moved, and she'd put his letters into her hope chest. They weren't gushy love letters like Henry had written her, but they were tender and loving in their own way.

She imagined Henry's letters were more like an explosive fire—instantly overwhelming and burning everything around, then snuffed out just as quickly. Nothing left but ashes—just like their relationship.

Walt's letters were like a slow-burning ember she hoped with careful tending would grow and provide just the right amount of heat to comfort her and last a lifetime.

She laid the letters aside and sifted through her other treasures. The

Royal Dalton china from her mom's mom was stacked on one side. Her grandmother had passed away when Nancy was ten. The set was white with a pale yellowing gray band adorned with pink, yellow, pale blue, and brown flowers. Next to the china lay the tablecloth and fabric napkins embroidered with gray scallops that her father's mother had made. They matched the china. She imagined her treasures gracing Walt's table in the dining room of their new home.

Moisture filled her eyes. Lately, it didn't take much to make her cry. So many wonderful things were happening, but she kept waiting for the other shoe to drop. She didn't feel worthy.

She caught sight of the Bible lying on the floor next to her and recalled the things she'd discussed on the phone with Walt about Psalm 103. She was surprised when he said he was glad God took Brenda away from him. Knowing that Walt had struggled with the same sin encouraged her that she would be able to accept God's forgiveness for hers. It also gave her hope that he really had moved past his loss of Brenda.

She reached for the Bible and flipped to Psalm 51, curious about what she would find. Skimming through it, she wondered how Walt knew just what she needed. Verses ten through twelve seemed to be written for her—"Create in me a clean heart, O God, and renew a right spirit within me. Cast me not away from your presence, and take not your Holy Spirit from me. Restore to me the joy of your salvation, and uphold me with a willing spirit."

"God, that's what I want," she whispered into her empty room. She couldn't remember if she had confessed her sin to God. Since returning home the first time, she'd been so wrapped up in her broken heart and later the pregnancy. Again, she skimmed over the words in the Psalm, then closed her eyes. "Like David says in verse two, 'Wash me thoroughly from my iniquity, and cleanse me from my sin.'" *Please, Father, forgive me. Help me to move past this.* She opened her eyes and silently prayed through more of the passage.

Pulling the Bible to her chest, she leaned back against the hope chest, letting the words of the scripture wash over her. Peace filled her. *Thank you, God.*

Chapter Fourteen

"Here's more cornbread for your bowl." Lucille dumped the pan of cornbread into the giant bowl of bread and cornbread Nancy was breaking into pieces.

"It smells delicious. Your cornbread makes the best dressing." Nancy's mouth watered as she thought about their Thanksgiving meal the next day.

"I made extra to go with the ham and bean soup you're having for dinner tonight."

"I'm going to miss your cooking when I move, but not as much as I'll miss you." Nancy's heart did a little flip at the thought that she would be married in only a week and a half. She still had a hard time wrapping her mind around it. Walter Moore would be her husband. *Swoon.*

"You'll have to drive home regularly. Or have that handsome husband of yours bring you around if he can't part with you. It's not like Greenville is on the other side of the country."

"If he can't part with you" stuck in her mind. Maybe one day that would be the case. She'd been praying and asking God to show her how to be a good wife so he would love her in all the ways she hoped.

"That would be nice." Nancy set aside a small piece of cornbread she'd saved and pushed the large bowl forward. "Does this look like enough for the dressing?"

Lucille glanced at the bowl from the stove where she was sautéing celery and onions. "I think that's got it."

Overwhelming hunger hit Nancy. She grabbed a spoon from the utensil drawer and snuck behind Lucille to spoon out some of the aromatic deliciousness from the pan.

Lucille turned with a hand on her hip. "Missy, you know better than to sneak up on me like that. When everyone complains there wasn't enough onion and celery in the dressing, I'm giving them your name." She chuckled. "You just ate before you sat down to work on the bread."

Nancy shrugged and spoke with her mouth full of the sautéed vegetables and cornbread. "It's gooood." After swallowing, she added, "How am I supposed to work around all this food and not be constantly hungry?"

"If you keep it up, you'll have hips like these." She patted her hips before turning back to the stove.

"Lucille, you are beautiful," came Mrs. Wilson's voice as she joined them in the kitchen. "And look who I picked up."

Lucille's daughter, Yvonne, and Kathy trailed behind Mrs. Wilson.

"Betty, I'm glad you had better luck getting Yvonne out of bed than me." Lucille raised a brow at Yvonne.

"Mo-o-o-m, I didn't want to leave the house before eight a.m. on my day off from school."

"I don't blame you," Kathy said as she walked up and hugged Lucille. "Mmm. College cafeteria food is nothing like your cooking, Lucille."

"I'm glad. Now, you ladies can get to work helping with some of this cooking." Lucille handed Kathy and Yvonne aprons, pointed to piles of vegetables on the counter, and assigned each woman a job.

Nancy picked up the peeler and started working on the sweet potatoes.

"How are you feeling about the wedding plans?" Yvonne asked as she sliced and peeled apples.

"Mom and Mrs. Grace have pretty much taken care of everything, so I'm not too worried. You know my mom." She glanced across the room and winked at her mom. "She's good at planning events. It's been nice, since I've been busy with work."

"I do know your mom, and even without much time to plan, it's gonna be outta sight."

Nancy laughed and gave Yvonne a side hug. "I'm going to miss you. After I move, I'll make sure your mom knows when I'm coming to town so we can get together." Yvonne was like another little sister who she'd watched grow up. "I'm glad you're spending Thanksgiving with us."

"Me too, sis." Yvonne bumped hips with Nancy. "But I'm sure you're anxious to get to the wedding next week. It's about time you two got married. You've only been pining after Walt forever."

"That's what I said," Kathy chimed in.

Two hours later, the ladies sat around the kitchen table, eating apple hand pies they'd made with the scraps of pie crust, when they heard a knock on the front door.

"Now who would be botherin' us when we finally got a chance to sit down?" Lucille pushed back her chair.

"Don't you move, Lucille—you've been on your feet the longest. I'll get it." Mrs. Wilson checked the clock. "It's still a bit early for Grace. She had teachers' in-service until two."

"Hi, Mrs. Betty, is Nancy home?" Walt's voice was muffled, but Nancy easily recognized it.

"Of course. We're all in the kitchen."

"It sure smells good in here. You've been busy."

Butterflies inside of Nancy desperately tried to escape as she waited for Walt to come into view.

"A meal like we have planned for tomorrow takes many hands."

The second Walt entered the kitchen, their eyes met and everything else faded. He came straight to her and pulled her into a tight hug when she stood. "I've missed you."

She buried her face in his chest and breathed him in as his hand slid from her hair to her back. The butterflies continued their flight.

At the sound of someone clearing their throat, Nancy stepped back. She looked up at him, and he winked.

"Do we need to give you two some privacy, or do you think you can wait another week until the wedding?"

Nancy's face went red at her sister's words.

"Kathy, don't embarrass your sister. Walt, why don't you join us and have an apple hand pie?"

He slid in a chair to Nancy's left and placed a hand on her thigh, hidden by the table. She looked over at him. *What does this mean to you,* she asked with her eyes. His response was unreadable, yet his touch ignited something inside she thought had died when she first returned from London. The entire time they sat at the table, his hand remained on her thigh, sending heat throughout her body. Periodically, he glanced at her and grinned. Each look made her heart soar. Would his touch always feel this way after they were married?

Thanksgiving morning, Nancy smiled as she stretched in bed and thought of the day to come—good food, time with family, and time with Walt. A savory aroma wafted into her room. In seconds, happy thoughts dispersed when a wave of nausea hit her. She reached for the glass of water on her bedside table before nibbling on a cracker. Closing her eyes, she took deep breaths. As the rumbling eased, she ate more of the cracker. Within minutes, she could sit up, and tucked the crackers into the drawer before heading to the bathroom. With Kathy home and even Lucille around, she hid evidence of her pregnancy. So far, she'd managed to avoid detection. There had been a few close calls on days she'd vomited, but she'd discovered that running the tub faucet covered the noise.

Once she made it to the kitchen, she found it bustling with activity.

"Good morning, dear," her mother called as she pulled something from the oven.

"Good morning, everyone." Nancy scanned the room. Lucille stirred gravy on the stove, and Grace made rolls across the room.

"There's breakfast casserole and bacon on the table." Lucille pointed to the kitchen table.

"Thanks."

Grace looked up from the rolls and said, "Walt is at our house, in charge of getting casseroles in and out of our oven if you want to join him after you eat."

Nancy's face warmed as she looked at her soon-to-be mother-in-law. "Yes, I'll do that."

"I guess I shouldn't call it our house anymore, now that Walt is gone and the two of you have your own home. Are you and your mom still planning to go Monday to get things unpacked and start decorating?"

"We are." Nancy smiled at the thought of their new home. She'd never dreamed they would find a home with so much character.

Nancy found renewed energy and hurried to eat her breakfast so she could spend time with Walt. She was both excited and nervous whenever she was with him.

After brushing her teeth, she waved goodbye to the ladies and went next door. Anticipation filled her as she knocked on the door. This was another chance to show him what a good wife she would be. But the moment she saw him standing at the entrance, all her courage fled.

His face lit up as he took her in. "Good morning."

"Good morning," she croaked out. Why did her mouth choose now to go dry? She swallowed and tried again. "I heard you were in charge of the casseroles going in and out of the oven, so I came to keep you company and help."

He bit his lower lip and nodded while reaching for her hand. "How did you sleep?"

"Good."

He raised a brow. "Really? I worry about you. One of the ladies at the bank here in Greenville used to complain that she had trouble sleeping."

She shook her head. "I've not had that yet. I've heard some women have to go to the bathroom a lot, but it hasn't hit me at night. The materials I received also said I might have some round ligament pain in my second trimester, which can cause discomfort while sleeping as well as during the day, but that's a month away."

"Good. I don't like the thought of you being uncomfortable the whole time. Did you get sick this morning?"

"Just mild nausea, and it went away with the crackers and water. It's rare now that snacking before getting out of bed doesn't stop it."

He led her to the sofa in their family room, laid a large fluffy pillow over one of the armrests, and guided her to sit. "Why don't you lean back and stretch out your legs? I'll rub your feet."

She sat but was hesitant to give him her feet. "It's not like my feet are swollen. Are you sure you want to do that?"

"I'm sure. I want to do something nice for my fiancée. If you're patient, I might even massage your shoulders."

As he worked on her feet, she felt her eyes growing heavy. A loud buzz startled her, and she threw open her eyes.

"Sorry. That's the casseroles. I need to check on them." He stood and leaned down to kiss her on the forehead.

In her dreamy state, she almost grabbed onto him and pulled him to her lips. But even in her dream state, she worried she'd scare him off before the wedding.

"I'll be right back," he assured her.

Did he see the longing in her eyes? She tried waking herself as she listened to him washing his hands and removing casseroles from the oven.

"I didn't mean to fall asleep during our time together," she said when he returned and settled beside her. She tucked her legs under herself.

"It's okay. I wanted you to relax." He ran a hand through her hair, and she tensed.

"What's wrong?"

If she only knew the answer to that question. One minute, she was ready to kiss him, and the next, she flinched. Lately, her emotions had been a jumbled mess. When he showed her affection, was it friendly affection, or was it leading to something more? She knew what *her* heart wanted.

"Sometimes when I look at you, I see fear in your eyes. Or worry. Maybe both. Are you having second thoughts about our marriage?" He placed a hand on her chin and gazed into her eyes.

"I . . ." She looked away. "I know you would keep your promise and never make me feel like a burden, but I worry I am."

His thumb slid to her cheek and caressed it. "Never. I'm twenty-nine years old and have had every opportunity to marry before now, but I believe God has kept me single for you." He leaned his forehead against hers, and her heart nearly stopped.

He continued to rub his thumb on her cheek, and their breaths mingled. Time slowed. She closed her eyes and waited.

Releasing her, he pulled away. "But, Nancy, I won't make you marry me. As much as I believe we are meant to be together, you have a choice."

Her heart stuttered at the loss. She met his gaze to read what was etched across his face. He was all in. In a battle of wills, she stared him down, silently telling him to set himself free. But the look in his eyes didn't change. It spoke of promises, protection, and love. She knew he loved her as a friend and sister, though she hoped for more. One day. Maybe it was selfish, but she wouldn't be the one to stop her wedding this time.

"I choose you."

He smiled. "I choose you too. See, we're already in agreement. We may not have the romance that some start with, but we have a better foundation than many—a strong, solid friendship."

She nodded as he pulled her close. It hurt to be reminded they were only friends, but she trusted him to be faithful and would redouble her efforts to get him to see her as more.

When he leaned back, his mouth pulled into a slow grin. "So tell me, future wife, what are your plans for the last week before our wedding?"

"You already know about Monday, when your mom is joining my mom and me to take some things to Columbia."

"Yes, and I get to take you ladies to lunch. Don't forget."

She nodded, the tightness in her chest easing. "Next Thursday, I have a girls' night with Donna, Elaine, and Gail."

"Do I need to worry?" He raised a brow and bit back a smile.

"Ha, ha. Later in the week, I'm having my last dress fitting, and hopefully I'll get everything else packed."

"Sounds like a busy week." He rubbed his chin and examined her.

"Do you remember the time when you were . . . I think nine, because I was sixteen and driving. Anyway, you were panicked because you had a softball game and your parents couldn't take you because your sister broke her arm falling out of a tree. They had to take her to the emergency room."

Her heart skipped a beat as the memory surfaced. "I do. You had a girl with you, and when you offered to drive me to the game, she whined that you were supposed to take her on a date and she wasn't dressed to sit outside for a ballgame."

Walt chuckled. "That's right."

"What was her name?"

"Who knows."

"I recall she came with you to get me, but you took her home after dropping me off for warm-ups."

He nodded. "Do you remember what I said?"

Nancy shrugged. "I was nine. That part is hazy."

"A lot of it's hazy for me, too, but I do remember telling you I would always be there for you."

She searched her memory and did recall something like that. "I know I always felt I would be okay with you around. You were my safe landing."

He reached for her left hand and ran his thumb across her engagement ring. "I'm still your safe landing. At sixteen, I may have said those words carelessly, but I mean them now. I will always be there for you. You have no need to worry about my commitment to you and our marriage."

She nodded, and he wrapped an arm around her. She still wondered how he could give up so much for her, yet with all of his promises and affirmations, she didn't think he would let her down.

Another buzz sounded in the kitchen.

"The casseroles are done. As wonderful as it is having you all to myself, we should get these over to your parents' house." He stood up and checked his watch. "My brother should be here soon with his family. The kids can't wait to see you. They're excited about being in the wedding. Pete said they've been practicing calling you Aunt Nancy."

"Your niece and nephew are adorable. It's going to be hard

following in the footsteps of Uncle Walt. I've seen how they worship the ground you walk on."

He grinned and walked backward. "I think with some convincing, they'll realize you're just as great. And once they find out you're carrying their cousin, you'll likely be more popular than me."

Nancy touched her stomach and frowned. "It will still be a few months before we share information."

"I promise." Walt made a motion of zipping his lips before turning into the kitchen.

Chapter Fifteen

"And now you may kiss the bride."

Nancy panicked as Walt searched her face before drawing near. At the last second, he shifted his head and kissed her cheek.

"That was pathetic, bro," came Walt's brother's voice from behind. "I hope you'll put on a better show at the actual ceremony tomorrow."

Nancy's cheeks felt like they were on fire, and she quickly turned, avoiding Walt's gaze as he guided her down the aisle.

During the rehearsal dinner at their favorite Italian restaurant, Nancy tried making sense of her feelings. She was really marrying Walt, but what would happen after the wedding? What would she do when they were alone together? Would she panic every time he drew near like she did at the rehearsal? He looked like he wanted to kiss her, but was it for the same reason she wanted to kiss him? Did she really want to know how he felt? Did it matter? If she threw herself at him the way she desired, would it scare him away?

She smiled and made small talk during the meal, never revealing her worry. Presenting herself as the happy bride was exhausting. Walt kept eyeing her and patting her leg.

As they walked out of the restaurant, he pulled her aside. "Let's take a drive. There are Christmas lights to see."

Nancy nodded and followed him to his car.

"Look." Walt pointed as they drove past the courthouse.

Nancy looked up at the tree covered in lights. A star topped it, and at its foot stood a wooden nativity. "It's beautiful."

Walt reached for her hand. "I'm looking forward to spending our first Christmas together. The way our families have always spent the holidays together has meant the world to me, but we'll have fun making our own traditions."

Nancy examined his silhouette. "I'd like that. There are so many things like creating our own traditions that I haven't thought about. I feel like I'm unprepared."

He pulled into a parking spot and turned to her. "What are you unprepared for?"

"Being a mother . . . a wife."

"I think you'll do just fine at both." He reached for her chin and cupped it. "There is one thing we can do to help you along." His eyes dropped to her lips. "It will also help the wedding go smoother tomorrow."

Her heart raced.

"I'd like our first kiss to be in private. The idea of standing up in front of everyone doesn't seem right. Wouldn't you agree?" His thumb caressed her chin.

She'd wanted this for so long, but now that it was happening, a rush of emotions overcame her. *Don't cry, don't think—just act.* She nodded.

"May I kiss you, Nancy?"

She nodded again and clenched her hands. It felt like her heart would beat out of her chest.

With his free hand, he unclipped his seatbelt and slid across the bench seat, his eyes never wavering from hers.

When his hand moved from her chin to her cheek, she closed her eyes and took a deep breath, not wanting to forget a single thing about this moment. Time slowed, and she felt his heat as he leaned in. The first touch of his lips was soft and gentle. He pulled back, and she held her breath. Just as her eyes fluttered open and her heart faltered in disappointment, his lips touched hers again. This time, it was firmer. His hand moved to her hair and pulled her closer. The kiss sucked her remaining breath away and left her dizzy yet hopeful it would never end.

She placed her hands on his shoulders to steady herself. Her whole body heated in spite of the chill in the car. She lost all sense of time and space. When he pulled back this time, he leaned his forehead against hers. Her body melted into the seat, committing the kiss to memory. Not wanting to break the magic of the moment, she didn't say a word.

He leaned away and once more cupped her chin. When he held her gaze, his pupils were dilated, and he gave her a small smile.

She would treasure that kiss forever. She'd been kissed a few times, and none of them compared. Once more, questions plagued her. Was it as meaningful to him? Did he want to kiss her again as much as she did? Or did he only kiss her to make their wedding kiss less awkward? Despite all her questions, no words left her lips.

His words broke the silence. "I . . . Thank you." He slid back behind the wheel, buckled, and started the car, his hand on hers the whole time.

Thank you? For the rest of the drive home, both remained silent. Once parked, he guided her to her front door.

Taking her hands in his, he tugged her to him and leaned back against a column. "This is the last time we have to say goodbye like this and go our separate ways."

She looked up at him and wondered what their future goodnights would be like. They had separate rooms set up in their new home.

He tucked her hair behind her ear, then traced her cheek with his fingers. His thumb slid across her lips, and his eyes held the same look as they did after their kiss. He leaned down, and she closed her eyes, waiting for his kiss, but his lips landed on her cheek. He kissed her repeatedly, trailing them down her cheek, across her jaw, and right next to her mouth. There he stopped. He lifted his head, and she felt a kiss on her forehead before he kissed her hair. She wanted to beg him to kiss her on the lips again.

"I can't wait to marry you tomorrow."

Her heart raced. She couldn't wait either. If he knew how long she had hoped for this, he might run for the hills. She searched for the right words and finally settled on, "You're going to be an amazing husband and father."

Something flashed in his eyes and he smiled, but it didn't reach his eyes. He pulled her hand to his lips and kissed her knuckles. "Close your eyes."

"Why?"

His smile was sincere this time. "You'll see."

After she closed her eyes, he flipped over the hand he'd just kissed and pressed something into it.

"Okay. Open them."

When she did, she saw a square package wrapped in white paper with a gossamer bow on top. Her hand began to shake, and she tried to steady the package with her other hand. An image of the pendant Henry gave her came to mind.

"Here. I'll help you."

Walt carefully unwrapped the box, exposing a jewelry case perfectly sized for a necklace. He helped her open it, and there lay a beautiful pearl necklace, just longer than a choker.

She let out a breath. "It's beautiful." The flawless pearls were a rich off-white color with an iridescent shimmer. Thankfully, it was nothing like the gold necklace and large red jeweled pendant from Henry. She shook her head and dispelled the thoughts of Henry. "Walt, you're too good to me. Thank you."

He lifted the necklace from the box, unclasped it, and placed it around her neck. The smile that filled his face lit up the night brighter than the front porch lights. Taking her hand in his, he walked her to the door.

"Will you wear it tomorrow?" She nodded. "Get some rest. Tomorrow's a big day. I'll meet you at the end of the aisle at two." He turned the doorknob and opened the door for her.

She stepped inside and turned back.

"Goodnight, beautiful." He winked but didn't turn away.

"Goodnight." She closed the door and touched her pearl necklace. Walt held her heart in the palm of his hands, and she knew he would keep it safe as much as possible. No one was perfect.

Softly she placed one foot in front of the other and stepped towards the stairs.

"Nancy?"

"Mom?"

Her mother came around the corner in her night robe. "Come sit with me. It's our last night before you're a married woman."

"I'd like that." She followed her mom to the living room and snuggled next to her on the sofa.

"I know this isn't happening the way you dreamed of when you were younger, but you are going to be a good wife and mother. And I can imagine you're anxious about how things will go with Walt. Give it time. You two were made for each other."

Footsteps at the entrance drew their eyes up.

"Do you have room for a third?" her dad questioned as he walked in.

"Of course." Nancy patted the spot beside her.

"Nancy, make no mistake, we are proud of you. We all do things we regret. God can take our weaknesses and turn them into strengths. We've been praying for this day since you were born. I have every confidence that Walt will be the husband I have hoped and prayed you would find. We love you so much."

Her father pulled a letter from his pocket. "I wrote you a letter. I'll not read it all to you, but I do want to read the scripture. It's a prayer and a charge.

"And so, from the day we heard, we have not ceased to pray for you, asking that you may be filled with the knowledge of his will in all spiritual wisdom and understanding, so as to walk in a manner worthy of the Lord, fully pleasing to him: bearing fruit in every good work and increasing in the knowledge of God; being strengthened with all power."

He continued his prayer and finished it with the reference. "Colossians 1:9-14."

Tears slipped down Nancy's face, matching both her father's and mother's. "Thank you."

"We won't keep you up, dear. But I want you to know that I'm honored to walk you down the aisle." Her father wrapped Nancy and his wife in a hug.

Approaching the mansion housing the Greenville Art Museum, Nancy caught a glimpse of the castle tower in the back section just before her father turned the car into the driveway. As the road curved, the two-storied, white-columned mansion came into view. The Christmas wreath hanging on the arched front door and topiaries on either side, wrapped in ribbon, added to the allurement of Gassaway Mansion. It was a beautiful setting for a wedding. Again her inadequacies left her feeling unworthy of such a lavish celebration.

At the rehearsal the night before, she'd taken in every detail of the rooms that would house the wedding and the reception. Wood wainscoting, an intricately-carved fireplace surround, and an enormous two-story window set the scene for the ceremony. With the art-filled walls, it had the ambiance of a posh social venue. The large entry hall that was set up for the reception was just as elegant.

"I still can't believe you're marrying Walt." Kathy's voice pulled Nancy out of her thoughts. "There were times I secretly wished you would marry someone else so I could have a chance."

"What? You never mentioned you had feelings for Walt." Nancy leaned closer to her sister in the backseat of the car.

Kathy patted Nancy's arm. "Don't get all twisted up over it. He never meant that much to me. It was more like a passing fancy. How could I not have those thoughts, with you and every friend I ever brought home going ga-ga over him all the time? He was always meant to be yours. Deep down, I knew that."

"Okay. You had me worried. I love you, and I don't want there to be anything like that coming between us." She leaned back into the seat.

"Kathy." Their mom turned around from the front. "Don't get your sister upset on her wedding day. This is no time for jokes. One day, you'll understand how anxious a woman is on her wedding day. The smallest thing can send you over the edge."

"Yes, ma'am."

Their father's gaze met Nancy's in the rearview mirror, and he gave her a wink as he parked the car. "It's going to be a beautiful wedding, and in a few hours, our Nancy will be Mrs. Walter Moore."

Nancy swallowed. It sounded strange to her ears, though she had secretly scribbled it on her notebooks more times than she could count through the years. She scanned the property as she took her father's hand and stepped out of the car. This was it.

He pulled her into a tight hug. "I love you, my dear."

"Don't mind me if I sniffle as we walk down the aisle," Mr. Wilson whispered in Nancy's ear as they watched her sister walk down the aisle to the processional music.

Walt's niece and nephew stood before them, giggling. They were adorable in their little outfits. Petey wore black dress pants and a black suit vest with a bow tie over his white dress shirt, and Laura had on a lacy white dress. They were a good distraction from her nervous thoughts. While getting ready earlier, she'd had to stop several times and take deep breaths to keep from hyperventilating.

She touched their shoulders. "It's almost your turn."

The wedding coordinator walked up and guided the children to the entrance of the room.

Nancy's father turned to her. "My precious girl. I wouldn't want to hand you over to a lesser man. I'll be praying for the two of you. I trust God to guide you both."

"Thank you, Daddy." She leaned on his arm and blinked back the moisture in her eyes.

"This way." The coordinator guided them closer to the entrance as the wedding march began playing.

She glanced up at her father one last time when they were positioned at the entrance. When she turned to face the front, her breath caught in her throat as she met Walt's eyes. His face lit up, reminding her of his bright smile the night before. She focused on his face as she and her father walked towards him.

She trembled when her father passed her to Walt, and he grasped her hands. Once again, their eyes locked, and everything else faded away. When Walt squeezed her hands and looked at the pastor, she realized the pastor had already shared scripture with those gathered. Walt guided her to the prayer bench borrowed from their church, and they both kneeled while music played softly.

Walt leaned in, pressed his forehead against hers, and spoke softly. "Father, thank you for the gift of each other. You are a good God who gives good gifts to his people. Help me lead and love Nancy the way Christ leads and loves the church. Show us how to stand firm in you and protect our marriage. Help our marriage grow into more than we ever imagined it could be, and help it be centered on you. Thank you for bringing Nancy into my life. Help her always feel loved and cherished. In Jesus' name, Amen."

The prayer couldn't have been more perfect—even if they were romantically in love. Nancy pulled the embroidered heirloom handkerchief from the center of her bouquet and dabbed her eyes.

"Are you okay?" He touched her chin.

She nodded. She wanted to tell him how beautiful the prayer was and how it made her feel cared for, protected, and wanted, but all she could say was, "Thank you."

He helped her up and guided her back to the pastor, who continued the ceremony. Nancy's chest tightened as they said their vows, yet she was overjoyed once they were done.

"I now pronounce you man and wife."

It didn't seem possible that Walter Moore was her husband.

"You may kiss the bride."

Heat rose to Nancy's face as she looked from Walt's eyes to his lips. Their kiss the night before left her longing for more, and she'd looked forward to this all day. He gently wrapped a hand around the back of her neck and pulled her close as he leaned down. Her eyes fluttered closed as his lips met hers. The same spark and heat she'd felt before ignited. All too quickly, he pulled back, and she recalled they were standing in front of nearly fifty people.

"I now present to you Mr. and Mrs. Walter Douglas Moore."

They turned and looked out at their friends and family. Her eyes scanned the room. The string quartet on the balcony began playing the recessional music, and Walt tugged her forward.

She was sure she looked like a crazy person, smiling from ear to ear. Clinging to Walt's arm, she glanced up at him, and he looked just as happy. Was it possible he was happy about their marriage? She still wondered about his willingness to marry her, but right now, she would bask in the joy that she had just married the man she'd dreamed of marrying since she was a child.

Two hours later, their wedding guests waved them off. They were alone in his car and driving to *their* home. It seemed impossible that a few minutes and a few words forever changed their lives.

The tension and excitement of the day caught up with Nancy, and she yawned. Her eyes blinked and she tried to keep them open, but the rhythmic vibration of the car didn't help. "Sorry, it's not the company."

Walt reached for her hand and interlaced their fingers. "My mom warned me how stressful a wedding day can be for a woman and that it might wear you out." His eyes flashed in her direction before moving back to the road. "I know with our situation, it might be especially stressful, and you have a little peanut demanding much of your energy." His thumb caressed her fingers in reassurance.

His touch renewed her energy. "Thank you for understanding." She twisted her body to watch him. "Right now, I'm okay, despite the yawn. I'm hungry, and that trumps sleeping lately."

"Do we need to pull over so we can get food out of the picnic basket our moms sent with us?"

"No, I can make it the rest of the way to Columbia. Thank you though."

"It will be nice to have you in our home. I've felt bad enjoying it all by myself after all the work you and our moms did to make it feel homey."

"It does feel homey." An image of their new home flashed before her eyes and made her smile. "I know it's not cold enough yet, but I can't wait to use our fireplaces." They had arranged cozy sitting areas in front of the fireplaces in both the living room and the study. She waited for Walt's response, and he bit his lip. "What are you making that face for?"

"Nothing."

"Mm-hmm. I know that look. You're up to something."

"Patience, wife."

Her breath caught. She loved the sound of that.

"Wake up, sleepyhead."

"What?" She wanted to keep sleeping, but her husband, Walt, needed her. She blinked. Oh. It was a dream. Outside the car, homes in their new neighborhood flew past.

"We're almost there, and I wanted to give you a couple of minutes to wake up."

"Thanks." She sat upright and stretched.

The car turned the corner, and their home came into view. It was as picturesque as she remembered.

When he pulled into the driveway, Walt turned to her and grinned. "Don't move." He jumped out of the car and helped her out. Wrapping an arm around her, he guided her to the front door, then stopped. "Wait right here." He ran to the door, unlocked, and opened it. When he returned, he lifted her into his arms, bridal style.

Nancy gasped. She'd wondered if he would carry her over the threshold. It seemed like a silly tradition, especially for them in their circumstance, yet she'd still hoped he would. It shouldn't surprise her. So far, he'd done everything she would hope for with a traditional marriage for love.

He carried her through the entrance and into the living room, where he placed her on the sofa. In front of the sofa, she noted their coffee table had been moved, and in its place was a beautiful arrangement of blankets and pillows facing the fireplace.

"What is this?"

He attempted to hide his grin. "I thought we could eat our dessert in front of the fire. There's a starter log in there. It should be enough to give us a cozy feel but not heat up the house too much. I planned for us to eat our meal at the dining room table first." He gestured to the dining room. "But if you'd prefer, we can eat it all on the floor in front of the fire."

"That's why you had that look in the car." She turned and peeked into the dining room, and it looked like it was set. "What did you do in there?"

She stood and walked to the dining room, where she was greeted with a fully set table for two. He had used the linens from her hope chest, paired with their fine china, crystal goblets, and silver place settings. There were even crystal candlesticks in the center with candles waiting to be lit. "Oh, Walt. This is . . . it's just so thoughtful. Of course I want to eat our meal in here."

"Good." He walked up to her and placed a kiss on her forehead. "I'll be right back. Make yourself comfortable, and we'll eat soon."

Walt made two trips to the car and brought in their luggage and the picnic basket. When he called her to dinner, he had lit the candles and set out the food. It was a light meal of items that didn't require heating—shrimp cocktail, finger sandwiches, a garden salad, and a fruit salad.

After Walt prayed for their meal, they dove in.

"I know this isn't a gourmet meal, but eating in our own dining room on our china with you for the first time makes it the most special meal I've ever had."

Nancy rubbed her chest. "Walt, thank you for making everything so amazing. You keep surprising me."

"This is day one of the rest of our lives together. I don't want you to ever feel like our marriage is less than you had hoped. Give it time. I know something wonderful is growing between us."

Her heart leapt.

Half an hour later, Nancy was comfortably situated on the floor in front of a flickering fire. Walt appeared with two plates of sliced lemon meringue pie.

"Lucille," Nancy said knowingly.

"Yep. She also sent an apple pie. She said that one would freeze if we wanted to save it for later."

"Might be a good idea. If the two of us try to eat both pies before they go bad, I'm going to look like I'm much further along than I really am." She patted her belly.

Walt laid the plates down and joined her. "You'll be beautiful when you begin showing."

"We'll see." She shook her head. "At this point, I just look bloated when I'm in my underwear."

Walt's eyes drifted to her stomach before color filled his cheeks. He quickly looked down at his pie and took a bite.

With the awkwardness of their first night together as man and wife, that might not have been the best choice of words. A bite of pie was a good idea. The tang of the lemon made her mouth water as it hit her tongue.

"We can take our time leaving tomorrow. We don't have anything scheduled until dinner at the bed and breakfast. With it being Sunday, not much is open, but it will be a good day to walk around and see some of the architecture. I ordered us a map and marked the most scenic areas. We could also drive out to the beach if it's nice."

"Mmm, I'd like that." The combination of the heat from the fire, a full belly, and thoughts of walking along the beach relaxed her. But the tension in her neck and shoulders remained. She set her fork down and reached up to squeeze the muscles on either side of her neck.

"Let me help you with that." Walt took his last bite of pie and slid next to her. "May I?"

A refusal was on the tip of her tongue, but she didn't argue. He was trying to make everything special, and she didn't want to take away his joy. "Thanks."

He had her shift so her back was to him as he leaned against the sofa with his legs on either side of her. The second he touched her shoulders, electricity radiated from the spot. He began to press and knead her shoulders, and she sank back against him. "Mmm, Walt, this . . . is just what I needed." Why had she considered telling him no?

As he worked her muscles, Walt described some of the sites he had researched for their Charleston visit. She tried paying attention, but her eyes kept drifting shut.

"Nancy?"

"Mm-hmm."

"Nancy, let's get you upstairs."

"Mm-hmm." A bed would be nice. This bed kept moving. "Walt?"

"Yes."

Her eyes were so heavy, but she finally managed to open them. Walt's face was right next to hers. "Oh." She glanced around and realized he was carrying her up the stairs. "You can put me down. I can walk."

"I've got you. We're almost there." He set her down just outside of the master bedroom.

"Thank you." She was now fully awake, and her heart raced. Maybe he wouldn't notice the flush on her face in the dim hall light. What would he expect on their wedding night? Just because they had married for the baby didn't mean he might not have expectations. She had heard that many guys didn't need an emotional connection to want sex.

"Nancy." He ran his fingers across her cheek. "We'll take things at your pace. But maybe we can practice with a kiss again."

Yes, please. She nodded and closed her eyes. She felt his lips gently touch hers first, then his hands touched her cheeks and slid into her hair. The kiss intensified, and she lifted onto her toes to get closer. His arms slid around her back and pulled her in tight. She felt lightheaded, but his sudden release pulled her back to reality, and her eyes popped open. How had he moved so far away that quickly?

"Goodnight, wife. I . . . goodnight."

"Goodnight." She watched as he entered his room and shut the door. He never turned back.

Shaking her head, she stepped into the master bedroom and dropped to the bed. She loved him, and it was hard waiting for those feelings to develop in him. Did he still see her as a little kid? *Stop it*, she silently chastised herself. He had been romantic all day. There was no reason to let this bother her. That kiss didn't *feel* like one he'd give a little kid.

He had always been a man of his word. They had their whole lives to figure this out. She could be patient—at least, she would try.

Chapter Sixteen

alt's lips felt warm, and Nancy never wanted to stop kissing him. He pulled away. Where did he go? She tried to see, but it was hazy in the dark. *Walt*. Her words were muffled.

She blinked. Where was she? With a sigh, she realized it was a dream, and she was in bed in her new home. She took in the room. It was larger than her bedroom at home and had an attached bathroom. It wasn't as ornate as the rooms on the main level, but it still had beautiful wood trim. The large pair of windows looked out onto the balcony and a grassy area beyond. She hoped to one day enjoy mornings sitting out there with Walt.

Squeezing her eyes shut, she recalled how quickly he recoiled from their kiss. Before that, she had thought he was beginning to have romantic feelings for her. Today was a new day. She sat up, and nausea took hold. As she reached for her crackers on the nightstand, she remembered she'd not had a chance to unpack her saltines and had been too out of it to pour herself a glass of water. Yet there on the nightstand was a container of saltines, a glass, and a water pitcher. How could she doubt Walt's intentions? He had been nothing less than amazing. Unfortunately, it was too late for the saltines, and she darted for the bathroom.

After getting to know their new toilet, she brushed her teeth and sat back on the bed, munching crackers.

A soft knock drew her attention to the door. "Are you okay?"

"Yes, I'm eating some crackers now to help. Thank you for setting them out."

"You're welcome. Can I come in?"

"Um." Nancy glanced down. She only wore a thin nightgown. "Just a minute." Thankfully, her robe was packed on the top of the suitcase. She quickly pulled it on, smoothed out the bedcovers, and sat on the bed. "Okay."

He opened the door and joined her on the bed. "Sorry you're feeling bad. I don't really know how morning sickness works. Are you hungry, or is your appetite ruined? I can make breakfast if you'd like."

"I'm starving." She reached for another cracker. "But you don't have to make me anything. I can fix something or just eat cereal."

"No, ma'am. You sit right here." He patted her leg. "Or come down and watch if you want, but I'm doing breakfast. My mom made some cinnamon rolls, and I can scramble eggs in no time. Plus we have the fruit they sent. Would that work?"

"It sounds nice. Thank you. I'm not going to know what to do when you go to work and I'm on my own for meals."

"I might just have to come home every day for lunch to make sure you're fed."

"Or I can have lunch ready for you. Now breakfast is another thing. Don't expect me to climb out of bed and whip you up something. I was barely able to make it to work on time the last few weeks with this nausea."

"Well then, I can make the breakfasts and leave some for you when you're not able to get up before I leave." He leaned over and kissed her on the forehead. "Good morning, wife. I should have said that first, but I was distracted with worry." He stood up. "Come down when you're ready. We can eat and then get on the road so we have plenty of daylight to sightsee."

As they sped down the interstate, Nancy flipped through the pamphlets Walt had collected about historical places in Charleston. "I'd like to tour at least one of the historical homes. From the pictures, the interiors remind me of England."

"I imagine so. This town was originally designed by British citizens."

Nancy chuckled. "True. I hadn't thought about that." She checked her watch. "We should be approaching our exit."

For the next few minutes, Nancy navigated, until they pulled in front of a beautiful white clapboard home. The front was graced with a balcony-covered bay window and a large wooden door painted Charleston green to match the shutters. It held a festive Christmas wreath of magnolia leaves with a large red velvet bow. A columned side porch with a balcony on the second floor overlooked a gated garden. Both the porch and balcony had garlands strung along iron railings.

"Walt, it's beautiful. Thank you for setting this up in spite of me telling you I didn't need a honeymoon."

He gave her a slow grin. "You're more than welcome. Let's go meet the owners."

Walt helped her out of the car and up the stairs of the grand home. The door opened before they knocked. They were met by a woman with graying hair who stood several inches shorter than Nancy.

"Mr. and Mrs. Moore! It's so good to have you join us. I'm Ruth Beaumont, and this—" She turned her head just as a stocky, graying man came up and smiled. "This is my husband, Charles. We're honored to host y'all for your honeymoon. Nancy, you just follow me to the parlor, and we'll let the men get your bags."

"Thank you, Mrs. Beaumont."

"Now, I'll have none of that Mrs. business. Call me Ruth." Ruth grabbed Nancy's hand and led her down the hall.

Nancy was so busy processing being called Mrs. Moore, she hardly noticed the details of the home. Once they were seated, she caught a glimpse of Walt with a suitcase through the bay window. Her heart fluttered.

"How about some sweet tea?" Ruth pointed to a mahogany sideboard where a pitcher of tea and several glasses sat.

"Yes, ma'am. That sounds nice." While Ruth poured the tea, she glanced around the room. The furniture was all finely detailed and polished mahogany, and elaborate white molding decorated every doorway, window, and the ceiling. "This reminds me of London. Is the furniture from England?"

Ruth smiled and handed Nancy her tea before joining her on the settee. "This house was built in 1784. We've collected furniture from that time period in the Sheraton style. Some is from England, but Charleston was an epicenter of furniture makers during the eighteenth century, so some are locally made. There are also pieces made in the northern colonies. You've been to London?"

"I have." Her mind drifted to Henry, but Walt's arrival in the parlor chased away the sad thoughts.

Walt's eyes met Nancy's, and he winked. "Our bags are in our room." He turned to Ruth. "The room is perfect. Thank you."

"Wonderful. I was just getting acquainted with your lovely wife, and she was telling me about London."

Walt's brows raised. "Oh?"

"Yes. She said the room reminded her of London."

His eyes shifted back to Nancy, and his brow furrowed.

"Mrs. Beaumont—I mean, Ruth—said some of the furniture is from England, so I imagine that's why."

"And Charleston was filled with loyalists during the Revolutionary War. They had close ties to England, so it was highly influential on the design of the homes and furniture. But enough about that. Your husband called ahead and asked me to put together lunch. I have she-crab soup and toasted ham and Swiss ready. How's that?"

"It sounds like it will hit the spot." Nancy stood, glad to change the topic from England. "I'd love to freshen up first."

"Charles, why don't you show her the room while I set everything out." Ruth took Nancy's empty tea glass before guiding them to the foot of the steps.

"I'll take her. Your husband showed me the room already." Walt placed an arm around Nancy's waist and pulled her close.

Ruth winked. "Of course. You two lovebirds don't want us bothering you every second. When you're ready, you'll find the dining room next to the parlor. Just ring the bell sitting on the table, and we'll serve you. Charles, come help me, please." She tugged her husband down the hall.

As they ascended the stairs, Nancy's heart beat rapidly. Walt had said there was an extra bed, but unless the area was split into two rooms, it would be awkward. Maybe it was a good thing. He might see her in a different light. Despite being sleepy the night before, she recalled he had said they would take things at her pace. That was a lot of pressure. How would she know when he thought of her differently than in the past? Could she tell him she was ready for more now? Or maybe she would show him and kiss him first. She glanced at Walt and blushed at her thoughts.

"Here it is." He opened the door to a room that would fit in any historical English home from the late 1700s. The mahogany canopy bed drew her attention with its elaborate bedding. It was covered with a cream toile decorated with blue pastoral scenes. The same fabric covered the canopy. In the center of one wall, a fireplace was surrounded by marble and a carved mantle. French doors led to the side balcony that she had seen when they first drove up.

"Walt, thank you for this. It's beautiful." The reality of all he had done to make their honeymoon special overcame her, and she turned to embrace him. He hugged her back, but not with the intensity of the night before. Rather than dwell on his response, she pulled him out to the balcony. "The courtyard is lovely too. The whole house is." From above, she could better see the symmetrical design of the garden and pathway that radiated from a fountain in the center.

A slight breeze blew their way, and Nancy shivered. When Walt didn't make a move, she wrapped an arm around him. "I'll need my jacket when we go to the beach."

"You still want to go? It will be chilly with the ocean breeze."

"It will be worth it. Besides, it's sunny out, and that will help. The shade here makes it feel colder." She was hoping for an excuse to snuggle close to him.

"Then we'll go to the beach after lunch." Walt's smile looked forced.

"I'll pop into the bathroom, then let's eat. The she-crab soup sounds delicious." She lowered her voice. "And I know the baby is only the size of a grape, but she's making me hungry nonstop."

This time, his smile was full and genuine.

The soft clip-clop of horses' hooves echoed through the streets as the carriage driver led Nancy and Walt down Meeting Street towards St. Michael's Church. There was the iconic steeple. Nancy had seen it a few times before, but something about snuggling under a wool blanket with Walt gave it an importance it had never held before. Like most of the other buildings in the area, it was decorated for Christmas with wreaths and garlands.

"Do you think we can do this again tomorrow after dark? I'd love to see the Christmas lights."

Walt turned his head, and they were face to face. "I . . . yes, we should do that." He glanced at her lips, then turned away.

She'd made several attempts to get him to kiss her during their quick trip to Sullivan Beach. So far, he'd been a perfect gentleman. Her goal became to get him to kiss her at least once, not counting a bedtime kiss. It almost seemed as if he'd withdrawn more since their kiss the night before. She didn't know what to make of it, and she was scared to ask. She didn't want to hear how he was working up to viewing her as more than a friend.

Maybe he wasn't comfortable kissing in public. The image of him kissing his high school girlfriend from the tailgate of his dad's truck came to mind. He wasn't worried about it back then. Had he changed since becoming a Christian? No. She remembered seeing him kiss his college girlfriend Brenda too.

As they turned onto Broad Street, their driver pointed out City

Hall. Its unique pair of circle windows on the ground level drew her attention away from Walt's indifference.

"Don't you think this looks like it's straight out of a Dickens book?"

"It does have that effect." His brows pinched together. "Does it bring back bad memories when you think of England?"

She thought back to her time in England and with Henry. "You know, it doesn't cause me pain anymore to think of Henry. For a while, I forced him into the recesses of my mind—separating him from memories of my time there whenever England was mentioned. But this time, it didn't bother me. Not like it used to. I'm mad at Henry, but I'm glad I'm not married to him. That would be worse. It's good I learned his true colors."

Walt placed a hand on her cheek and smiled, but his brow remained furrowed.

She reached up and pressed a finger to the space between his eyebrows. "I'm going to be okay. I'm happy things worked out the way they did." She saw her opportunity, wrapped a hand around his neck, and leaned in for a kiss.

He pulled back and frowned. "I don't want to take advantage of you."

"This is my pace." She pulled him back down and kissed him soundly.

It didn't take long for him to reciprocate. Everything else faded away. When they pulled back, Nancy snuggled into his side. "I love you" was on the tip of her tongue but never escaped. As she gradually became aware of their surroundings, she noticed they were on East Battery Street with a view of the water.

They arrived back at the bed and breakfast just in time for dinner, and the Beaumonts served them again. Nancy was glad their hosts didn't join them. She was still lost in their romantic bubble. The elegant silver candelabras alongside the silver, china, and crystal added to the romance. Above them hung a crystal chandelier, and the mahogany table was polished to bring out the rich tones of the intricate inlay.

After a filling meal of crab dip, roasted oysters, poached pear salad, and shrimp and grits, they invited the Beaumonts to join them for dessert. When Nancy declined coffee, Ruth offered a hot cup of winter rose tea. She said she made it herself with rose petals and peppermint from her garden. It complemented the pecan pie nicely.

They learned that Charles owned the Charleston Gazette, which fascinated Nancy. Charles had inside information on so many topics. He told them that earlier in the week, the U.S. had started something called the EPA, the Environmental Protection Agency. They had fun guessing what that might entail.

"Since you are our only guests this first night and honeymooners no less, you can choose if you'd like us to leave breakfast outside of your room by a certain time or if you'd like to eat downstairs any time after eight," Ruth said as she cleared the dessert plates from the table.

Nancy and Walt glanced at one another, and he raised a brow. When Nancy shrugged, Walt suggested they come down for breakfast at nine but have coffee for him and more winter rose tea for Nancy waiting outside their door at eight thirty.

This time when they ascended the steps to their room, Nancy was more hopeful about things moving along in their relationship. Once he gave into the kiss on their carriage ride, he'd been less standoffish and even seemed to enjoy their touches and cuddles.

In the bathroom, Nancy rushed to change, remove her makeup, and brush her teeth. While she waited for Walt to get ready, she sat at the antique mahogany secretary and wrote in her journal. She rubbed her belly and thought about the child one day reading to see that despite having a biological father who didn't claim her—or his—mother, Walt had stepped in like a white knight, and Nancy had loved him for years. She was determined to finally tell him either tonight or the following night that she loved him, before they returned home. He might not say it back, but at least he would know how she felt.

While she finished writing, Walt appeared in the doorway of the bathroom. When she stood, his eyes roamed her body from head to toe, and though she wore a full-length gown and robe, she felt exposed. *This is marriage*, she reminded herself. *Leaving yourself exposed.*

Her heart raced as she moved towards him and leaned for a kiss. When he returned her kiss, she relaxed and wrapped her arms around him. The kiss became more desperate than any of their previous kisses, and his hands moved from her shoulders to her waist. When they finally took a breath, she reached for his hand and tugged him towards the bed.

Like a statue, Walt didn't budge, and when she met his eyes, he shook his head. "I don't think we're ready for that."

"But it's our honeymoon. I'm ready, I promise."

Walt pressed his forehead against hers and groaned. "Not tonight, okay?"

Though it hurt, she decided not to push further. She backed away and climbed onto the big bed. He had insisted on taking the daybed even though he looked like a giant in it.

Nancy lay in bed, running through the day's events until she couldn't stand it anymore. "Walt, why did you marry me?"

She was met with silence and guessed he was asleep.

"Have you ever felt like God was speaking to you?" His voice was low but clear.

"I don't think so."

"The first time you told me about your pregnancy, I thought I heard God tell me to marry you." She heard him shift in the bed. "I didn't say anything to you right away, because my first thought was that I was losing my mind or it was my imagination running away with me. But as I prayed about it that day, inside, I knew God was confirming it. When I got the job in Columbia, it was like another confirmation. I knew if I didn't follow God's lead, everything in my life would be wrong. It might not make sense to others, but I trust God."

It wasn't the confession of love Nancy wished for, but it was touching. "That's sweet. I'm trying to trust God in all of this too. I think I'm mostly there."

"I know this is an unusual circumstance for marriage, but we've always been close. We're getting there, but I don't want to rush things."

Nancy wasn't sure how to respond. She didn't want to rush him, but she was ready for more. Each time she kissed him today, he had seemed a little more responsive, so she determined to keep showing him instead of just telling him she was ready. "Thanks." *I guess.* As she drifted off, she prayed that God would help her to show Walt how she felt.

As Nancy washed her face for bed, she recalled her earlier kiss with Walt. It had only been a peck and happened in the ground level hallway of the Hayward Washington house, underneath the mistletoe. They were part of a tour group. The guide was speaking and the others had walked ahead when Nancy stopped Walt, pointed to the mistletoe, and stole a kiss.

The rest of the day, Nancy was ineffective in getting Walt's attention other than hand-holding. Though he did wrap an arm around her and pull her close during their evening carriage ride. That was romantic—sipping hot chocolate in the back of the carriage, snuggled under a blanket while viewing Christmas lights and decorations.

She closed her eyes and blew out a breath. It was the last night of their honeymoon. She had hoped to tell him she loved him, but the opportunity never arose. With a quick application of face lotion, she was ready to face the man she loved . . . in their honeymoon suite. Thoughts of returning home and sleeping in their separate rooms lingered in the back of her mind. She shook her head and opened the door. Walt met her at the door with an armful of clothes and his toiletry kit and leaned down to kiss her forehead before taking his turn in the bathroom.

Part of her wanted to go straight to bed rather than set herself up for more disappointment, but instead she again sat down at the secretary and wrote in her journal. She recalled the couple with their toddler who joined them on their second historical home tour. They made such a sweet domestic picture with the husband holding the sleepy little girl while the wife folded her arm around his.

Nancy blinked back tears. As she squeezed her eyes shut, warm, strong arms wrapped around her shoulders.

"Today was nice." Walt leaned down and kissed the top of her head.

Her eyes remained closed, and she nodded. His hand wrapped around hers, and he tugged her up. When her eyes found his, she saw longing just before he leaned down and touched his lips to hers. His relentless kiss left her feeling like she was spinning.

"Nancy," he said against her lips.

She pulled back slightly, and his eyes reflected the dazed state she felt.

He spoke again. "Do you still think you're ready?"

Her heart raced, and she nodded. He lifted her and carried her gently to the bed.

Chapter Seventeen

The smell of eggs and bacon pulled Nancy from a sweet dream. The details of her dream were vague but happy. She remembered she and Walt were madly in love and happily playing with a little girl on the beach. As it faded, reality replaced it and memories of the night before woke her fully. She blinked and found Walt setting up their breakfast on the small table next to the window overlooking their balcony and the garden.

He looked her way and smiled, causing heat to rush to her face. Just as quickly, her shoulders tensed and she worried he might tell her it had been too soon.

In three steps, he was beside the bed and leaned down to kiss her on the lips. When his fingers tangled with her hair and he let out a sigh mirroring the one in her head, she relaxed.

She'd not said she loved him, but she would soon. For now, it was enough to know they had turned a corner in their marriage.

Nancy felt peaceful during their ride back to Columbia. She'd been excited but anxious when they first left for their honeymoon and never dreamed it would turn out so well. All day, Walt had been playful and attentive. Gone was the hesitancy of before.

When they pulled into their driveway, Walt turned and grinned. "Don't move. I'm carrying you over the threshold."

"Again?" Nancy giggled at his silly grin.

He nodded and wiggled his eyebrows. "It's different now." He popped out of the car, swept her into his arms, and lifted her up. Key in hand, he managed to open the door without releasing her. Once inside, he set her down and drew her into a long kiss.

She inhaled deeply and savored the moment, holding him tightly.

"You go relax while I get the bags."

She shook her head. "I need to stretch, and I'll pour us some sweet tea."

"Perfect." He pecked her on the nose before turning back to the door.

She poured their drinks and set them on the coffee table in front of the sofa. Taking a sip, she looked around and imagined little ones filling the house. She chuckled at the thought that they might one day have more children.

"I've got everything in." Walt broke into her thoughts, and she turned so she could see him. He bit his lip and held up his suitcase. "Are you okay with me moving into the room with you?" He moved closer to the sofa, and his jaw tensed.

Smiling, she stood up and kissed him. "Yes. I want you to." She patted the sofa. "Why don't you sit down and have some tea, and then we can both go up and move your things into the master bedroom."

He dropped the suitcase, sat down, and pulled her into his lap. "Perfect." He pecked her lips and reached for a glass of tea.

Hand in hand, Walt and Nancy explored their neighborhood after a late lunch. The trees were bare, but there was still plenty of green on the bushes. Most of the homes looked like they were built around the same time as theirs, but a few looked newer.

"This week, I'll work on decorating for Christmas," Nancy said as she admired the decorations on the homes. "We have a magnolia tree in the side yard that I can pull leaves from to make a couple of wreaths like the one at the bed and breakfast. I'm sure the fabric store has some big red ribbon."

"I like that idea. You've already made our home cozy on the inside. I trust whatever you want to do."

"Thanks." She recalled the happy family the day before. "Do you remember the little family that had the toddler on the tour with us yesterday?"

"I do."

"They called her Julie. I've been thinking that would be a nice name if we have a girl."

Walt chuckled. "You're determined it's going to be a girl, aren't you?"

Nancy shrugged. "Maybe. Not that I have anything to do with it. I do like that name, though. What do you think?"

"I like it, but it's not up to me."

Nancy pulled him to a stop. "Walt, look at me." He turned to her, and she lowered her voice. "You have every right. You are her—or his— father. That is part and parcel of us getting married. I don't want this to be an issue every time we have to make a decision. You're my husband and the head of our household."

Walt nodded and reached for her hands, which she didn't realize she'd folded into fists. When she relaxed them, he placed her hands on his waist and wrapped his arms around her. He leaned down and whispered, "You're right."

She lifted her head and kissed him, then reached for his hand and tugged him along. "Glad that's settled."

As they turned the corner back to their street, Nancy noticed their next-door neighbor wrapping garland around her front porch railing.

He whispered, "That's Mrs. Butler. I forgot to tell you about her.

She's a widow and invited us to her church." He waved when the white-haired Mrs. Butler turned towards them.

"Hi, y'all." Mrs. Butler stepped down from her porch and met them on the sidewalk. Turning to Nancy, she reached out a hand. "Welcome to the neighborhood. I'm Fanny Butler. Your husband told me you were to be married this past Saturday. Congratulations. It's so nice to have another young couple join the neighborhood. It's Nancy, right?"

"Yes, Mrs. Butler." Nancy shook Mrs. Butler's hand as she examined her. She was about Nancy's height of five-five and looked well put together with her chin-length bouffant. She looked older than her mother.

"No pretense is needed, dear. Call me Fanny." Fanny still held Nancy's hand and clasped it with her other. "I just know we're going to be good friends. In fact, you should join me on Monday mornings at ten. I have a women's Bible study at my home. It will be a great way for you to get to know some ladies."

"Oh, I . . ." She glanced at Walt, wondering how much he knew about her and if she should accept the invitation. He just smiled. "Yes, sure. That sounds nice."

"Before I forget, I made an apple pie for the two of you. I made it this morning and wasn't sure when you would be in. Give me just a minute, and I'll go get it."

As soon as Fanny closed her door, Nancy peppered Walt with questions. "She seems nice. Is she a nice lady, or do you think I need to worry about her? You said she's a widow. Do you think she'll be nosing around because she's lonely?" Nancy was a little worried about someone figuring out their secret. Mrs. Butler seemed to know so much about them already. "I wonder what her pie is like. Have you heard if she's a good cook? I'm spoiled with Lucille's pies."

"Yes, I think she is a sincerely nice neighbor. No, I don't think you need to worry. Let's see, what else? Oh, no, I don't think she'll be overly nosy. I've only seen her twice. She's gone a lot. And yes, she's a good cook. She brought me a meal when I moved into the house. It was a delicious chicken, broccoli, and rice casserole covered in cheddar cheese." Walt licked his lips.

"You like that kind of casserole?" Nancy made a mental note. She was going to have to come up with a selection of meals to cook. She didn't feel comfortable using Walt's hard-earned money to hire a maid. She planned to do everything herself.

"I do. I like lots of things. But you don't have to cook all the time if you don't want to."

"I'm not expecting you to come home and eat sandwiches or boxed cereal, and I certainly wouldn't expect you to come home after a long day of working and cook. I can cook—I just have to figure out meals for two that we both like." She thought about the many meals their families had eaten together. They usually had a tableful of food, and though she paid attention to him, she never paid particular attention to what he ate. Why would she, when his handsome face was much more interesting?

She was so caught up in her thoughts and staring at her handsome husband, she didn't notice Mrs. Butler walk back up.

"I hope you enjoy it. A friend gave me the apples from a farm on the outskirts of town. He sells his apples, too, if you want local apples. He has several kinds of trees. I made this with Golden Delicious, and it is delicious, if I do say so myself."

Walt took the pie, and Nancy peeked under the foil.

"It looks delicious, Mrs. Butler. Thank you."

"Now I told you to call me Fanny, and I meant it." The older woman placed a hand on her hip.

"Okay, Mrs.—sorry, Fanny. It might take me some time to remember."

"I'm just giving you a hard time, though I do sincerely mean it. Now if you want to warm the pie, I suggest putting it on a pan in a 350-degree oven for about fifteen minutes."

Her eyes shot to Walt's arm around Nancy, and she smiled. "I won't keep the two of you. By the way, I invited your husband to visit my church. It's the one three blocks over. We have quite a few couples around your age. Oh, and here's my card." She pulled a calling card out of her pocket and turned it over to where she had written her phone number. "Please don't hesitate to call me if you need anything. I can tell you where to get the best produce, who the best plumber is, or whatever you need."

Nancy examined the card with the elegant engraved script. *Mrs. Fanny Butler.* "I'm so glad to meet you. Thank you for making us feel welcome and for feeding my husband before I moved in. This seems like a lovely neighborhood."

"Oh, it is, and it will be even better with the two of you." With a wave, she was off.

"She's a talker, but she does seem nice." Nancy turned to the walkway of their home.

"She definitely has that southern charm. With us being new here, I'm sure it will be invaluable to have a neighbor who's so helpful. It makes me feel better about you being home alone during the day too."

As they entered the house, Walt started towards the kitchen before turning back. "Want some pie?"

Nancy glanced at the pie and then smirked. "Only if I get to snuggle with you on the sofa while eating it."

He laid the pie on the counter before turning to sweep Nancy into his arms. "You make a hard demand, Mrs. Moore. But if I must, I must. Shall we heat it?"

She shook her head. "That will take too long."

"Your wish is my command. Cold pie it is. I could warm up some milk while I slice it. That will only take a couple of minutes."

"I guess I can wait for that." Nancy played with the ends of his hair and stared into his brown eyes before lifting up and kissing him.

After a few seconds, he pulled back. "If you keep doing that, we won't get any pie."

She shrugged playfully and turned away. "I'll leave you alone then."

He reached for her arm and pulled her into one more kiss. "I wish I had scheduled a longer honeymoon."

"Me too. I don't want to think about you being gone all day tomorrow."

As Nancy drifted off to sleep that night, she smiled to herself. She had finally said "I love you." It happened when they were in the throes of passion and she couldn't stop the words from escaping. To her delight, he said it back.

Chapter Eighteen

Swedish meatballs, steak Diane, beef bourguignon, chicken Kiev, chicken a la king, chicken broccoli rice casserole . . . Nancy sat at the kitchen table, working on a list of recipes to make for Walt. She grabbed her grocery list and added the ingredients for the recipes to the fruits, vegetables, and other staples already listed.

Setting it aside, she hopped up to set the table while humming a Beatles song. Walt had promised to pick up sandwiches and bring them home to eat together for lunch. Things were more perfect than she ever dreamed they could be.

She laid out her moss-green napkins and matching placemats with her white Corelle plates ringed with a cute little floral design in a color slightly darker than the napkins. While she poured their drinks, she heard Walt pull into the carport and rushed to meet him at the door.

"Honey, I'm home," he called out as he opened the door. His smile widened when he saw her standing there.

"Hi."

He leaned down and greeted her with a lingering kiss. "I could get used to welcomes like this. You're the best sight when I walk in the door." He set the bag of food he held on the table in the hall, wrapped his arms around her waist, and swung her around.

"What did you bring us?" Nancy tried to peek into the bag as she led him into the kitchen.

"A Reuben for me and a turkey club for you."

"You remembered, although lately I've had odd cravings. Did it come with a pickle? That's something I've been craving too."

"Yes, it came with a pickle." He kissed her nose as they entered the kitchen. "Doesn't this look nice? Thanks for making our lunch special," he said, gesturing to the set table. "Mmm. I smell cinnamon. You've been baking too?"

"No, there's barely anything in the pantry. I wrapped two pieces of Mrs. Butler's pie in foil, and they're heating up in the oven."

"I bet it's even better warm." He laid out their food, then prayed. "Tell me about your day."

"I've been planning meals and organizing the kitchen. I hope you don't mind that I switched some things around from the way you had them."

"Of course not. Mmm, this Reuben is perfect. Just the right amount of sauce and sauerkraut."

"Mine's tasty too. You'll have to show me where you got them."

"This café is close to my bank. I can pick up from there when I come home for lunch or even for dinner, if you're not feeling well. Plus, there's a diner close to work that I hear has great food too."

"Perfect. I can also pick up food and come to you for lunch sometimes so you don't always have to spend your time driving home."

"It's not a long drive. I can easily get to you."

"Yes, but I want to see where you work. I could bake some cookies to share with your coworkers and bring you lunch. I plan to go to the grocery store after you leave. I have the ingredients for oatmeal raisin and chocolate chip cookies on my list."

"Both of those sound delicious. Why don't we wait a bit before you come visit me? I'm still figuring things out."

"That's fine. I've got plenty to keep me busy here. But I don't want to wait too long to visit you at work. I'd like to be able to imagine where you are when you're gone."

Walt nodded. "I'll let you know. In the meantime . . ." He pulled her into a hug and kissed her. "I like coming home to you and having our privacy."

"Walt." She pulled back and covered her mouth. "I had a mouthful of food."

"Sorry. I couldn't help myself."

"Tell me about your day. Better yet, describe where you work so I can imagine you there. Since someone won't let me come visit."

"It's not that I won't let you. It's just . . . never mind." He ran his fingers through his hair. "I have a corner office that's in the back of a large open area. It's filled with a desk and credenza and two guest chairs. Beside my office is a conference room, then there's an assistant manager, and beside him is the loan officer. We have a receptionist outside of our three offices. There's an open space with a table for people to write out their checks for deposit or fill out withdrawal forms. Then the three tellers are on the opposite side from the offices, behind a counter. They also have a drive-through that they service."

"You spend most of your time in your office?"

"About half of my time is there. I also have meetings in the conference room and outside of the bank."

"Okay." She smirked. "I'll just have to wait and see for myself. My cookies might actually win you favor with your staff. You should be begging me to come."

"I'm sure your cookies will be a hit. I've always been fond of your cookies." He winked.

Nancy's heart leapt as she thought of the times she'd tried impressing him with her baking skills in the past. It was nice to know it had an effect.

Nancy had a bounce in her step as she pushed her cart through the grocery store. It was a momentous occasion to be making her first trip to the grocery as a married woman and preparing to make her first home-cooked meal for her husband. Her husband, Walt . . . A little girl's dreams came true.

Internally, she sighed. Even when they were planning the wedding, she struggled to grasp that it was really happening. Things had come so close with Henry. Until they said their I dos, she'd worried history would repeat itself—this time with the groom running away. Yet here she was. Even their honeymoon turned out more perfect than she'd anticipated. She'd thought it would take months to get where they were, but everything fell into place.

She scanned her list as she strolled down the produce aisle. Carrots. She eased her cart towards them. Just as she reached for the last bunch, a sandy blonde-haired woman who had been eyeing the celery grabbed them.

"Oh. I . . . I thought you were getting celery." Nancy was annoyed but didn't want to make a scene. She didn't know anyone in town but Mrs. Butler, and she should give this lady the benefit of the doubt. Maybe she didn't see Nancy reaching for it first.

"Sorry, I'm distracted and rushing around here. My almost eight-year-old is sick in the car, and I'm picking up the ingredients for chicken soup."

"Poor thing. By all means, you keep the carrots. I don't have to have them for dinner tonight."

"Thank you so much!" The woman tossed the carrots and celery into her cart, grabbed an onion, and hurried off.

In just six and a half more months, Nancy would have her own little one to worry about. She glanced down at her belly. It was hard to imagine a life was growing in there. Some of her clothes were getting snug in the middle, but for the most part, she looked the same.

Nancy marked the carrots off her list. They were her last item. She could ask Walt to stop by when he was coming home another day if she really needed them. Crackers! She'd forgotten to add them to the list and was almost out. She studied the signs at the end of the aisles, trying to figure out which one held the crackers. They were on the same aisle as the prepackaged cookies, and she was relieved to find the saltines in stock. They seemed to have the best effect on her nausea.

"Looks like we have the same idea again," said the blonde from earlier. "My son insists on having saltines with his chicken noodle soup. I'm just glad my work let me have the day off so I could stay home with him."

Nancy smiled, mostly because she was thankful there was more than one box of saltines. Otherwise, she might have had a battle on her hands. Not knowing her way around town, she wouldn't have wanted to risk not finding saltines. Morning sickness was no joke. It wasn't even confined to first thing in the morning. She often found herself nibbling on the crackers multiple times between meals.

Slowly she perused the rest of the aisle to see if anything else struck her fancy now that she had all the important things. It would take a few more trips to get a better grasp of where to find everything in the store.

Somewhere between the Apple Jacks and Cocoa Krispies cereal, Nancy realized the blonde woman seemed familiar, but she couldn't quite place her. The woman was stunningly beautiful, though the dark circles under her eyes showed that she was exhausted. She imagined it was from staying up with a sick child. Had she and Walt seen her while touring the town with the real estate agent? She shook her head. Maybe she'd see the woman again.

She hurried down the aisle with thoughts of getting home and making the perfect meal for Walt of chicken Kiev, a salad, scalloped potatoes, and chocolate pots de crème. She'd found an easy recipe for the chocolate dessert in a newlywed cookbook her mom gave her and couldn't wait to try it out.

When Nancy got in line to check out, the woman from earlier walked past with a bag of groceries, and Nancy waved. "I hope your son gets better quickly. Maybe the chicken soup will hit the spot."

"Thanks."

"By the way, I'm Nancy—Nancy Moore." Her new name was going to be hard to get used to. "I'm new to the area, but you look familiar to me."

The woman pursed her lips and tilted her head. "I agree, there's something familiar about you too." She snapped her fingers. "You're Walt's new wife. I work with him at the bank, and we go way back. Nice to meet you. Sorry I don't have time to talk more now. I'm sure I'll see you around." She turned and started to walk off, then stopped and looked back. "By the way, I'm Brenda Charles."

Walking to the car, Nancy tried to recall how she might know Brenda. Charles didn't ring a bell. She'd known some Brendas through the years. It wasn't until the grocery bagger finished loading her bags into the trunk that it hit her. It was Walt's Brenda from college—and he'd not told her Brenda was working with him.

The entire car ride home, Nancy tried to imagine why Walt hadn't told her. The only reason she could imagine was that he still had feelings for Brenda. It made sense. He'd had a long relationship with her and had bonded with her physically—a lot, apparently. Nancy remembered how devastated he'd been after the breakup.

She recalled their conversation before getting married, when he revealed his past with Brenda. Working with her must have made him feel guilty. She hated the thought that he'd been with someone else intimately, but before seeing Brenda in person, it was easier to handle. The thought of seeing Brenda regularly changed things. She didn't want to see Brenda, nor did she want to see them together, and she definitely didn't want them working together. Could Brenda be why Walt didn't want Nancy going to the office? The longer she thought about it, the more worked up she became.

"Maybe there's a perfectly good explanation," she huffed out. She recalled Brenda talking so sweetly about her son. Hopefully Brenda was happily married and it was a nonissue.

When she pulled into the driveway, anxiety hit her again. She laid her head against the steering wheel. "God, please help me. I felt so insecure coming into this marriage but thought I had moved past that. And regardless of whether he still has feelings for Brenda, he deceived me by not telling me she was here—and works with him. Just help me. I'm so tired of being stressed, and I know it's not good for the baby." She rubbed her belly.

Reluctantly, she got out of the car. Her special dinner didn't seem so special any more. Reaching into the trunk, she balanced two bags in her arms and made her way to the house just as Mrs. Butler pulled up and jumped out.

"Let me help you with those groceries."

Mrs. Butler was one of the most energetic women Nancy knew. And that wasn't even taking into account her age. "Thanks, Mrs. Butler." The truth was, what little energy the baby left her with had now largely disappeared along with her recent revelation.

"I'm going to have you remembering to call me Fanny soon enough, dear." She'd already grabbed the last two bags, shut the trunk, and was walking in behind Nancy.

Nancy forced a smile. "Fanny. Hmph. I'll keep working on it."

"Nancy, you've been crying." Fanny laid the bags onto the kitchen counter.

Reaching up to touch her face, Nancy found that it was wet. "Oh . . . I . . . I guess so."

"Let's get these groceries put away, and you can come over to visit. I'll pull out a plate of cookies and we can drink hot tea or coffee. Your choice."

"I don't know." She didn't want Fanny to think badly about Walt. All of this might be nothing, and besides that, she barely knew the woman.

"You don't even have to talk about what's bothering you. I'd just like to get to know you better. Besides, I sort of have an ulterior motive."

"You do?" Nancy felt a frown form on her face.

"I heard you are something called a . . . what is it?" She pressed a finger to her chin. "Oh, yes, a paralegal."

Nancy nodded.

"Yes, well, I have a ministry to women in difficult circumstances, and they sometimes need a lawyer, but the lawyer who is helping me doesn't have enough time to do it all. It would be very part-time if you're interested. Oh, I'm getting ahead of myself."

Nancy was immediately intrigued. Maybe this was an opportunity to keep doing what she loved—at least until the baby came.

After they'd put away the groceries, Fanny again invited Nancy to her home. The design was similar to Nancy and Walt's house, but most of the wood trim was painted white, and it was filled with antiques. Nancy stopped and examined a dark wood bookcase with glass doors and an intricate inlay of lighter wood.

"My parents collected antiques and gave me a love for them. Some of what we—" Sadness flashed through Fanny's eyes. "I—have was theirs, but much of it, Floyd and I collected." She pointed to a picture frame sitting on the counter. It showed Fanny and a white-haired man smiling at one another. She didn't look much different in the picture. "He died three years ago from a heart attack. We were married forty-nine years."

"I'm so sorry. I can't imagine how hard that was."

"It has been hard. We went through a lot together. I'll share that with you sometime. Why don't you make yourself comfortable while I get out the cookies?" She pulled out a chair from the kitchen table for Nancy. "Do you prefer hot tea, coffee, or sweet tea?"

"Hot tea. Do you have Earl Grey?" Though she really craved the winter rose tea that Ruth Beaumont had sent her home with from the bed and breakfast.

"I do. I'll just be a minute putting the water on, then I'll let you sample some of my cookies."

"Thank you." Nancy watched Fanny flit around the kitchen. She poured water into a kettle, then pulled cookies from a tin and arranged them on a platter. When Nancy looked down, she noticed an open Bible and book sitting on the table.

"I think you'd like this book," Fanny said as she laid the platter of cookies down and reached for the book on the table. "It's a book of faith-filled poems with scripture interspersed." She flipped it over. "Oh, and the author is from London. I met her in New York when I was there for training with my ministry and she came to hear what we were working on. Her husband owns a publishing house out of London, but they recently opened a New York branch. Her name is Margaret Corbyn. She also has a series she's working on called Willowland."

As Fanny spoke, recognition dawned on Nancy. "Yes, I know her. Well, maybe I shouldn't say know her, but I met her in London. She was signing books for her latest Willowland release. I have the signed copy at my house. I haven't read my book yet. I had a lot going on soon after meeting her and forgot about the book until I packed for the move."

"She's a lovely young woman and such a strong Christian. We went to lunch, and I had the opportunity to meet her husband Graham and their daughter Tracey. In fact, they donated to my ministry to help get it off the ground."

Nancy was intrigued. "What is the ministry? You mentioned I might be able to help with my skills as a paralegal."

Fanny smiled, but it was tempered, creating worry lines on her face. "It's called New Hope Pregnancy Center."

Nancy's heart fluttered. Had Fanny guessed at her situation? She thought back to what might have given her away. Walt wouldn't have said anything.

"Its purpose is to help women in crisis pregnancy situations carry their babies to term and not get drawn in by those who tell them abortion is a better option. I know what you're thinking. Yes, abortion is illegal here, but it still happens. We help the women get the support they need—sometimes it's financial, sometimes it's emotional, or it may be medical—but it's always spiritual. There is a spiritual battle at hand over the lives of these babies and the hearts of these women."

Fanny's eyes teared up. "We always point them to Christ. We do Bible studies with the ladies and help them find local churches."

Words escaped Nancy, and her throat constricted. After taking a sip of her tea, she managed to say, "How would my skills help?"

"There are so many things at play causing them to be in crisis. In some cases, there might be an abusive boyfriend or even husband. We sometimes have to have charges brought against them to keep them away from harming the woman, or it might involve making sure the abusive person has no custody rights when the child is born. In a few cases, the parents of the pregnant woman are the problem. We have also facilitated adoptions. As you can imagine, there's a lot of paperwork and research involved with each case. Our lawyer does the work pro bono, but often it's more than he has spare time for. We have the funds to pay you, and you could work as much or as little as you would like. There's room in the lawyer's office for you to work and have access to everything you would need."

"I . . . wow." The woman who gave her the abortion brochure at Planned Parenthood popped into her mind. What if she had given in? This precious life she was carrying would be another statistic. This was an opportunity to help other young women know they could make it through and carry the child to term. "Yes. I mean, well, I guess I need to talk with Walt first, but I'd like to." Walt . . . She'd almost forgotten about Brenda.

She glanced at her watch. "I need to get home and make dinner."

"Don't worry about that. I made you a chicken, broccoli, and rice casserole. It just needs to go in the oven for thirty minutes on 350. I also made angel biscuits and peach cobbler. You can reheat the cobbler."

"Mrs.—sorry, Fanny—you didn't have to do all that. Though it sounds amazing."

"I enjoy it. It's more fun to cook for other people, since there's just me here. It's better for me, too—otherwise I'd just make one meal for the whole week and get bored with it."

"Thank you. You've made us feel so welcome." She thought about all the food Fanny had listed out. "What are angel biscuits?"

Fanny's face lit up. "A little bit of heaven. You'll love them. They're like a cross between biscuits and yeast rolls."

"That sounds delicious." Nancy eyed the assortment of cookies. She'd been listening so intently to Fanny that she'd forgotten they were there.

"Go ahead. I make up batches of different cookies and freeze them, then bring out an assortment each week to share with my Bible study ladies and friends." She pointed to the cookies. "There are Russian tea cookies, hello dollies, spritz cookies, molasses cookies, chocolate crinkle cookies, and lemon snowflakes."

Nancy hardly knew where to start, but if she didn't nibble on something soon, nausea would set in. She picked up a lemon snowflake, and the burst of lemon danced on her tongue. "This is delicious. I'd love to have the recipe."

"Of course. In fact, I'll put what you don't eat from the platter into a container and you can try them all. I'm not one to keep my recipes a secret. You can have them all." Fanny walked to a cabinet and pulled some cards and a pen from the drawer. When she sat back down, Nancy noticed the cards said From the Kitchen of Fanny Butler.

While Nancy ate cookies, she watched Fanny's elegant cursive letters fill the recipe card. After two small cookies, she was done. The unsettled feeling from her earlier revelation returned, and she regretted the second cookie.

Nancy pushed back from the table. "I should go. Thank you for the cookies and making dinner for us. And also for the recipe."

"You're welcome, dear. Before you leave, would you mind if I prayed for you?"

Blinking back the moisture filling her eyes, Nancy shook her head.

Fanny came around the table and laid a hand on Nancy's shoulder. "Heavenly Father, you are so good, and I trust you have a good plan for Nancy and Walt. I pray that you would bless their marriage. Help them as they adjust to marriage. You know what is bothering Nancy. Please give her peace and wisdom. And thank you for blessing me with them as neighbors. In Jesus' name, Amen."

While Fanny prayed, calm overcame Nancy. "Thank you. That was beautiful."

"I'll continue to pray for you." Fanny stood up. "Just give me a minute to get a tote to put all of the food in."

"Honey, I'm home."

Nancy took a deep breath and made herself busy in the kitchen.

"Something smells delicious." Walt walked up behind Nancy and kissed her on the cheek. "I missed you."

She remained silent. Biting her lip, Nancy removed the casserole and placed it on the table. She'd already set everything else out, so she sat down.

"Nancy? Is something wrong?"

"Why don't you pray, and then we can talk."

Walt's brow pinched, and he bowed his head and prayed. After saying "Amen," he looked up. "Did something happen? Why didn't you call me?"

"Go ahead and start eating." She gestured to his food. When he took his first bite, Nancy finally spoke. "I met one of your employees at the grocery store today."

He quickly swallowed. "O-kaay."

Nancy leaned back and crossed her arms. "It was Brenda Charles."

The color drained from Walt's face. "I'm sorry. I was going to tell you."

"She's the reason you didn't want me to go visit you at work?"

He nodded.

"Have you met her husband? Does he know you were the one she dated before?"

He shook his head and looked down.

"You haven't met him, or he doesn't know?"

His eyes snapped back to hers. "She's not . . ." He pressed his lips together and looked away. "She's divorced."

"Divorced?" It was as if the air had been knocked out of her, and Nancy gasped for a breath. She pushed back her chair, stood, and raced to the bathroom, thankful she'd only had cookies and tea in the last few hours.

"Are you okay?" Walt asked from outside of the bathroom.

Nancy rinsed out her mouth and ignored him. Why had she let things go this far? She should have known his swooping in and marrying her was too good to be true. He still had feelings for Brenda. Sinking to the ground, she touched her stomach and silently cried.

"Nancy, speak to me . . . please. I'm so sorry I've hurt you. I promise there is nothing going on, if that's what you're thinking." He was silent for a moment, then spoke again. "Please let me in. Please let me explain."

Closing her eyes, Nancy tried to think of what to do but her thoughts were muddled and the floor was uncomfortable.

"Nancy, please."

She blinked and realized she'd started drifting to sleep. Struggling to her feet, she dabbed her face with a tissue and reached for the doorknob. After a fortifying breath, she opened the door and Walt nearly fell on her. Without looking at him, she pushed past and said, "We can talk in a while. Right now, I need to lie down. I'm not feeling well."

"Okay." She heard him following behind her as she walked up the stairs. "Can I get anything for you? Do you need more water for the pitcher on your nightstand? Crackers? A cool compress for your head?"

"No. Thank you."

"Okay. I'll clean up dinner, and we can reheat our food later."

"Go ahead and eat without me, please." She hurried to the room and shut the door, hoping he didn't follow her. She didn't want to see his face, and she wasn't in the mood to talk. She knew they should talk things out, but the afternoon's stress had caught up with her and she could barely think straight.

It took all her remaining energy to brush her teeth, wash her face, change clothes, and climb into bed. Her body began to shiver, and she arranged an extra knit blanket on her side of the bed. Her eyes drifted to Walt's side—the side he slept on the night before. Tears started again, and she wondered if this was the beginning of the end.

She felt so tired and needed to close her eyes for just a few minutes. Maybe after resting, she could figure out what to do next. *God help me.*

Chapter Nineteen

The stairwell leading to the bathroom wound up and up, and Nancy's hunger grew while trying to reach it. Arriving at a landing, she saw a door and sighed in relief. Swinging it open, she found . . . a closet. So she continued up more stairs. Then more.

Her hunger and the need for the bathroom increased. At the top of the stairs, she saw an open door revealing the long-awaited bathroom. As she approached, the bathroom door slammed shut. She jumped and fell backward on the steps, yet never hit the hard stairs.

Her eyes flew open and worked to adjust to the dark. Had she passed out? She searched around for the stairs and was relieved to instead find she was in her bed. Nancy exhaled and sank into the softness.

She did have to go to the bathroom, though. Since about the time she found out she was pregnant, she'd had quite a few dreams incorporating a never-ending hunt for a bathroom. At least she never found it in the dreams. Her stomach growled on the way to the bathroom, and as soon as she relieved herself, she sat back down on the bed to have a few sips of water and two crackers. The clock read five fifty. If she hurried and dressed, she could go downstairs and get something more substantial to eat before Walt went down for breakfast.

She hadn't planned to go to sleep without letting him talk, but now that she was awake and hungry, she felt even less prepared to face him.

Once dressed, she tiptoed to the door and quietly opened it, nearly tripping over something on the ground.

"Nancy," came Walt's groggy voice.

"Walt?" She looked down and found him lying on the floor with a pillow and blanket. "Did you sleep here?"

He blinked and looked around. "Yes. I need to talk to you." He stood up, wrapped his arms around her, and kissed her hair. "I'm so sorry," he whispered. "Let me make you breakfast, and we can talk."

"I . . . Okay." Why fight it? Following him downstairs to the kitchen, she was curious to hear what he'd say.

She'd fallen asleep before thinking through her options. The last time she ran from a man, she found out she was pregnant, and he didn't want her back once she came to her senses. This time, she was already married. Leaving would be more difficult. Not that she wanted to. Her stomach growled again, reminding her that it wasn't wise to make important decisions when hungry.

While Walt scrambled eggs, Nancy buttered the piece of toast he'd made her, then topped it with strawberry preserves. It tasted delicious as she washed down the first bite with a sip of milk.

A few minutes later, he brought two plates of eggs to the table and joined her. "Let's eat, then talk. We both need nourishment after last night—especially you, since you're eating for two."

She nodded but remained focused on her food. This morning, her hunger overcame the voice inside screaming to shut everything down.

After he prayed, they began eating in silence. A few minutes later, he cleared his throat. When she looked up, she noticed he had already eaten his eggs and toast, though she still had several bites of eggs left.

For the first time since he sat, she examined him. The dark circles under his eyes caught her attention, and she felt a mixture of worry and gladness that he was affected as much as she was.

After she took her last bite, he spoke up. "I can only imagine what you're thinking." He ran his fingers through his hair. It was bunched up on one side and flopped back as if he'd not touched it.

What was she thinking? She hardly knew anymore.

"Brenda wasn't working the day I came out here for the interview. I saw her name on the list of employees, but with her new last name, I had no idea it was her. I always imagined she still lived in Charleston after making such a big deal about me moving there."

"You didn't know . . ." She worked to piece together the timing of things. "Until after you asked me to marry you?" The realization stung. She wanted to run crying out of the house. Or maybe yell at him. But she took a deep breath and forced herself to remain calm. "And she's not married . . . Walt, why didn't you say something? She was the love of your life. You didn't have to marry me. I would have figured something out." Moisture pooled in her eyes, and she blinked it back.

"No, Nancy. Don't think that way. This"—he waved a finger between the two of them—"is what I was supposed to do. I know it is. And I love you. I've told you I do."

She fiddled with the napkin. "Like a sister. That's not the same. I told *you* I didn't want to keep you from real love."

"You didn't. And no, I don't love you like a sister." He stood, slid next to her on the bench seat, and wrapped an arm around her waist. "The things we've done since the honeymoon are not things I would do to a sister if I had one."

Tears surfaced again. Everything in her wanted to believe him.

"Please give me a chance to show you how much you mean to me. I'm sorry I kept it from you. I was worried you would have doubts about our marriage, but I didn't know how to approach it before or after the wedding."

She wanted to believe him. She had to try. "Okay."

"Good. Why don't you come out to the bank today for lunch, and I'll introduce you to everyone. We can go eat at the cafeteria across the street."

She nodded, but her heart wasn't in it.

Nancy rushed to place the last few raisin oatmeal cookies in the tin before leaving to meet Walt at work. She was anxious about seeing

Brenda again and still not sure how she felt about Walt keeping things from her.

At least she knew he liked her cookies. Not that something like that should make a difference. She stopped and hugged the tin to her chest. What was she doing? How did she get here? Once again, Walt said the right things, but did he mean them?

He said he loved her, but after the rejection from Brian in college and recently from Henry, she wondered if long-term romantic love was possible for her. Maybe something about her scared men off.

She looked at her watch. There was no time to worry about it. If she didn't leave now, he wouldn't have time to go to lunch with her, since he had a meeting afterwards. Gathering her things, she stopped by the bathroom once more to check her hair. She may not have had his full attention before, but she would do her best to get it.

Walt's bank was only ten minutes away, but that was enough time to get worked up. What did one say to the woman her husband was intimate with for years and brokenhearted over? Especially when one's husband only married one out of pity, though he would deny it.

She pulled into the parking lot. The bank was in a modern one-story building, unlike the bank where he worked in Greenville with its large columns out front. The entrance of this one was almost completely glass, and the roof was made up of different sections set at odd angles. It was unusual but striking.

After parking, she reached for the cookie tin and noticed her hands shaking. She placed them in her lap and took several deep breaths before stepping out. When she entered the bank, she found the modern design continued inside. She was met with a sleek cranberry- and tan-colored seating arrangement to the left and several desks with matching partitions to the right. A medium wood-colored counter with several tellers stood straight ahead. Employees greeted her as she entered.

She approached the counter and asked a middle-aged-looking lady with a nameplate that said Wanda where Walt's office was.

"Do you have an appointment?" Wanda questioned, and her eyes fell to the tin of cookies.

"I'm meeting him for lunch." Then she remembered this woman had no idea who she was. "I'm his wife."

"Oh, Mrs. Moore. It's so nice to finally meet you. Walt speaks highly of you. Let me show you to his office."

"I can find it if you'll just point me in the right direction." She remembered she was holding the tin. "And these are for the office to share. Oatmeal raisin cookies."

"How nice. Thank you. I'll put them in the breakroom." Wanda reached for the tin. "Walt's office is in the left corner there behind the cubicles." She pointed to the corner of the large space. "His assistant has a desk just outside of his office, so you won't miss it."

"Thank you, Wanda. It's nice to meet you too." She said hi to the other two ladies behind the counter before turning to find Walt's office.

She wound her way past the cubicles and came to a desk that must belong to his assistant. As she walked past it, she noticed the nameplate said "Brenda Charles," and her heart sank lower. She peeked around her desk, through his open door, and saw Brenda standing next to Walt's desk, pointing to something on a piece of paper. Brenda smiled and giggled as Walt spoke to her. She looked elegant in her smart business suit. They made a handsome pair, and guilt welled up inside Nancy.

Walt glanced up and saw Nancy. A frown flashed across his face before he replaced it with a smile, winked, and waved her in.

Looking up, Brenda's brow furrowed before her mouth lifted into a smile. "Oh, hi. So nice to see you again, Nancy."

Nancy forced a smile. "You too." Was it bad if she didn't really mean it?

"Nancy and I are going out for lunch. Can you take care of this, Brenda?"

"Certainly. Enjoy your lunch." Brenda grabbed the paper and slipped past Nancy. The smell of fancy perfume trailed behind her.

Nancy watched Walt put some papers away in a file while the sun shone through the window, highlighting his square jaw and broad shoulders. He was the most handsome man she knew. What was she doing here as his wife?

Walt moved to stand in front of her before she could speak. He wrapped his arms around her, kissed the top of her head, and just as quickly, released her and tugged at her hand. "Thank you for coming.

Mmm, you smell like cookies," he whispered into her ear as they approached the door.

"I brought oatmeal raisin cookies, and Wanda took them to the breakroom." While she made the cookies, she'd imagined they might remind Walt why he chose her, but now eau de cookie didn't seem as enticing as the lovely scent Brenda wore.

From the corner of her eye, Nancy noticed Brenda watching them exit.

Once outside, Walt looked down at Nancy. "I was worried you might not show."

"I guess I'm a glutton for punishment" was out before Nancy could check her words.

"I hope it's not punishment to be with me, but I deserve that." He pointed to the cafeteria across the street. "Come on—their lunch specials are great."

Lunch was filled with small talk and served with a side of awkward silence as they ate. After finishing, Walt hurried her back to the bank, saying he wanted to officially introduce her to everyone else. There were a lot of new names, but in her unsettled state, she doubted she would remember many other than Brenda and Wanda.

Once again, she returned home with tears in her eyes, and once again, she found Fanny working on something outside and watching.

"Nancy, would you mind helping me with these Christmas lights? I can't quite get them right on these bushes."

"Sure."

Fanny likely noticed her red, swollen eyes but didn't comment.

"My Bible study is tomorrow at ten in the morning. Why don't you join us?"

"I don't know . . . I—"

"It's a great way to get to know people, and I'll have my cookies and tea. Speaking of, it's cold out here. Why don't you pop in for some hot tea?"

No, thank you was at the tip of her tongue, but her longing for a distraction took over. "Okay. Thank you."

As they entered the house, Fanny stepped around some infant toys.

"Do you have grandchildren?"

"Oh no, I mentor a young lady, and she brings over her baby when we meet."

Nancy settled into the same spot at the kitchen table where she'd sat the day before while Fanny brought over her platter of cookies and a ceramic teapot filled with Earl Grey tea.

When Nancy had a mouthful of what Fanny had called lemon snowflakes, Fanny spoke up. "Floyd and I don't have any children."

"Oh." Nancy wasn't sure what to say. From the frown on Fanny's face, she imagined something tragic had happened.

"The truth is . . . six months *before* our wedding, just after our engagement, I found out I was pregnant. My dad was a state senator, and my parents convinced me to have an abortion to protect his image. It damaged my uterus and left me unable to have more children."

Nancy drew in a breath.

Tears slid down Fanny's face. "It never gets easier to say." She reached over and patted Nancy's hand. "Don't fret, dear. I've made peace with God about it. I know this is a heavy topic when you barely know me, but I felt God nudging me to tell you.

"Anyway, regardless of the fact that my parents coerced me to do it, I know it was wrong of me. There's hardly a day that has passed when I haven't thought of that child. It took me many years to get to the point that I could talk to God about it. I had hidden the sin away, but it was burning a hole in my soul.

"When Floyd and I first married, things were okay, but once we realized I couldn't get pregnant as a result of the abortion, resentment welled up inside both of us. Each of us blamed the other. I was mad at him for getting me pregnant, mad at my parents, and felt useless as a wife. He was mad at me for letting my parents determine our future and mad at himself. We almost divorced. But God intervened and placed someone in my life to point me to him and help me understand that forgiveness was possible, even for that. It took years before the pain from that situation became the ministry I have now, yet God was laying the foundation."

Nancy quietly sipped her tea through the whole story, entranced by all that Fanny had gone through and brokenhearted for her at the same time. She wondered how she and her husband worked through such difficulties and if it were possible for her and Walt.

"I suppose there is something God wants you to get from my story. I've learned not to argue with him when he prods me."

"Thank you for trusting me with this. From the way you speak of your husband, I never would have imagined you had such a difficult start to your marriage."

"It's only through the work of God that we got through it."

"What made the difference?" Nancy wondered if there was some formula she could apply to her own marriage.

"We were five years into our marriage when I accepted God's forgiveness, and by then there was a lot of damage to our marriage. But when I turned the abortion over to God, my attitude in life changed dramatically. I got back into church and became active there, but also my feelings towards Floyd began changing. I forgave him and was able to love him even though he still had deep-set anger towards me. He noticed how I changed, and my friend's husband offered to mentor him. It wasn't quick, but Floyd eventually forgave me and repented to God for his part in the pregnancy. He became active in church and a spiritual leader in the home—praying with me and leading us in Bible studies."

Could God really turn around such a broken situation? Nancy had neglected her personal study of the Bible lately. "Speaking of Bible studies, I'd like to come tomorrow."

"Wonderful. And I don't know if you've had any thoughts about helping with my ministry, but if you are interested, we can have a quick lunch after the study and then I can take you by to meet the lawyer I work with. You can see his office and meet his other staff. Maybe that will help you decide."

"I'd like that." Nancy wanted to help, and though she'd not mentioned it to Walt, she imagined he wouldn't mind her checking it out. Glancing at her watch, she stood. "I'll need to get home to start dinner."

"Great. I'll see you tomorrow." Fanny followed Nancy to the door. "Nancy, I'd like to pray for you. Is that okay?"

"I'd appreciate it. Thank you." She turned to the door.

"I mean right now. I'd like to pray over you."

Nancy turned back and walked to Fanny, feeling slightly uncomfortable.

Fanny laid a hand on her shoulder and closed her eyes. "Father God, you are all-powerful, all-knowing, and with us at all times. Thank you for bringing this young family into my life. I lift up Nancy and her new husband Walt to you. I don't know what is going on with Nancy to make her sad, but you do. I pray you would give her wisdom if there is a decision to be made, and I pray you would provide what she needs. I also ask you to give her peace. Above all these things, I pray you would bless their marriage. Bring them closer to you and to each other, and protect them from attacks of the accuser. In Jesus' name, Amen."

"That was beautiful." Nancy dabbed at the moisture trying to escape from her eyes. She leaned forward and hugged Fanny. "I needed that." When she released her, Fanny squeezed her hand.

As Nancy ambled back home, she processed Fanny's story. It was different than Nancy and Walt's situation, but just as serious, maybe more.

She'd decided on making steak Diane for dinner. The recipe looked fairly straight forward. An hour and a half later, the table was set and the food was ready just in time for Walt's arrival.

At ten minutes past the time she expected him, she began to worry. As upset as she was about him hiding the situation with Brenda, none of it mattered compared with his safety. Just as she was about to call his office, she heard his car pull up. Some of her tension dissipated as she rushed to the front door. Hopefully, there was a simple explanation.

She flung open the door and was surprised to see him holding a beautiful bouquet of red roses.

"Hi. Sorry I'm late, but I wanted to surprise you with these." He was trying.

"They're beautiful. Thank you." She wanted to forgive him immediately but was happy to let him work to prove himself.

"Something smells wonderful." He leaned in and kissed her on the lips.

Regardless of not wanting to let him off too easily, she lost herself in the kiss.

Walt pulled back and rested his forehead on hers. "I don't want to stop kissing you, especially after the tension of last night and today, but I'm sure you worked hard on dinner and don't want it to get cold. Also, I have an important phone call to make after we eat. We need to keep working through things, and unfortunately, our time together will have to wait until after that call."

She wondered what was so important—especially since he didn't offer an explanation. The situation with Brenda was still a barrier between them, and she was anxious to discuss it further.

Nancy hurried into the kitchen to get the food to the dining room table, where she had set out the fine china. She didn't want the meal she'd labored over to be rushed. She also worried she wouldn't have enough time to tell him about the job with Fanny's ministry. Even though part of her wanted to go behind his back and take the job, as her husband, it was only right for him to know.

About halfway through the meal, Nancy broached the subject of the job. She explained about the ministry and her understanding of how she could help. "Fanny is taking me to the law office tomorrow after Bible study and lunch."

"Bible study?"

"Yes, she leads a ladies' study at her home and invited me."

"I'm glad you'll have the chance to meet some ladies at the study. But as for the law firm, I thought you didn't want to work."

Nancy pressed her lips together and thought about what to say. "I'm not sure I'll do it, and if I do, it would only be part-time. After the baby, I don't know if I want to work at all. But I would like to have the chance to consider it. I hadn't imagined my career being cut short like this." She pointed to her belly.

"And the work would be for a good cause. She helps the women at New Hope Pregnancy Center see they have options that will allow them to keep their babies and not have abortions. It hits home with me. It's hard to believe I considered an abortion. I was scared, embarrassed, and brokenhearted. Because of my distress, it seemed like my only option. I'm still not sure why I admitted it to you. I guess I was hoping you would talk me out of it. I'm thankful you did."

"I am too." Walt moved his chair so he was close enough to reach for her hand. "You've been through a lot these past couple of months, and

I'm glad to be the one who stepped in. You've always been a good friend to me, and it's fitting that we're family now." He frowned and pushed back from the table. "I'm truly sorry I didn't trust you enough to tell you about Brenda. I want us to be able to trust each other. I keep messing things up."

She nodded and looked at their hands. Trust was what she wanted too.

Walt stood. "I need to go make this call, and then we can work on figuring out how to move past what I've done." He leaned over, kissed the top of her head, and picked up their plates.

When he opened the dishwasher, Nancy popped out of her seat. "You can't wash the good china in the dishwasher." She pulled it from his hand. "I'll wash it."

"No, you cooked. I'll wash them when I'm done with the call."

"It's fine. I've got it. You go on."

"Okay. Thanks." He turned to walk towards his study.

Forty-five minutes later, Nancy sat on the living room sofa reading *Emma*. For some reason, that was her go-to book when she felt unsettled. She recalled reading it the day she met Henry. She'd felt out of place in England, but her book was a familiar comfort. She'd read it so many times, she could quote much of it. Sometimes she picked it up just to read a specific part somewhere in the middle. Growing up, she'd imagined Walt as her Mr. Knightley.

Today, she wanted to start at the point when Mr. Knightley confessed his love for Emma. Walt had told Nancy he loved her, but she still wondered if it was a romantic love. After finding out about Brenda, she had the feeling that when they rushed into the physical side of things, it created a false sense of romantic love on his part. And what's worse, she worried he might just as quickly realize he didn't love her that way and decide she was more like a friend to him. He'd commented on it during dinner. She rubbed her forehead. How could they fix something that was so broken?

Nancy glanced back down to the book. She had reread the same sentence five times and still wasn't sure what she had just read. Her tangled thoughts made it difficult to concentrate. Once more, she skimmed across the page, but this time, it was the sound of Walt's steps nearing that distracted her.

"Sorry that took so long." He rubbed the back of his neck and sat down next to her on the sofa. His brow was knit, and the edges of his mouth slanted into a frown. "I . . . um . . . it was your dad. I told him what I did regarding Brenda and asked for guidance on how to make things better."

His words grabbed Nancy's attention. With her father being Walt's mentor for so many years, it made sense he would talk to him, and she trusted her father to give good advice. But it also made her somewhat uncomfortable for her dad to know too many details about their marriage.

"What did he say?"

"He said we should go back to sleeping in separate rooms for a time. He thinks we rushed things physically and we need to give ourselves more time to let the romance in our relationship grow naturally. He mentioned I Corinthians 7:3-5. It's about the husband and wife . . . abstaining for a time that they devote to prayer."

"Oh." Something inside her knew her dad was probably right about it, but she also dreaded being separated from Walt in that way. What if that made it easier for him to think of Brenda? Now she wished they hadn't rushed the physical part.

"He also suggested a Bible study for us to do together every day. I had meant for us to continue studying the Bible together but have let it slide. I'm sorry. I've gone about all of this wrong."

"No. We're both figuring things out."

"So will you agree to this with me?"

For a moment, she sat there silently, wishing there was another solution. "Yes," she finally agreed.

"I do love you, and we're going to come through this better than ever."

I hope so. She forced a smile, but words never came.

That night, Nancy felt even less settled than she had the night before. While she lay in bed, the emptiness and silence of the room echoed in her head, creating so much noise, she couldn't relax. Earlier, after their talk, Walt read some scripture with her and prayed for their marriage and her potential job. God's Word silenced the chaos inside for a time, but now it was back in full force. *God, please take it away. Heal our marriage.*

Chapter Twenty

"So who is this lawyer you'll be working for?" Walt asked as he pulled on his jacket and grabbed his keys to leave for work.

"I don't know his name."

"Without knowing who it is, I feel uncomfortable. Your dad is an upstanding man, but some lawyers are worse than the people they try to get out of trouble."

"I can't imagine he would be volunteering his time for a cause like this if he wasn't a good person."

"Maybe, unless he's the type who thinks he can earn his way back into God's good graces by doing good deeds. I worry about you."

"I don't think Fanny would be working with him if she didn't trust him, nor do I think she would have him around traumatized women. But don't worry, I'll keep my wits about me when I meet him."

"Okay, okay." He chuckled. "Well, I'll be at work if you need to call me to come save you." He winked. "Actually, though, I would love it if you would ask Fanny his name and give me a call with the name of the law firm before you leave. That way I have an idea of where you are. With the pregnancy, I don't like not knowing."

"I understand." She leaned up towards him for a goodbye kiss and closed her eyes. When he placed a kiss on her head, she pulled back in disappointment.

He touched her chin. "I do love you. Why don't you ask the ladies for restaurant recommendations? I'd like to take you on a date tonight."

"Okay." Stepping back, Nancy leaned against the doorway. "Have a good day at work. I'll let you know the name of the law firm before we go."

"Thanks."

She watched and waved as he got in his car and drove away. Taking a step back with Walt physically felt like they had stepped back emotionally too. She was ready to be on more solid ground with him.

Fourteen women filled Fanny's home, including herself. Nancy looked around the dining room at the broad mix of ladies. A few seemed close to Nancy's age, including one who looked like she walked there from Woodstock. Most of the women appeared to be about her mom's age, though some were likely as old as Fanny, whom she'd learned was seventy.

While they ate cookies and chatted, a middle-aged red-headed woman named Edna approached Nancy and introduced herself. After only a few minutes, Nancy could tell she was a talker. If Nancy wasn't careful, Edna would have her telling her life story within the first five minutes of meeting. Nancy did manage to find out the name of a couple of good restaurants for dates during their conversation.

Once Fanny gathered them into the living room, Nancy sat next to a woman named Marie who looked close to her age and was also pregnant. When Nancy asked Marie how far along she was, she said seven months, but that was all Marie said. She noticed Marie didn't speak to others or make eye contact unless she was spoken to. Nancy didn't see a wedding ring on her finger and wondered if Marie had gotten involved in the Bible study through the pregnancy center. She imagined some of the women's stories were much more complicated than her own. Yet if it weren't for Walt, she, too, would be pregnant with no ring on her finger.

Fanny opened the Bible study with prayer and then had them turn to the book of James. She explained that they would be methodically going through all five chapters. Nancy flipped through it and noted it was short. She had never participated in a study like this. Though she had read quite a bit of the Bible on her own and grown up going to Sunday school, she hadn't looked at the book of James closely. Fanny had told her to bring a highlighter and pen to mark things in her Bible as well as a notebook. Writing in her Bible was a new idea to Nancy, but she liked the idea of marking it to help her remember what she'd learned.

The first few verses seemed to have been written specifically for her, yet left her with questions. She silently reread the words of James 1:2-4.

"Count it all joy, my brothers, when you meet trials of various kinds, for you know that the testing of your faith produces steadfastness. And let steadfastness have its full effect, that you may be perfect and complete, lacking in nothing."

Fanny handed a dictionary to one of the women to look up the word *steadfast*, and they learned it meant endurance.

Nancy was stuck on the idea that trials could bring joy. She had her share of trials over the past few months, and it wasn't the trials that brought her joy. As she thought about it, it dawned on her that Walt was always the one who brought her joy. Each time, he surpassed her expectations, and her joy increased. But when she realized she had overestimated their relationship, her joy diminished. Right now, she was experiencing that diminished joy.

"I don't understand how trials bring joy," Nancy asked.

Fanny smiled at her. "That's a good question. First, let's look at Galatians 5:22-23. Why don't you find it and read it to us, Nancy."

"Okay." Nancy was curious as she found the book of Galatians. "It says, 'But the fruit of the Spirit is love, joy, peace, patience, kindness, goodness, faithfulness, gentleness, self-control; against such things there is no law.'" She'd read and heard those verses numerous times through the years. They were all good things to want in her life.

"Those are the fruit of the Spirit. The Spirit is the key. This fruit grows in the lives of Christians because they have the Holy Spirit inside of them, gradually changing them to be more like Christ. Since the fruit comes from the Holy Spirit and not naturally, it's going to be different than it would be in the life of a non-Christian. I imagine we all know people who are not Christians who have many of these characteristics in their lives." Fanny looked around the room, and the women nodded.

"But the difference is that with worldly love, we love when something pleases us, with worldly joy, we are joyful when everything is going well, we have peace when things are calm, et cetera. With the Holy Spirit, we can love our enemies, sing when in prison like Paul, or have peace in the storms of life. Irene, would you look up and read Hebrews 12:1-2?"

"Sure." She flipped to the passage. "'Therefore, since we are surrounded by so great a cloud of witnesses, let us also lay aside every weight, and sin which clings so closely, and let us run with endurance the race that is set before us, looking to Jesus, the founder and perfecter of our faith, who for the joy that was set before him endured the cross, despising the shame, and is seated at the right hand of the throne of God.'"

"Thank you. Jesus endured the cross for the joy set before him. What do you think that joy was?"

The room grew quiet, but eventually, one of the ladies spoke up. "Being back in heaven with God the Father?"

"I'm sure he was looking forward to that. What was the reason he died?"

"To save us from our sins," a lady named Ruby spoke up.

"Yes. To save us. And what is the result when we are saved?"

"We go to heaven," someone quickly answered.

"True, and we will be with Jesus when we go to heaven. The Bible calls God's people the bride of Christ and Jesus the bridegroom. Like a groom waiting expectantly at the front of a church, longing for his bride, Jesus is longing for the day that we will be with him face to face and without the separation of sin. Each of us is so precious to him that he endured the cross with joy because he is looking towards that day. When he was on that cross, he saw each of you." She leaned forward, pointed a finger to one of the ladies, then swept it around so it pointed at each woman in the room. "And knew the suffering was not only worth it, but it brought him joy."

Settling back in her seat, Fanny's brow creased. "And from what

I've heard, women experience a similar feeling when they give birth. They experience pain and yet all the while, have joy at what is to come. This is a different joy than the typical earthly joy we speak of. As I said earlier, it is a joy that comes through the Holy Spirit. So getting back to our original verse—those trials that test our faith produce steadfastness, or as we learned, endurance. Our faith will be perfected and endure. This can bring us joy because just as Jesus on the cross looked ahead to that day when we would be with him, we can also look ahead with joy to that day. When we suffer in this world, our attachments to it lessen, and hopefully, our longing for him increases."

Nancy's heart raced. Was it possible her trials could bring her closer to God? She'd been through so many trials lately—losing Henry, finding out she was pregnant, and now being unsure of where she stood with Walt. It seemed that trials would be an ever-present part of her adult life. She longed for real joy. Was it truly within her grasp? She wrote down all of the verses Fanny mentioned so she could go back through them and work on gaining that joy.

By the end of the study, Nancy had three pages of notes, and excitement bubbled over within her. She still looked forward to her meeting with the lawyer, but she would be counting the minutes until she could go back home and study her Bible. In all her years of being a Christian, how had she missed that it held so much wisdom?

Once all the other ladies had left, Fanny offered Nancy a bowl of beef and vegetable soup for lunch. It tasted delicious, like everything Fanny made. She was glad for the one-on-one time with Fanny so she could ask her about some of the things discussed during the study.

After a quick call to Walt, Fanny drove Nancy to Rutledge and Rutledge Attorneys at Law to meet Arthur Rutledge. It was a father-son firm specializing in family law. Nancy would be working with Arthur, the father, if she took the job. As they drove into the office parking lot, she realized it was only a few blocks from Walt's office. Thoughts of meeting him regularly for lunch flashed in her mind and made her smile.

"Arthur is such a dear. I think you'll get along well with him," Fanny said as they walked to the building. "He can use all the help you're willing to give, but don't feel like you have to do more than you like. Of course, if you don't want to do this, I won't be offended one bit. So don't worry about hurting my feelings."

"Thanks. I'll keep that in mind." She couldn't imagine not wanting to at least try. The idea of getting back into the legal field excited her, and she'd entered it in the first place wanting to help women.

They walked through the door and were greeted by a middle-aged woman with short brown hair sitting behind a traditional wooden desk.

"Good afternoon, Mrs. Butler. Mr. Rutledge Sr. is expecting you. You can go directly to his office."

"Thank you, Theresa. Now I know I've told you to call me Fanny. You don't have to be so proper. And it makes me feel old." Fanny's eyes creased as she smiled and chuckled. "Theresa, I'd like to introduce you to Nancy Moore. She's considering helping me out with the pregnancy center by working with Arthur to take some of the work off his plate."

"So nice to meet you, Nancy." Theresa ran around the desk and shook Nancy's hand. "He could definitely use some help, and he's easy to work with. I hope it works out."

"Thanks. Me too."

As they walked around the corner, Nancy heard a loud voice through the door. "No, she won't take a penny less!"

Fanny smirked and shook her head before knocking on the door labeled Arthur Rutledge, J.D., Esq. "He drives a hard bargain with some of these men who try to get out of doing their duty when they leave their wives, or in the case of the pregnancy center, when they leave someone they got pregnant caring for a baby alone."

"Then we'll see him in court!" The sound of a phone receiver slamming into its base echoed in the hall. "Come in," he said in a calmer voice.

Fanny opened the door and led the way.

"Mrs. Butler. It's always good to see you. Is it that time already?"

"Indeed, it is, Arthur, and I've brought Mrs. Nancy Moore."

The first things Nancy noticed upon entering the office were the piles of paper on the man's desk. Her eyes worked their way past the clutter to the jovial-looking white-haired man she assumed was Mr. Arthur Rutledge.

"Hi, Mr. Rutledge, I'm Nancy Moore." She held out her hand as she leaned over one of the shorter piles.

Mr. Rutledge followed Nancy's line of sight to his desk and grimaced. "Sorry." He walked around and shook her hand. "My wife's always after me to clean this up, but the one time I let her help me organize, I missed appointments and deadlines for days, because I couldn't find a thing. I work best with the piling system." He pointed to the filing cabinets lining the side wall. "Only completed cases go in those, and Annie does that. I'm sure I'd mess it up if I tried."

"Well, whatever your system, it works." Fanny turned to Nancy. "He's never let one of the clinic's clients down yet."

"I normally meet with clients in the conference room, but if it's okay, I'd like to meet in here so I have access to my files as I explain how you can help."

"That's fine." Nancy looked down at the chairs in front of Mr. Rutledge's desk. One had a pile of folders on it.

"I'll get that." Mr. Rutledge mumbled something as he shifted it to his credenza. "Okay, ladies." He waved them into the chairs. "And by the way, Nancy, don't let my wreck of an office worry you. If you decide to help, you'll be working in my wife's office next door. It's as neat as a pin. She comes in a few hours a week to do the books. She's mostly flexible with her hours, so you can decide when you want to be in, and she'll work around it."

"That sounds good." That relieved Nancy. She didn't imagine she'd work well in such a chaotic environment as Mr. Rutledge's office.

Half an hour later, Nancy had a good idea of what the job required, and it was everything she'd hoped for. Mr. Rutledge introduced her to Annie, who assisted both Mr. Rutledge and his son. Between the work and the kind staff, Nancy knew she wanted to take the job and told Fanny and Mr. Rutledge so.

Just as they were saying their goodbyes and turning to leave, a man entered the office, causing Nancy to do a double take. His blond hair and blue eyes were similar to Henry's. But on her second glance, she noticed he wasn't as tall, nor was his jaw quite as squared. And compared to Henry, his facial features were quite plain. Relief filled Nancy, which both surprised and satisfied her.

"You're just in time, Michael. Mrs. Butler and Mrs. Nancy Moore were about to leave. Mrs. Moore is the one I told you was considering helping me with the pregnancy center work. She's decided to take the job and will begin next Monday."

Michael's face lit up. "Of course. I'm glad I made it in time. So good to meet you, Mrs. Moore." He reached out and shook her hand.

"You too, Mr. Rutledge."

"You can call me Michael. Everyone here does. It's less confusing than having two Mr. Rutledges." Michael leaned closer. "And I don't want to be called Junior." He winked and released her hand.

"Okay, then. Michael it is." Nancy smiled.

Michael placed a hand on his father's shoulder. "Don't let his sometimes gruff demeanor scare you away. He's a good man and makes sure the women from Mrs. Butler's center get treated right and are provided for by these deadbeat fathers."

"That's what I keep hearing. I'm glad to know there are good people out there." Looking between the two men, she saw a resemblance. They both had kind eyes and were about the same height and build, minus a few pounds on Michael's side. "I'll see you on Monday then." Nancy waved at Theresa, who was seated behind the desk, and the Rutledge men before following Fanny out the door.

On the way home, Fanny thanked Nancy profusely for her help and reminded her that if she changed her mind, to not hesitate and let her know. She also pointed out several sights on their ride home.

Just before Fanny pulled onto their street, she changed the subject. "The early days of marriage are difficult. You have two imperfect people trying to learn to live together and learn to communicate. You also have the everyday ups and downs of life coming at you, and you're having to learn to work through them together. There may be days when you say things or do things you don't mean, and the same for him. Give each other grace."

As she turned the corner, she smiled softly at Nancy and patted her shoulder. "I learned these things the hard way from nearly fifty years of marriage. I told you how we had a rough start, but if we can come back from that, I think any marriage centered around Christ can succeed." They pulled into the driveway, and once she'd parked, Fanny turned again to Nancy. "Do the two of you have a relationship with Christ?"

"Oh, yes, ma'am." Nancy was a bit taken aback by her straightforwardness.

"Good. There is no reason to doubt. Again, I learned the hard way that Satan would have God's people doubting God could truly forgive them for this thing or that. He's real good at paralyzing us so we don't grow in our relationship with God and we don't help anyone else learn about God through us. But we have something He doesn't—the Holy Spirit in us. When we get into God's Word each day, we'll find we're giving the Holy Spirit more opportunities to pour into us than we are giving to the prince of this world to attack us. And don't forget the power of prayer. You may think God doesn't care about the details of your life, but he does. If he knows how many hairs are on your head like Jesus tells us in the gospels, he certainly cares about all the other details, big and small."

Nancy swallowed and tried to keep the threatening tears at bay. How did Fanny know just what she needed to hear? She truly seemed to be in touch with God. Nancy wanted that too. "Thank you," she said in a hoarse whisper.

"May I pray for you?"

"Of course."

Fanny laid her hand on Nancy's and said a sweet prayer for their marriage and that Nancy would draw near to God and lean on him for all her needs.

When Nancy stepped out of the car, her thoughts were swirling. She wanted to open her Bible and dig some more into God's Word, and she also wanted to pray for her own marriage. In some ways, it felt like she was fighting for her marriage, but it may have been more of a battle inside herself to trust that God was giving her good gifts in spite of making wrong choices with Henry.

Once inside her house, she grabbed her Bible and notes from the study and climbed onto the window seat in the cozy nook of the living room. Hugging the Bible to her chest, she gazed into the yard. Even with the leaves gone and the grass browned, it was a lovely place. The garden was so artfully arranged that it still held beauty, and the wooded lot beside their home created a perfect backdrop for pondering important things.

She let the tears flow freely. They were a mixture of happiness for her blessings and worry for her future with Walt. A future she desperately wanted to trust God with.

It took a few minutes for Nancy to let all of her emotions out, but when she finally did, she opened her Bible and began to study. Periodically, she stopped and prayed. It felt like a conversation between her and God. It was intimate and wonderful. Was this a taste of the joy that they had spoken of in Bible study? She wanted more. It was as if she'd eaten a delicious meal that left her completely satisfied yet looking towards the next meal. Warmth filled her body—a happiness she'd not felt in a long time. *Thank you, God.*

Suddenly, she felt so tired. Glancing at her watch, she saw she had an hour before Walt would be home. Since he was taking her out, she didn't need to rush to make dinner. Maybe she would just rest right here for a few minutes. She arranged the pillow behind her and slid down to rest her head on it. She'd get ready for their date in a few minutes.

Chapter Twenty-One

"Nancy? Are you okay?"

She felt Walt run a hand up and down her arm. Opening her eyes, she glanced up to find her handsome husband staring down at her, and she smiled. When his relaxed smile matched her own, she sighed.

"Tired?"

She nodded and stretched. "I was." He brushed the hair back from her face and caressed her cheek. "Mmm. I feel better now."

"Would you rather I go and pick dinner up for us?"

Pushing herself up, Nancy shook her head. "Not at all. I learned of some good restaurants today, and I want to go the Italian one."

"Then that's what we'll do."

"I just need a few minutes to freshen up."

"What's the name, and I can call ahead."

"Villa Tronco. They say it's been around for years and is delicious."

"Villa Tronco it is. I'll go find it in the Yellow Pages." He leaned down and kissed her forehead, then helped her up.

Nancy hurried as fast as she could, not wanting to waste a minute of their date night. She was still on her high from her time with God earlier and couldn't wait to share that with Walt.

She touched up her eye makeup, brushed her teeth, and changed into a different dress before running back down to meet Walt.

He was sprawled out on the living room sofa, reading the newspaper. Folding it, he laid it aside and made a slow perusal of her. "Just checking out the dress." He winked.

She shook her head and smiled. "I won't make you sleep in the extra room anymore if you don't want to."

He ran a hand over his face and groaned. "What was I thinking when I committed to doing that?"

She shrugged and sashayed by him towards the door. Looking back over her shoulder, she winked.

"Hold on!" He ran up and tugged at her arm.

When she turned, he held out a dark blue book and a bouquet of pink flowers mixed with a few red roses and ivy.

"The flowers are beautiful." She read the title of the book. "*Starry Night: Christmas Advent Devotional*. This is so thoughtful."

"It's for us to read together as we prepare for Christmas. It's focused on the life of Christ from Genesis to Revelation."

"Christ in Genesis?"

"Mm-hmm. I scanned through it and think we'll learn a lot from it. It's easy to get distracted by all the commercial things at Christmas."

She nodded. "I'd like going through it with you. And I love these pink flowers. What kind are they?"

His eyes fixed on hers. "Camellias."

"They're wonderful. So many petals arranged perfectly."

He nodded. "I picked each part as a message to you. During Victorian times, flowers and plants were used to send secret messages."

"Ooh. How fun." She spun the bouquet around. "What do these mean?"

"We can stop by the florist tomorrow and get the book so you can look them up."

She placed her free hand on her hip. "You won't tell me?"

"I think it will have more meaning if you look them up yourself."

Nancy rolled her eyes. "I'm guessing the roses mean love."

He shrugged. "Here." He pointed to the table in the hall. "I've already filled a vase with water so we won't be delayed for dinner. We have a reservation in . . ." He checked his watch. "Twenty minutes."

Nancy arranged the flowers in the vase and then leaned in to kiss Walt. He turned so her lips hit his cheek. She wanted to fuss at him, but instead said, "Thank you."

"How did it go at Rutledge and Rutledge?" Walt asked once they were on the road. He reached over and took her hand.

"Oh, Walt, it's going to be perfect for me. I'll work Tuesday, Wednesday, and Thursday for now, from eight thirty to twelve thirty. If I decide to change to fewer days, that's fine too. They are happy to get any help they can. But next week, I plan to go in Monday, Tuesday, and Thursday because Mr. Rutledge will be taking his wife out of town for their anniversary."

"So you've already accepted the job?" Walt pulled his hand back and placed it on the steering wheel.

"I did."

"I wish you had called me first. Not that I would have said no, it's just . . . I don't know. It seems like the right thing to do now that we're married. It's a big decision, and I hope we will make those together in the future."

Nancy picked at her fingernail. She'd not even been married a week, and things were already falling apart. "I'm sorry," she said softly. "This is still new to me. I didn't think it would matter, since we'd already discussed it and Fanny insisted that I can back out altogether or reduce my time if I want." She sniffed back tears and felt Walt's hand on hers.

"I'm sorry. I didn't mean to upset you. I'm not mad, just disappointed. We're both figuring this marriage thing out. Obviously, I'm not the best example myself." He rubbed his thumb in circles on her palm, then lifted her hand to his lips and kissed her wrist.

"I also wanted to give them an answer since he was going out of town next week. This way, he can have things ready for me on Monday."

"It will be fine. Next time something like that happens, though, you can call me at work. Just tell my assistant it's time sensitive so she'll know to pull me out of a meeting if necessary. If for some reason I'm out of my office, I'll trust you to make a wise decision."

"I can do that." The moment she said it, she remembered she would be talking with Brenda if she left a message. She wished she could get past the worry of them working together. Recalling her earlier time with God, she determined to spend some dedicated time praying about it.

He pulled into the parking lot of an adorable building composed of two sections—a tall section with a large arched wood garage door on the lower floor and a trio of windows on the top level, and a short section painted red with green doors and windows in the center. They looked like they were from the early 1900s.

Walt escorted her inside, and they were led to a table in a large rustic room. The floors were brown terrazzo, and some of the walls were aged brick while others were old wood. It wasn't anything fancy, but it smelled delicious.

"It seems like a homey place." Walt glanced around the room.

"According to the lady who told me about it, it's a Columbia staple that's been around since 1940. The family who owns it started cooking for World War II soldiers of Italian heritage stationed here. That way, they could still get a familiar home-cooked meal. Isn't that sweet?"

Walt's eyes found hers, and his smile grew. "I like that." He looked down at the menu. "Should we share two dishes?"

"Absolutely!"

By the time the waitress walked away to turn in their orders, Nancy was more than ready to tell Walt about the ladies' Bible study and her time.

"This morning, I had the Bible study at Fanny's, remember?"

"Mm-hmm."

"There were fourteen ladies from around my age to older than Fanny. We're studying the book of James, and Fanny is teaching us to study it on our own. It's unlike any Bible study I've done before. She had us look at verses from different parts of the Bible to help make sense of the ones in James. We also looked up definitions for words that might not be clear."

"Did you like it?"

"I loved it. At first, I wasn't sure about it. It seemed like such a clinical way to look at things. Not that I've ever minded studying. I've just never looked into the Bible this way. This method really helps make sense of things. It's making it come alive for me. It's hard to explain. I'll have to get out my notes and show you."

Walt reached across the table to squeeze her hand. "I'm kind of jealous. Would you ask her if she knows of a study like this for men? I'll have to double down on my own study so I have something more to offer to you spiritually."

"You're already way ahead of me. But I have to say, it's getting me excited to study on my own. When I came home this afternoon, I looked again at my study notes and at some of the cross references, like Fanny had mentioned. I had sweet time alone with God. That's how I fell asleep in the window nook."

Walt's smile grew mischievous.

"What?"

He shook his head. "You looked so adorable curled up and sleeping before I woke you."

Nancy propped her chin on her hand and examined him. She wasn't sure adorable was how she wanted him to think of her. How could she turn this date around so he thought of her romantically?

"I'm stuffed and sleepy," Nancy said as they entered the house. "I can't believe I ate the spumoni. I should have stopped after the meal."

"You said you still had room." Walt chuckled and held her at the waist so she wouldn't fall as she leaned over and took her shoes off.

"I was wrong. It wasn't like the lasagna and scallops with fettuccine didn't fill me up."

"I know you're sleepy, but if you want to stay up a little longer, we can get ready for bed, then meet up in the living room. I'll give you a foot massage or a shoulder massage. Whichever you'd prefer."

"Deal. I can stay up for that."

It was tempting to slip into her silky nightgown and robe, but she decided to play nice and chose a pants and top set with her quilted winter robe. It was a flattering style she hoped might help him keep seeing her as more than his friend and roommate.

As she walked down the stairs, the sound of Bing Crosby singing "White Christmas" traveled from the living room. Nancy's heart leapt, and she picked up her pace.

When she came around the corner, she found Walt standing over the record player, looking at the record cover. He turned around and bit back a grin before laying the cover down.

"Care to dance, wife?" He held out a hand.

"I'd like that, husband." She approached and took his hand. He quickly swept her into his arms. Clumsily, she followed his lead before she realized the problem. "I don't know that fuzzy slippers are the best for this."

He lifted her chin and looked into her eyes. "I won't complain one bit if you step on my toes, and if you trip, that gives me a reason to catch you." He followed it with his signature wink.

Her heart was doing funny things again.

When the song ended and "God Rest Ye Merry Gentleman" began to play, he led her to the sofa.

"Are you a little more awake?" He helped her get comfortable and covered her with a throw from the back of the sofa.

"I am. And dinner finally settled too."

"Good. Any issues from your pregnancy lately? You've not said anything."

She shook her head. "Nothing major. The nausea has eased up. The biggest thing I noticed is tiredness. I don't want to get up in the morning, and after lunch, I get sleepy. I also have to go to the bathroom more than I used to."

"I'm glad there's nothing serious. You have a doctor's appointment next week, right?"

"Next Wednesday. I made it for twelve fifteen so you can come if you want."

"I'll be there." He reached for her hand and rubbed circles on it. "I was thinking we could do our Christmas devotional book now. Maybe if we do two or three of the devotions a day, we'll get caught up soon. The lady at the bookstore recommended it, and it looks like it's very in-depth —not just a quick, fluffy thoughts."

"I'd like that. After seeing how much more I understand when I take the time to do in-depth study of the Bible, I want to do more."

He lifted the devotional book from the coffee table, wrapped an arm around her, and began to read. Within a few minutes, they'd finished day three and covered numerous verses in the Old and New Testaments.

Walt closed the book.

"Just one more?" Nancy asked.

"We'll save some for tomorrow and Sunday. I have a feeling we'll be caught up by then. Was there anything that stood out to you?"

"So much. For starters, it's interesting to think of Jesus being in existence since the beginning. We focus so much on his birth. But those John 1 verses make it clear he was there in the beginning."

Walt nodded.

"I've also never thought about Jesus being referenced in Genesis 3 and 'he shall bruise your head' talking about Jesus destroying Satan. Right there, in the beginning, God had a plan. It's comforting."

"Mm-hmm." He squeezed her shoulder. "Day three hit me hard when it pointed to Genesis 22, where Abraham was called to sacrifice his only son as a test. His faith must have been so strong. He had no idea that at the last minute, God would provide a substitute. I had forgotten that Hebrews 11 says he trusted that God could bring his son back from the dead. It's a heart-wrenching picture of how God would later provide salvation through Jesus. As a future father, I can't even imagine . . ." He slowly shook his head. "And yet God did that for us. As broken as we are, he believes we are worth the life of his son."

Nancy looked up and saw moisture in his eyes. She leaned into him and placed a hand on his chest. She felt his heart pounding beneath her fingers. She never dreamed she'd get to marry a man who was so deeply moved by the things of God, much less the man she'd always dreamed of marrying. It may have hurt at the time to lose Henry, but she would forever be thankful that God had a different plan.

"So . . . I had some ideas for things to do tomorrow."

Nancy nodded. She'd not thought about how they would spend

their free time on the weekends. She imagined he'd want to do wood-working, but she'd have to come up with new routines. Her usual Saturdays had been spent with friends or her mom, but now she only had him.

Walt pulled an envelope from the coffee table and handed it to her. She'd not noticed it before. "Open it," he urged.

When she lifted the flap, she found two tickets. "*A Christmas Carol* tickets at Town Theatre. Oh, Walt, thank you." She wrapped her arms around him. "I've always loved that play around the holidays."

"I haven't forgotten. I still remember when you were little and climbed onto my lap when the Ghost of Christmas Future appeared on stage."

"You'll never let me live that down, will you? You remind me of it every Christmas." She tried to pull back, but he hugged her tighter.

"It was sweet. You buried your face in my chest, kind of like you are now, and made me tell you when it was gone. How old were you? Four . . . five?"

"Two."

"You were not two. We didn't move next to you or know you until I was ten . . . so you were three. This was at least a year later, so you had to be four or five."

Nancy pulled back and put hands over her face. "It's embarrassing."

"I choose to disagree. I didn't fully appreciate having you lean on me for comfort back then, but I still loved that you looked up to me."

She uncovered her face and examined him. Sometimes he said things that had her thinking they were getting back to where their marriage needed to be.

His smile turned into a smirk, and she smacked him on the bicep. He had her hanging onto his every word . . . and muscle. That was one solid muscle. She pretended she was patting the spot she'd smacked, but she really wanted to feel his bicep again. Yep, solid. What had he just said?

Before she could remember, he slid her bangs back and kissed her on the forehead. Now she was thoroughly disoriented.

"I also thought we could pick out a Christmas tree tomorrow, and Sunday, we can decorate it. I saw some boxes of ornaments in the guest room closet."

"I brought them from home. Sorry, are they in the way of your clothes?"

"I don't have that much. It's fine. Especially since some of my out-of-season things are in your closet."

She wished he'd called it *their* closet. Hopefully they'd rectify that soon. The thought made her face heat.

"I brought my ornaments and ones your mom gave me. We still might not have enough to cover the whole tree."

"Let's add ornament shopping to our list for tomorrow."

"Let's also go by the florist so I can figure out my flower message."

"That's right." Walt grinned and tapped his chin. "I left you with a mystery."

Nancy couldn't hold back a yawn. "Somebody promised me a massage for staying up, and I'm cashing in. Shoulders, please." She turned away from him and pointed to her shoulder.

He reached up and squeezed her shoulders before sliding his hands across them and pressing into her muscles with gentle rhythmic pressure.

She yawned again, barely getting her words out. "This is wonderful." The pressure on her shoulders eased. He placed a kiss on her neck and then another.

"Walt," she whispered. "Will . . . will you sleep in our room tonight?" Her face heated as she asked, but at least she didn't have to look him in the eyes.

He pressed close to her back and tightened his grip on her shoulders. "I want that, but I also want us to work on our relationship a little more before we add *that* back in."

She sighed. "I thought it was usually the woman who was a tease."

He chuckled. "I'm sorry, beautiful, that's not my intent. We'll get there soon, I promise. I want our marriage to stand the test of time with a strong foundation. We've gone about things somewhat backwards, but I think . . . I hope if we take this time, it will pay off in the long run. Do you trust me?"

His hands slid up and down her arms, and her heart replied with somersaults. "Yes."

Chapter Twenty-Two

"Walt, can you put this angel ornament up in that spot on the tree? I can't quite reach." Nancy pointed to an empty spot on the upper portion of the tree.

Walt winked, took the ornament, and climbed the ladder. "Here?" He held the ornament over a spot.

Nancy stood back and took in the Christmas tree nestled in the corner of their living room and nodded. "That's perfect. I think that's the last of my angels." She sifted through the box that previously held the twenty-three angels her parents had given her throughout the years for Christmas. It was strange to think this was her twenty-third Christmas. Nothing but tissue was left in the box. "Yep, that's it for angels."

"How about we put on the tinsel before hanging the rest of the ornaments? That way, the tinsel won't cover them."

"Good point. I guess that's why my dad always brought it out first." She pulled the tinsel packets from the bag of Christmas items she'd purchased and handed him one.

She let him reach for the higher section of the tree while she carefully laid the strands across the lower branches. "Christmas Time is Here" from her *A Charlie Brown Christmas* album played in the background, and her heart hummed in happiness.

"I wonder what Julie will think of all the decorations next year. She'll be so small, but she may enjoy the lights and colors."

"I still think you're having a boy." Walt chuckled. "But I do look forward to celebrating Christmas next year with a little one." Walt stepped down from the ladder and pulled her into a hug from behind. He lightly laid a hand on her belly. "You're still so tiny. It's hard to believe a little person is in there."

"It is. Even after all of the nausea and other signs, I'll be glad to get blood tests back from the doctor confirming everything is still okay."

"I agree." Walt tugged her back from the tree. "How did we do? Any spots need more tinsel?"

Nancy tapped her chin. "Maybe just up there." She pointed.

Walt climbed up the ladder with a handful of tinsel, pulled out some strands, and leaned towards the tree. "Here?"

"A little to the left."

He shifted his hand. "Okay, has this got it?"

She shook her head. "Up just a touch."

Again he moved in that direction. "Here?"

She tapped her chin again and couldn't hold the smile in.

"You're pulling my leg." He jumped down from the ladder and tossed the handful of tinsel on her head. "Yep, that's the spot."

Giggling, Nancy threw it back at him, and he lunged at her. Sweeping her in his arms, he gently laid her on the sofa and tickled her ribs.

"No fair." She tried wriggling out of his hold. "You know my most ticklish spot."

"And I've had years of practice." He kissed her neck and trailed more kisses up to her cheek, then to the edge of her mouth before he pulled back suddenly. Shaking his head, he stood up. "Sorry." He ran his fingers through his hair and walked across the room to their last two boxes of old ornaments from each of their homes. "Why don't we put these up?"

Nancy reluctantly stood up and took her box. She carefully lifted the ornaments out and sorted through them. She smiled when she spied a fake piece of mistletoe. Pushing it aside, she pulled out one of her favorite ornaments and flipped it over. "To: Princess" was written in blue marker.

"Do you remember giving this to me?" she asked, holding out the figurine ornament of Bob Cratchit holding Tiny Tim on his shoulders.

He walked over, touched the ornament, and smiled. "I do. It was a couple of years after you hopped onto my lap at the play."

"I was seven when you gave it to me." She pointed to the spot where she had written her age in red next to the word *Princess*. "You stopped calling me Princess." She tried to remember when he'd last said it to her. "I was in high school. I think it was the summer you moved back home from Clemson." She bit her lip when she remembered that was the summer Brenda broke up with him. Did it have something to do with that? She saw something flicker in his eyes. Was it sadness?

Walt's hand moved from the ornament to her cheek, and he smiled softly. "You were getting too old for me to call you childish nicknames."

She looked down at her feet and dug her toes into the rug. "I liked it. I felt like something changed between us that year. Even though I was there for you after losing Brenda, you somehow seemed more distant."

He caressed her cheek and shook his head. "I'm sorry. I was going through a lot. I would go back to calling you that, but I feel like I should call you my queen now that we're married."

She remembered the mistletoe and said, "Hold that thought and stay right there." Leaning down, she found the small branch and held it behind her back. "Close your eyes."

His brow furrowed. "What are you up to?"

"Just do it. Please."

"Only because you said please." He winked and shut his eyes.

She held up the mistletoe, stood on her tiptoes, closed her eyes, and leaned in to kiss him on the lips. When he gripped her shoulders and pulled away, her eyes flew open and found his hooded.

"Nancy." It sounded like a groan.

"Please. I want to kiss my husband."

She'd barely uttered the last word when he pulled the mistletoe from her hand and crashed his lips into hers. The kiss was searing, and she nearly lost her footing.

"You can't say sweet things like I'm your queen and not expect me to kiss you," she mumbled against his lips.

The side of his mouth curled up, and he gave her one more peck. "Nancy Jane Wilson Moore, you're going to be the death of me."

"Is that a good thing?"

He grinned and shook his head. "That remains to be seen." Pointing to his box on the floor, he said, "We have some more decorating to do."

"You're changing the subject. I think the flowers you gave me mean it's a good thing."

He raised an eyebrow.

"Let's see . . . ivy means affection, friendship, and fidelity. Next, there were the red roses, which mean I love you."

He nodded and held back a smile. "I've told you that."

"And finally—the pink camellias mean longing for you." She wiggled her eyebrows.

"You've found me out." He bent down and kissed her on the lips. It was slow and gentle, but when she leaned in for more, he pulled back. "I'm hoping we can wait until next weekend before we . . . before I move back into your room."

"Our room."

"Yes, our room. If we keep kissing like this, I don't know that I'll make it. If we can hold back for this one week, it can make a difference in the future of our relationship. I'm trying to do the right thing."

Nancy bit her lip. The thought that he struggled flattered her, and she understood he wanted them to bond in other ways first, but she really liked kissing him, and she already loved him in every way possible. Waiting for him to catch up was hard.

"I know . . . I'll try to be more patient. At least I start work tomorrow. That will be a good distraction."

"We'll make it. I am happy you'll be able to continue doing something you love."

Nancy's heart lightened at the thought. "It's amazing how God worked it out. I always imagined using my paralegal skills to help women, and when I thought I'd never have the chance, God dropped this right into my lap."

There was a glint in Walt's eyes as he smiled and nodded. "I know what you mean."

She thought about the way he had moved up in the bank over the last few years. "He has blessed you with jobs too. It's a good feeling. Not everyone gets to do what they love for a living."

He squeezed her close and ran his fingers through her hair before releasing and tugging her to the last two Christmas boxes. "Speaking of jobs, we should get busy so you can get a good night's sleep."

"Actually, tomorrow I'm going in later, since Mr. Rutledge has court in the morning. I'll eat lunch early and go in about noon. In the future, I won't go in on Mondays."

"That means I won't get to have lunch with you." Walt frowned.

"What if I swing by your office afterward? I'm only staying until three or three thirty tomorrow."

"That would be nice. How about we go through each other's boxes of ornaments together? We can share where we got each one and what they mean to us."

She raised a brow. "I like that idea. We know a lot about each other, but I'm curious to find out which one means the most to you."

"Come on then. I want to show you the stars that a special someone gave me through the years."

"Surely you don't still have all of them." She recalled the stars she had made him through the years.

"Oh, yes. Every one, starting with the paper cutout you made in kindergarten."

"No way. Show me."

They huddled around his box, and he separated the stars she had given him.

"See. There are ten." He flipped one over. "You were fourteen when you gave me this one last."

She examined the silver star with "Nancy" etched into it and the date. "I still remember saving my allowance money for that. I was trying to impress you."

"As you can see, I was impressed enough to save it and all the others. Why did you stop?"

"I figured you'd had enough of a little kid chasing after you. And if you'll remember, you brought Brenda home that Christmas. I overheard you talking to her about marriage."

He rubbed a hand over his face. "I do remember bringing her. You know, she gave me several ornaments, too, but they all went in the trash. Yours are the ones I've saved."

"Aww. There you go again. Trying to make me swoon for you. You don't have to try hard."

"I don't?"

She shook her head.

Half an hour later, they finished their tree. Not every ornament made it on the tree. Some handmade ones from their younger years had seen better days, and they decided it was enough that they were preserved in the box. Only the handmade little paper star earned a spot despite its condition.

"You have a seat on the sofa, and I'll make you some of that hot tea from our honeymoon."

"Sounds wonderful."

"Why don't you check the TV Guide to see if there are any Christmas specials worth watching tonight? We'll also do our devotional."

Nancy took the TV Guide and *Starry Night* book from the coffee table. She noted that *A Charlie Brown Christmas* would start in twenty minutes, then flipped through the parts of the devotional they had already done.

The days depicting Jesus as a theophany in the Old Testament were interesting. She'd never thought much about Abraham meeting with two angels and God just before the incident at Sodom and Gomorrah. Could that have been Jesus? And what about the man who looked like the son of a god in the fiery furnace with Shadrach, Meshach, and Abednego?

Walt walked in with a steaming cup of tea. "One cup of winter rose tea for my bride."

"Why, thank you, dear. I have everything figured out. We'll do our devotional for day nine, then watch *A Charlie Brown Christmas.*"

"Ooh. We have a theme today with Charlie Brown."

"I guess we do." She flipped open the devotional book to day nine and handed it to him. "Here's where we are."

Walt wrapped an arm around her, and she snuggled into his side as he read the verse from Genesis 49 about the scepter not departing from

Judah. An image of Christ as king on a throne formed in her head, and her thoughts drifted. One day, all of God's people would celebrate in the throne room of heaven. From what she remembered, the descriptions of it in Revelation were beautiful in a way that was beyond comprehension.

She sighed. Though it started off terribly on Friday, it had turned into a good weekend.

Chapter Twenty-Three

Monday morning, Nancy stood in front of the mirror as she zipped up her skirt. Midway up, the zipper became stuck. She tugged it again with no success before looking down at it. She chuckled. "I have a pooch." Rubbing a hand over her belly, she marveled at her small baby bump. Anyone else would think she had put on weight. She slipped the skirt off and hurried to the closet to find one of her shift dresses. They were all loose enough in that area, they should carry her through a while longer.

She chose a navy dress and after quickly pulling it on, ran out to her car. Fanny waved from her front porch as Nancy pulled out of the driveway.

The day breezed past, working alongside Mr. Rutledge. He gave her several assignments to continue the following day. At three fifteen, they both agreed she was ready to work on her own while he was gone. She said her goodbyes and left for Walt's bank.

The thought of seeing Walt made her heart flutter as she approached the bank.

"Good to see you, Mrs. Moore." The brown-haired teller named Anna greeted Nancy. "I'm sure Walt will be happy to see you. He's had an interesting day."

"Oh, really?"

Anna smiled. "You'll see."

Nancy turned away, wondering about Anna's cryptic warning. Rounding the corner, she noticed Brenda's desk was empty and felt somewhat relieved. Even after Walt's assurances, a twinge of jealousy and insecurity remained.

As she approached Walt's office, she heard little boy giggles. "That's not a good horse name," said the little voice.

"Well, what is?" she heard Walt ask.

Nancy peeked through the open door and took in the scene of a little blond-haired boy playing with plastic farm animals on the edge of Walt's desk. Walt looked happy and relaxed. It made her heart glad. He was going to be a wonderful father for Julie—or possibly a boy, she conceded internally.

"Nancy!" Walt looked up, and his smile brightened further before he glanced back down at the boy. "Davie, I want you to meet my wife, Mrs. Moore."

The boy looked up, and his eyes went wide. "You're pretty."

"Why, thank you. And you're a little charmer, Davie. It's nice to meet you." As she stepped closer, she noticed a cast on Davie's left arm. "So, Davie, are you a new banker here, or did you come to take out a loan?"

He placed his good arm on his hip. "I'm just a kid. My mommy is the banker."

"Oh?"

She looked at Walt in question just as Brenda called out, "Davie, why don't you give Mr. Walt a few minutes alone with his wife? You can come out here to my desk."

"No, thank you. I want to be in here with Mr. Walt. He's lots of fun."

Brenda entered the office and gave Davie a stern look.

"Aw, Mom."

"Don't 'Aw, Mom' me." She pointed to her desk.

"Can I take the animals?" Davie questioned Walt.

"Of course. I bought them for you."

"Thank you!" Davie turned, threw himself at Walt, and gave him a one-armed hug. He scooped up the animals with his good arm and marched towards the door. Halting, he turned around. "Can I come in here again in a little bit?"

Walt bit back a smile. "We'll see. That will be up to your mother."

"Mom, I promise to be good," Davie said, then proceeded to her desk, where he dumped his animals.

"Sorry," Brenda told Walt as she closed the door. "You're a lifesaver."

Nancy sat in the chair across from Walt. "What was that all about?"

He stood and came around the desk. "No hug?"

"Why? You won't even kiss me. You probably think a hug is too much." She bit her lip to hide her smile.

"Hugs *are* nice. Kisses are nicer. I think you're safe from me here at work."

After making him wait with outstretched arms for several seconds, she stood and leaned into him, letting him pull her close. Before releasing her, he lifted her chin and gave her a quick kiss.

She returned to her seat, and he pulled the other guest chair close so their knees touched. He smiled, but his brows were furrowed. "As you can see, I've had a busy day. Just before lunch, Brenda received a call from Davie's school that he had fallen from the jungle gym at recess. Brenda had to pick him up and take him to the emergency room. She called the bank, saying she didn't expect to be back in until after two, because she had to pick up his medication and the crutches. It was in the opposite direction from the hospital and likely would have taken her an extra hour. Davie's dad couldn't help, so I offered to go pick the items up from the pharmacy."

"Oh." Nancy's stomach churned. "And the farm animals?" They were the only words that found their way out. Anything else might cause an argument.

"They were on sale at the pharmacy, and I thought they might help pass the time for him since she asked if she could bring him back with her while she finished work."

There were many things she wanted to say, but this wasn't the time or place.

"Okay. Well . . . I'm going to head home." She stood and walked to the door, needing to escape before she said something she'd regret.

His hand on her shoulder stopped her. "Nancy, I'm sorry. She's my employee. I would do the same for any of them."

She glanced back and nodded.

"I'll bring something home for dinner. Why don't you go rest?"

He meant well. He always did, but her hormones had her on edge, and this wasn't a good situation. "Thanks. See you in a bit."

When Nancy pulled into her driveway, Fanny was sitting on her front porch. She wondered if Fanny had spent the day outside.

"How was your day?" Fanny stood before her by the time she'd parked.

"Oh, work was good." Nancy realized she'd not even spoken to Walt about her work.

"The look on your face says it wasn't good."

Before Nancy answered, Fanny invited her in for tea, and she found herself sitting at her kitchen table with the now familiar plate of cookies. It was like having a grandmother next door.

"There's your real smile."

"You have a way of coaxing it from me, Fanny. Thank you."

"I'm just being a friend." She pulled her box of Earl Grey tea from the cabinet. "Your usual?"

"Yes, thank you."

Minutes later, they were quietly sipping tea. "I can tell something's troubling you, dear, and I don't want to overstep my bounds, but I'm here for you if you want to talk."

"Thank you." She smiled at Fanny before staring into her tea and mulling it over. An internal battle waged about whether to mention the problems with Walt. Maybe she could tell her part of it. Not the part about the pregnancy. She wasn't ready for that. And if she spoke to someone in her family or a friend back home, they might think badly of Walt. Maybe this would be a good outlet.

"I . . . yes, I think that would help me." She paused to think of what she wanted to say.

"Take your time. I'm in no hurry."

"Thank you. I guess I'll just dive in. A few days after returning from our honeymoon, I discovered that Walt's ex-girlfriend was his receptionist and assistant at the bank."

Fanny raised a brow.

"And . . . it bothered me that he had not mentioned it before. They had been very serious. He'd been her college sweetheart, and they planned to get married. She got mad at him for not coming home with her to live in Charleston the summer before their senior year and broke things off, saying they could reevaluate once school started back. At the end of the summer, she told him she was dating someone else."

She took a deep breath and shook her head. "I was there after it happened, and he was devastated. For a long time, I didn't think he would recover, so you can imagine the thoughts I had when she appeared in his life again. What really bothered me, though, is that she's divorced now. He assured me he has no lingering feelings for her, and I can't help but think he does, even if he doesn't mean to. I was there eight and a half years ago when she broke things off."

"Is there a reason you feel you can't trust him?"

She thought about him waiting so long before admitting he had slept with Brenda. Many times. That detail would always stick in her mind. "There was one other instance, just before we married, when he confessed something from his past to me. Something he intentionally kept from me weeks earlier." She wanted to stop there, but it seemed significant that both instances were related to Brenda. "It had to do with the same woman."

"Hmm. I can see how that would worry you." Fanny took a sip of tea. "So he was here working with this woman before you married?"

"He was."

"And yet he still married you."

"He did, but when he confessed . . . the first thing, he gave me the option to end the engagement. Maybe he was looking for an out."

Fanny frowned. A rare occurrence. "I don't know what the other thing was. That must play into your worry. I'm guessing whatever he said convinced you that he loved you, and you were the one he wanted to marry."

Nancy twisted her napkin. Maybe she shouldn't have brought up any of this with Fanny. She recalled the honesty Fanny had shown by admitting her own premarital sex and abortion. Scanning the room, she searched for words. Could she do it? Should she break her silence? *God, what should I do?*

Inside, she felt God nudging her. "Fanny . . . it might make more sense if I was completely honest with you." Her mouth went dry, and she took a sip of tea. "I'm pregnant, and it's not Walt's. He married me so I wouldn't be an unwed mother."

Fanny tilted her head and examined Nancy. "I've seen you two together, and that man is in love with you."

Nancy shook her head. "We've loved each other for a long time—as friends. Well, on his part. I've had romantic feelings for him since I was a child."

"Well, I still think he loves you romantically. Also, I am glad you didn't consider abortion."

"The truth is, I did consider it, though only briefly. But I feel bad that I even thought about getting rid of my baby." Nancy touched her belly.

"But you didn't. What happened to the father of your child? Do you not have feelings for him? Has he refused to accept responsibility for his child?"

Nancy pressed her lips together as she recalled how Henry had refused to see her in London. "I had planned to marry him. In fact, this child was conceived the night before our wedding." She went on to explain how his parents interfered, and finding Henry's father's letter. She even told her about the return visit with her parents and the letters and telegrams sent after she found out she was pregnant.

"I realize I made a huge error in judgment with Henry. He wasn't even a Christian. I don't know what I was thinking."

"That is quite a complicated situation."

Nancy nodded. "When Walt offered marriage, I tried to consider it carefully before accepting, but in truth, it's something I had wanted for for so long. I never dreamed I would have the chance to marry him.

Maybe I should have said no and not pulled him into my problems. Can you see why I'm concerned that I took a chance away from him to be happy with Brenda?"

"Did you both pray about it before the marriage?"

"I guess." She shrugged. "I mean, I did, but maybe I just imagined God gave me the go-ahead because that's what I wanted."

"I see." Fanny reached across the table. "Can I pray for you?"

"Please."

"Father God, please give Nancy comfort and wisdom that only you can. Help her know how much she is loved and treasured by you, the one who created her. And Father, strengthen their marriage. Help it to stand the test of time. In Jesus' name, Amen."

"Thank you."

"Nancy, as I was praying, I sensed the need to remind you of some things we sometimes forget when difficulties come. Your husband is human. Even the best of husbands will disappoint us at times. God is the only one who loves us perfectly. Our confidence must always be in him. Any person, even those we're not married to, may say or do something that has the power to tear down our confidence. But when we daily draw near to God and read his word, he will remind us that we are fearfully and wonderfully made just the way he intended. Place your confidence in Christ.

"There is no telling what may happen with this woman Walt works with, but in the same way, even men who marry the only woman they've ever loved sometimes end up straying. Do all that you can to strengthen your marriage. Be honest and open about your fears and ways you can both protect your marriage. And most importantly, go before the Lord daily in prayer for your marriage."

Something new stirred inside Nancy—it felt like hope. "You're right. I can do that. I can put my confidence in Christ, and I can protect my marriage."

"The next time something happens that gives you doubt, take it to the Lord in prayer, and as soon as you can afterwards, spend time reading your Bible. It will change your perspective."

Nancy stood. "I should go do that now before Walt comes home."

"Good idea. Oh, and . . ." She walked to a bookcase in the corner of the breakfast area and pulled out a book. It was the one by the British author they'd both met.

"Margaret Corbyn's book? The one with poetry?"

"Yes, you should borrow it. I think you'd enjoy it. It has a beautiful mixture of poetry and scripture she wrote in happy times and sad ones. It reminds me of the psalms in the Bible. She cries out to God with her hurts and moves into praise for his glory and greatness."

"That sounds like what I need. Thank you." Nancy walked towards the front door with Fanny following. "You know, Walt's my Mr. Knightley."

"Mr. Knightley?"

"From Jane Austen's *Emma*. We've known each other forever, and I want so badly for us to have that happily ever after."

"Nancy?"

"Yes?" Nancy looked at Fanny.

"Thank you for trusting me with something so personal. I'll be praying for your marriage."

"That means more than anything." Nancy waved goodbye and stepped onto the porch. She had work to do. The kind that would fortify her heart against lies that made her feel unworthy.

Chapter Twenty-Four

Nancy scanned the page of the legal digest, looking for every detail that could help her prepare for her client's legal case. She scribbled the information on her legal pad and turned the page. She'd found the perfect case law to help her client.

"Knock knock."

She glanced up to see Mr. Rutledge's son, Michael, standing in the doorway.

"Just thought I'd check on you to see if there's anything you need."

Nancy wrote down the last few words of her sentence before laying down her pencil. "Thank you. I think I've got it all figured out. I found the books I needed in your law library." She pointed to the pile of books scattered on the desk. "I don't see how Mr. Rutledge kept up with all of this and his other clients too."

Michael moved to the guest chair across from Nancy and crossed his arms. "That's why he was so quick to agree to work with you. When he realized how much experience you have, he knew you were just what he and Mrs. Butler had been looking for. He feared that if they brought someone other than an attorney in, they would need babysitting, and he has no time to spare."

"It was a God thing. I was looking for something part-time in

Columbia and wasn't quite ready to give up working as a paralegal completely."

"Well, I'm happy to have you around too. It's better than looking at my father's frowning face all the time. You're a lot prettier, too, and maybe with a lightened load, he won't frown so much."

She chuckled as he stood.

"I'll let you get back to it. Don't want to distract you when you're on a roll. I'm just next door if you need anything."

"Thanks . . . Michael. It feels funny calling you Michael when you're my superior."

"Superior." He shook his head. "Just think of me as a friend." He tapped the door and left.

Nancy stared at the open doorway, then shook her head and refocused on her case. She had just under an hour before she planned to wrap things up and leave to meet Walt for lunch.

Footsteps in the entry woke Nancy from her nap on the sofa, and she opened her eyes to see Walt coming around the corner.

"There you are." He glanced towards the kitchen. "Something smells delicious."

"Thank you. Salisbury steak is keeping warm in the oven."

"Mmm. I can't wait. I'm glad you had time to get off your feet. If it's ever too much, you can either call me to pick something up or open a can of soup, if you prefer. I'll understand."

"Thanks."

Walt reached down and picked up her fake pearl necklace from the coffee table. "I'm headed upstairs to change. I can drop this in your jewelry box."

She touched her neck. "Thanks. The beads are so large on it that they pressed into my neck when I lay down."

"We can't have that." He leaned down and kissed her on the forehead.

She got up, pulled dinner from the oven, and poured their drinks.

"Nancy?" Walt entered the kitchen, holding out his hand. "What is this? I've never seen you wear it. I didn't mean to be nosy, but it was hard to miss."

As she drew closer, she recognized the pendant necklace Henry had given her. "You're right. I haven't."

"It's beautiful. It almost looks real, but the jewel is too large to be a real ruby or garnet." He turned the pendant over in his hand. "We have our Christmas party planned for the office Friday. It will be an evening affair at an upscale restaurant in town. You could wear it with an elegant dress for that. Maybe I can help you pick a new dress out." His mouth drew up on one side, and he winked.

"I don't . . . Henry gave it to me for our wedding but wouldn't take it back when I offered it."

"Oh." His face dropped.

"Mm-hmm. So you can see why I don't plan to wear it."

"I do, but why keep it?"

"It seemed like the least I could do was to save it for my child. It's all she'll have from him. It's her heritage. Even if it's a boy, it will be something he can keep for his wife or children."

He nodded slowly. "Makes sense."

She took the pendant from his hand and laid it on the kitchen counter before wrapping her arms around his neck and leaning up to kiss him. It took him a few seconds to respond. But he finally wrapped his arms around her and deepened their kiss.

When he pulled back, he asked, "Do you miss him?"

She shook her head and tugged him to the table where their food waited. "You and I were meant to be."

The next morning, Nancy pulled a large book from a shelf in the office library and added it to the stack of several others she had collected for the day to help with her cases.

"Here, let me give you a hand," Michael said as he passed the doorway.

"That would be great. I would have needed to make two trips."

"It's no trouble." He let her lead the way to her office. "Should I put them here?" He held them over a bare spot on the desk.

"Yes, that's perfect. Thank you."

"Did you have a nice night yesterday?" He fiddled with a paperweight on the desk.

"I . . ." She thought about how her attitude changed from the time she drove home to the time after her Bible study. Even with the necklace incident, she felt like she and Walt were on more stable ground. "I did, actually. It was just a quiet evening. The highlight was watching a Christmas special."

He chuckled. "A quiet evening. Those seem to be long gone for me. I have a twelve-year-old daughter who loves drama and thinks she's an adult, and my boys are ten and eight and love to wrestle. That always ends with someone crying."

"Oh my."

He nodded. "I usually hide in my study, finishing up work and letting Dot deal with it."

"I'd love to meet Dot."

"She's a saint, that's for sure. You'll meet her at the Christmas party Saturday night at my dad's place."

"That would be nice. Your dad mentioned the party this morning. I'll check with Walt to confirm we can go."

"Sounds good. I'll let you get to the books." Michael tapped the pile before turning to leave.

Chapter Twenty-Five

Walt and Nancy walked hand in hand down the street in downtown Columbia, enjoying the Dickens festival the Saturday before Christmas. Victorian decorations dotted the area with wreaths on doors, bows on lampposts, garland, and even strolling actors dressed like they jumped straight out of *A Christmas Carol*.

Nancy drew closer to see the window display of a bookstore. It contained a Victorian-style dollhouse surrounded by Christmas-themed books.

"Walt, look." She pointed to a child's board book with the story of Jesus' birth. "We should get that. I'd love to have it for our little one." She whispered the last part so other pedestrians wouldn't hear.

He smiled and led her inside. A few minutes later, they left with the baby book and their own copy of *A Christmas Carol*. The smell of chocolate and sugar hit her as they exited, and she noticed a bakery two doors down.

The bakery had a Victorian-style Christmas village made of gingerbread in their front window. Walt took one look at Nancy's face and tugged her to the door of the bakery.

"How did you know I wanted to come in here," she said as they entered.

"Your eyes were as big as a kid's in a candy shop."

She looked around the store. "It's close enough."

There was an arrangement with several Christmas "trees" made up of different colored meringues, and the display cases were filled with an assortment of Christmas cookies, cupcakes, cakes, pies, and other goodies.

Nancy scanned the menu and saw they had hot chocolate with various topping options. She leaned into Walt.

"I'd like a cup of hot chocolate with candy cane and chocolate chips. But I need a minute to decide what type of treat I want."

The corner of Walt's mouth quirked up.

"Why are you looking at me that way?"

"Because you're adorable when you get excited about something." He leaned down to her ear. "If we do have a girl, I hope she's just like you."

Tingles shot through her body, and she wanted so much to pull him in for a long kiss. Instead, she settled for kissing him on the cheek.

He wrapped an arm around her and pulled her close as they continued to peruse the choices. She finally settled on plum pudding— the special of the day—in honor of Dickens. The lady behind the counter made sure she understood that it was an English dessert, which meant it was actually a dense cake. Nancy smiled as she told her she'd recently moved back from London, so she knew what it was. Walt chose a slice of Black Forest cake and promised to let her try it.

They found a small table near the window so they could watch the shoppers pass by.

"Walt, this cake is delicious. It has cinnamon and cloves and a hint of orange. Taste." She held out her fork with a bite.

He wrapped his hand around hers and fed himself as she watched, once more wishing she could pull him close and kiss him the way she wanted. It had been a week since he told her he'd consider moving back to her room, and she planned to convince him that tonight was the night.

She thought back to the evening before at his bank Christmas party. It had been perfect, mainly because Brenda wasn't there. Though she felt bad when she heard that Brenda's babysitter fell through and her ex-husband wasn't available. But it was nice to relax and get to know Walt's coworkers without worrying how she would react each time Brenda and Walt spoke to one another.

"Where's the bag with our new ornament?" Walt reached for the pile of bags they had set next to the table.

"I think it's in that one." Nancy pointed to a paper bag with snowflakes stamped on the outside.

"Here it is." Walt grinned as he unfolded the tissue paper that protected it and laid it on the table. "This is perfect."

"It is." Nancy admired the wooden ornament, which displayed a man and woman dressed in Victorian-style clothes standing next to a decorated lamppost. "The Moores' First Christmas, 1970." She read the words the artisan had painted for them out loud.

"It will fit in nicely with the Bob Cratchit and Tiny Tim ones I've given you." He held the ornament up. "Although it's too bad the artist didn't make ones with the Ghost of Christmas Past. That would look good on our tree too."

"Ha ha." She shoved at his side, and he pulled her chair close before wrapping an arm around her. "As if anyone would want that on their tree." She faked a shiver.

After a few more bites of cake, Nancy was done. "I can't eat the rest right now, but it's too good not to save. I'll ask them if they have a to-go box. Do you need one?"

"That's a good idea, but you stay put. I'll get them."

As Walt stood, he leaned over and gave her a peck on the lips. Her heart soared. Maybe if they hurried home, she could convince him to move his things into her room this afternoon. By the time they got back from the Christmas party at Mr. Rutledge's home, she doubted they would want to move things.

After boxing up the rest of their cakes, they headed out. She tightened her jacket. It was far from freezing, but there was a chill in the air. Walt pulled her close and rubbed her arms.

"Anything else you'd like to see?" he asked.

"I think I—"

"Mr. Walt!" A bright red jacket popped through the crowd on the sidewalk and wrapped its arms around Walt's legs. One arm was in a cast.

"Davie?" Walt looked down and patted the boy's head.

Davie craned his neck up at Walt. "Look at my cast." He lifted his arm. "My friends signed it."

"That's great."

"And I added the farm animals to the set I have at home. They—"

"Davie! You shouldn't run off like that. You scared me." Brenda jogged up to them, out of breath.

"But I saw Mr. Walt and had to say hi."

"I know you like him, but next time, tell me where you want to go, and be patient." Brenda looked up at Walt and batted her eyes. "I'm so sorry. It's hard to keep a seven-year-old boy still for long."

"No harm done." Walt chuckled. "It's good to see you again, Davie, but your mom is right. Something could have happened to you."

"But Mr. Walt, I'm almost eight. That's big enough to walk on my own," Davie announced.

"That's not for a while," Brenda said.

"My birthday is in February. That's soon. I looked at the calendar, and only one month is between Christmas and February."

"That's true, Davie. Your birthday will be here before you know it, but even at eight, you'll need to make sure your mom or the adult in charge of you knows where you are."

Brenda mouthed, "Thank you."

Davie frowned and stuffed his healthy hand in his jacket pocket before looking back up. "Did you have to stay with your mom all the time when you were eight?"

Walt bit back a smile and glanced between Nancy and Brenda. "When we were in busy public places like this, I did."

"What's a public place?"

"It's a place that is not private like your home or your friend's home. A public place is usually where there are a lot of people you and your mom don't know."

Davie looked around. "Yeah, I don't see anybody I know except you, Mr. Walt, and your pretty wife."

Walt laced his fingers through Nancy's and squeezed her hand. "She is pretty, isn't she?"

With a large grin, Davie looked up at Nancy and nodded.

"So, Davie, have you seen anything special while you've been out today?" Walt asked.

"I saw a Lite Brite at the toy store!" He pointed to the other side of the street. "And they let me try it out. That's what I asked my dad to give me for Christmas."

"A Lite Brite, huh? I think I saw a commercial about those. They do look pretty cool."

"They are cool! Mr. Walt, can I come back to the bank and visit you again?"

Walt looked at Brenda, whose cheeks colored. She shrugged.

"It will depend on your mom. How's your arm feeling?"

"It's okay. It itches sometimes, and I have a little stick I push down in it to make it stop."

"I can imagine that would be frustrating. Just make sure you follow the doctor's directions and listen to your mom so your arm heals correctly."

"Oh, I will." Davie stood up proudly.

Nancy felt like an outsider looking in at Walt's interactions with Davie. He was a funny and sweet little boy, and she could see how he had already endeared himself to Walt. It was Brenda's facial expressions that had Nancy concerned, though. Brenda looked entirely too enamored with every word from Walt's mouth. Nancy might have been dealing with jealousy towards Brenda, but she didn't think she was imagining Brenda's infatuation.

"We'll try to work out a time you can see Mr. Walt again." Brenda smiled up at Walt, then her eyes slid to Nancy and her smile faltered. She looked back at Walt. "We should let you two go. I'll see you Monday, Walt."

"Mom," Davie whined, "I don't want to go yet. Maybe I can walk around with Mr. and Mrs. Walt. They're adults, you know."

"I . . . uh." Brenda looked back at Walt.

"Sorry, buddy, but Mrs. Walt and I have to go home and get ready for a Christmas party."

"Oh." He kicked a piece of gravel under his foot.

"Maybe your after-school sitter can bring you by sometime soon."

Davie perked up and looked at his mom. "Can she?"

"Sure. Why don't you tell them bye, and we can go pick out a cookie from the bakery."

"Okay, I guess." He shuffled his feet again. "Bye, Mr. Walt and Mrs. Walt. Maybe I'll see you soon."

Walt leaned down and reached out to shake Davie's hand. "I'd like that. See you soon, then."

They all waved, and as they walked away, Davie called out, "Have fun at your party!"

"He's a cute kid," Walt said.

"He is."

"It wouldn't be so bad if we had a boy, would it?"

"Of course not. I just like giving you a hard time."

Walt chuckled. "You're funny, Mrs. Walt."

As they drove home, Walt was slower and slower to respond in conversation.

"Are you feeling okay?" Nancy examined him while he drove.

He nodded but said nothing.

"Did the cake not settle well?" Nancy had continued watching him. His face was tense and brow furrowed. He looked like he might be in pain.

"I don't know."

She reached out and squeezed his hand. He squeezed back, and they rode the rest of the way home in silence.

At home, she asked Walt if they needed to stay home and not go to her work party.

"I'll be fine, Nancy. I just need a few minutes, and then I'll get ready."

"Okay. Is there anything I can do?"

He shook his head and walked away, but she grabbed his hand and stopped him. Leaning in, she pecked him on the cheek.

"I love you," she said.

"I love you too."

When Walt came out of his room, he looked better and chatted a bit more with her on the drive to Mr. Rutledge's home.

The Rutledge home reminded Nancy of her parents' house with its stately front entrance and traditional decor.

Mr. Rutledge's wife, Helen, welcomed Nancy and Walt in. She had the same blonde hair and blue eyes as Michael and wore her hair much like Jackie Kennedy Onassis.

When they first arrived at the Christmas party, they found everyone milling around the living room, enjoying appetizers. Walt had not met anyone from the law office, and Nancy was glad she could introduce him to her coworkers and their spouses.

Annie and Theresa joined them almost immediately, and Nancy made introductions.

"Welcome. I'm Michael Rutledge." Michael approached Walt with his hand out.

Walt's face was tight, and Nancy guessed he wasn't feeling well again. But this time, she doubted it was from an unsettled stomach. He had a plateful of food and had already eaten several meatballs and crackers with cheese.

He looked at Nancy. "Is this the lawyer you work with?"

"No, this is his son I told you about. Though he is a lawyer and does work in the office."

"That's right. I had forgotten you mentioned a son." He smiled, but it looked forced. He shook Michael's hand. "Walt Moore. Good to meet you."

Michael placed a hand on Walt's shoulder. "I'm glad Nancy decided to join us. It's been a huge help for my father already. My mom was having a time trying to get him to cut back on the extra work, but he wanted to help everyone. Mrs. Butler is a good one too. She'd been trying to convince my father that he doesn't have to do it all. And I'm sure I don't have to tell you that Nancy's brightened things up at the office." He leaned in conspiratorially. "My dad can get kind of crotchety when things are looking bad for a case."

Nancy chuckled. "He doesn't seem that bad."

A brown-haired woman Nancy didn't recognize walked up to their group and laid a hand on Michael's shoulder. She was nice looking, yet wore a look of boredom.

"You must be the new girl," the woman said. "I'm Michael's wife, Dot. Did he tell you about me? I'm the one who runs the kids around and keeps up with his schedule. He's so busy and important. He's a lawyer, you know." She hiccupped after speaking and grabbed a glass of wine from a passing waiter.

"I think you've had enough, dear."

"Don't be ridiculous. The night just started."

"Yours didn't," Michael mumbled under his breath.

Dot looked away from Michael. "Oh, I should go say hello to Theresa. She's always the life of the party." Without saying goodbye, Dot walked away.

"Sorry about that." Michael frowned. "She's . . . well, there's not much to say."

He turned to Walt. "Do you golf? I don't have a lot of time for it, but I enjoy hitting the green when I can."

"No, it's not something I've ever taken the time for. I should probably learn. I hear it's a good way to get to know people in the community."

"I'd be happy to have you at my club any time. Just let Nancy know, and we'll set it up."

"Thanks."

Nancy noted the tension still present on Walt's face.

Mr. Rutledge cleared his throat and motioned for everyone to follow him to the dining room. It was a formal room with a large table set for the twelve in their group. The table was covered with a white linen cloth embroidered with a delicate garland design and accented with small red bows. Each place was perfectly set with china, silver, and crystal.

As they approached the table, Mrs. Rutledge explained that each couple was placed across from their spouse, and their seats were marked with place cards. Nancy was seated between Annie's husband, Tom, and Michael.

Mr. Rutledge thanked them all for their work before praying, then servers brought in a soup course of shrimp bisque. Nancy watched as Dot spoke incessantly to Walt. He nodded periodically and occasionally smiled, but Nancy noticed him clenching his jaw.

To her right, Tom discussed the state of his stocks and investments. Within minutes, she knew his top picks and how much they grew over the past week. It was interesting at first, but as a newlywed, she wasn't thinking seriously about how to invest their money.

"How has your weekend been so far?" Michael's question was a good excuse to bow out of the stock discussion.

"It's been busy. We had Walt's bank's Christmas party last night and went downtown to the Dickens festival today."

"It's a party weekend then?"

"It is."

"What did you think of the festival?"

"I loved all the decorations, but the strolling actors, musicians, and carolers made it stand out from other holiday festivals I've attended."

"It is a nice touch. This is the fourth or fifth year they've had it, and every year, it gets better."

"I'll be looking forward to next year."

On the other side of the table, Dot tapped her wine glass. "Waiter! Waiter! I need a refill." She huffed and looked around the room, which had become silent.

Michael slid his chair back and hurried around to his wife. When he whispered in her ear, she frowned.

"What? Why?" she responded to him.

Michael pointed towards the door to the hallway, and when she stood, he led her out.

Tom picked up where he'd left off with the stocks, and Nancy gently changed the subject to how they planned to spend Christmas just as they were served plates of prime rib and vegetables.

She'd barely started on her prime rib when Michael rejoined the group and silently began eating. A few minutes later, he whispered to

Nancy. "I convinced Dot to rest upstairs in one of the guest rooms. Maybe now your husband can eat in peace."

Looking across at Walt, she noticed he still looked miserable. She tried enjoying the rest of her meal, but it was difficult while seeing Walt so uncomfortable. As soon as everyone finished dessert and began to move from the dining room back to the living room, Nancy told Mr. and Mrs. Rutledge they needed to go.

"Walt, what's going on?" Nancy questioned as soon as they were on the road. "You've been quiet and moody all evening. Have I done something? Did you not want to go to my party?"

Walt glanced her way before refocusing on the road. "No, you haven't done anything wrong, and I did want to go to your party. It's . . . I've got something on my mind. I don't mean to keep anything from you, and I'll talk it over with you tomorrow. But tonight, I need to talk to God and sort some things out."

"I can't force you to talk to me, though I can't help but think it has something to do with me even though you say it doesn't."

He rubbed a hand over his face, then reached for her hand. "I love you, and that hasn't changed. Nothing between us has changed. And though this doesn't have anything to do with you, it could affect you. I just need to sort it out with God first. We'll talk after church."

When he said it did affect her, it sent her heart racing. He said nothing had changed between them, but maybe that was the problem. Something needed to change. Right now, they were only playing at marriage. She eyed his silhouette as they pulled into the driveway and silently entered the house.

In the upstairs hallway, she turned to go to her room when he pulled her to him and kissed her lightly on the lips. "I do love you. Please trust me." His voice cracked with the last few words, and he leaned his forehead on hers. "Please don't think you've done anything wrong or that I have a problem with you. We're going to get through this. I just have to wrap my head around it."

His ominous tone fueled her fears, yet she knew any answers would have to wait. She nodded and went to her room—their room. The room where she wished he was.

"God, I don't understand," she cried out softly. "Help me."

After getting ready for bed, she crawled in and grabbed her Bible. Over the past week, she had studied her Bible so much that it felt like an old friend. She came to the realization that her sense of self had become entirely tied to her relationship with Walt and his perception of her. But as she studied God's Word, understanding his greatness and power made his love and sacrifice for her all the more meaningful. She was precious to God—that was where her worth lay, and it was more than enough to see her through.

She rubbed a finger over the words "Holy Bible." God's love for her gave her more confidence, but she still longed to have a solid relationship with Walt. As she thought back over the day, it was obvious his attitude changed after they had the interaction with Brenda. He'd insisted things between them hadn't changed, but also said that whatever he was thinking affected their marriage. She rolled it around in her head, trying to discern what he meant.

She blew out a breath, then silently prayed. *God, please help me lay this down and trust you. Show me what I need to do, but help me not think that I can change Walt or make him feel any certain way. Also, be with him and help him sort through whatever is burdening him. I know you may have different plans, and I'm sorry if I jumped into our marriage too quickly, but I ask you to heal our marriage and grow it. I don't know what should happen, but you do. In Jesus's name, Amen.*

When she opened her eyes, she remembered the scripture Fanny had shown her in Romans 8, and she turned to it.

"Likewise, the Spirit helps us in our weakness. For we do not know what to pray for as we ought, but the Spirit himself intercedes for us with groanings too deep for words. And he who searches hearts knows what is the mind of the Spirit, because the Spirit intercedes for the saints according to the will of God. And we know that for those who love God, all things work together for good, for those who are called according to his purpose."

This was just what she needed to be reminded of. She also remembered their discussion about all things working together for good. *God, help me to trust you.*

Laying down her Bible, she spotted the book of poetry by Margaret Corbyn and picked it up. She'd read some of the poems and scripture in it and recalled how deep and meaningful they were. It was evident Margaret had faced challenges, but her faith had persevered and flourished. That was the kind of faith Nancy wanted—faith that drew nearer to God when difficulties arose instead of pulling away from him.

Randomly opening Margaret's book, she read a poem.

> Storm rages like tempest deep inside
> Ever eluding hope, it would seem
> Night darkened, nowhere to hide
> Smiling, pretending it was a dream
> Pain
> Loss
> Sorrow
> Devastation
> I look for peace in you
> And find the will to live
> Like the morning dew
> Hope only you can give

She'd felt many of these emotions over the course of the past two and a half months. She longed for that peace, but it eluded her. Just when she thought she had found it, a new storm hit. What would this storm be, and was it possible to feel peace in the midst of it?

Reading to the bottom of the page, she found a joyful scripture.

Oh, sing to the Lord a new song; sing to the Lord, all the earth! Sing to the Lord, bless his name; tell of his salvation from day to day. Declare his glory among the nations, his marvelous works among all the peoples! For great is the Lord, and greatly to be praised; he is to be feared above all gods. Psalms 96:1-4

It contrasted with the sadness of the poem. *I want that, God. I want to have so much joy, I can praise you when chaos surrounds me.*

Though her mind fought to worry and stress through the night,

God's Spirit reminded her that God had all power. Several verses Fanny had given her came to mind, and she turned to I Peter 5.

Be sober-minded; be watchful. Your adversary the devil prowls around like a roaring lion, seeking someone to devour. Resist him, firm in your faith, knowing that the same kinds of suffering are being experienced by your brotherhood throughout the world . . . To God be the dominion forever and ever. Amen.

"Amen," she said softly. *God, I don't know what's happening, but I feel the need to pray for strength. Please give me the emotional and spiritual strength I need for whatever this is. I pray the same for Walt. Amen.*

The urge to sleep overcame her, and she thanked God for it. When she'd first climbed into bed, sleep seemed impossible.

After turning out her light, she imagined Jesus sitting in the room and watching over her. *Thank you, God.*

Chapter Twenty-Six

The following morning, Walt and Nancy sat in the same pew they had occupied in the previous weeks. It was the church Fanny and some of the ladies from her Bible study went to.

When Nancy first saw Walt that morning, he had dark circles under his eyes and looked like he'd been crying, yet he insisted they attend church. She appreciated his determination to honor God, and that gave her hope for whatever news he would share later.

After singing several songs, the music minister encouraged them to take a few minutes and speak with those around them.

Janet, the lady in front of them, said hello, and her son spoke up and introduced himself. "I'm Tim."

"So nice to meet you, Tim. I'm Mrs. Nancy Moore, and this is my husband, Mr. Walt Moore."

"Can I call you Miss Nancy and Mr. Walt?"

She glanced at Walt and found his face blank. At least he wasn't frowning at the boy.

"Yes, that would be nice," Nancy answered for both of them.

"You'll be seeing a lot more of me," Tim said. "My mom said I can stay in big church now that I'm eight."

"Is that right? She must trust you to sit quietly and listen during the sermon."

Tim stood a little taller. "She does."

His mom looked at Nancy and winked.

"I think the pastor is ready for us to take our seats." Nancy pointed to the front. "I look forward to getting to know you better, Tim."

Once seated, she looked up at Walt to find him frowning, with his brow furrowed. When the pastor began reading the scripture for the sermon, Walt didn't open his Bible.

Nancy attempted concentrating on the pastor's words, but her mind couldn't stop drifting to Walt. First, he was affected the day before, after seeing Brenda and her son, and now after meeting another boy, he'd become more somber. Tim was the same age that Davie would be soon.

Something dark lurked in the back of her mind, and her heart raced. Surely not. She did some mental math, and her heart slowed. *God, please . . . no.*

Walt had said he'd broken up with Brenda eight and a half years earlier. It would have been May, if they broke up when Clemson let out for the summer. February would be eight years and nine months from that time. She worked the dates through her mind again and came up with the same thing.

Her gaze drifted to Walt. His face was still tense. Closing her eyes, she fought back tears. *God, help me. Holy Spirit, please intercede. If this is true, I won't be able to get through on my own.*

What would something like that mean for their already fragile marriage?

She felt the battle rage within, and her eyes fell to her Bible. Maybe this was all her imagination and she'd missed something with her calculations. Maybe Walt broke up with Brenda long before May. Until he told her what was on his mind, she would try not to panic.

Nancy sat quietly on their living room sofa while Walt paced without looking at her. After a few minutes, he sat next to her with tension continuing to roll off of him as he clenched and unclenched his fists.

"It's hard to know where to start." He stared at his clenched fists. "I'm not perfect, Nancy. But I may have gotten you into more than you bargained for."

Her heart slowed. *This is it. What will he choose?*

"I think . . . I think Davie might be my son." His voice was strained and ragged.

God, show me what to do. She laid a hand over his fist and squeezed.

"I'm so sorry." His eyes lifted to hers as he spoke. "You've gone through so much already, and now this." He rubbed a hand over his face. "I prayed through the night about it. But I've counted the months and years, and the last time . . . the last time I was with Brenda was in May. That was eight years and seven and a half months ago."

It was exactly what she'd imagined. She watched and waited for his next words.

"All I know to do is to talk to Brenda and have a blood test to see if he's mine. If he is, I have to be there for him. I won't do to him what Henry has done to your child. It's obvious Davie's dad isn't very involved in his life. He could use the stability of a man who cares for him." He shook his head. "I don't know. I'll have to see what Brenda says. I love you, and I don't want to call it quits, but I can understand if this is too much for you."

"I never took you for a quitter." The words were out before she could stop them.

"A quitter? Are you talking about our marriage? I told you I don't want to call it quits."

"Oh, I heard you. You said it as if you were giving *me* an out, but it sounded like *you* were looking for an out."

The furrow on his brow grew. "No, that's not at all what I meant. I guess . . . the truth is, I'm scared of losing you."

"Scared of losing me?" Nancy's voice softened. "I thought you were hoping I'd give up so you could work things out with Brenda." There, she'd finally admitted the worry that had been lurking in her mind all along.

He shook his head. "I've made such a mess of things—in the past and now. I may face lifelong consequences due to poor choices I made in college. But I need to correct a misunderstanding, and you may be the one rejecting me afterwards."

He tugged at the collar of his shirt. "Nancy, I love you, and not in a friend or sister way. I'm in love with every part of you. Your kindness, your wit, your cooking." He paused and gave her a small smile, but she remained stoic. "And I am and have been attracted to your beauty longer than you might appreciate."

She furrowed her brow, unsure of what he meant by the odd statement.

"I didn't tell you this before, because I worried it would scare you away."

"I don't understand."

"The real reason I got over Brenda was because I fell in love with you. All along, the one for me lived just next door."

She furrowed her brow as she contemplated his words. "You're saying you got over Brenda after we married, and you then fell in love with me?"

He bit his lip. "No . . . I fell in love with you when you were in high school."

Her eyes narrowed. "High school?" She examined his face for the truth. "Are you teasing me?"

Looking down at the floor, he rubbed the back of his neck and shook his head. "You were dating Brian, so it was a moot point. Not that I would have expected your dad to let a twenty-four-year-old date his seventeen-, almost eighteen-year-old daughter."

It still didn't make sense. Had she seen any signs? "I don't understand. I was always the one with the crush on you. I think I would have known if you were interested in me."

"I knew you had a crush on me when you were a kid, but it was obvious you'd moved on when you dated Brian. You two were inseparable. I kept waiting for you to realize he wasn't good for you, but when you did break up with him, you became a serial dater, then left for England, and here we are."

"I still . . ." She shook her head. "So you're saying you've been in love with me since I was sixteen?"

"Yes. Do you think I'm awful? And now I've possibly added another child to our complicated situation. I understand if you want to run far away from me, but that's not what I want. Not what I've hoped for."

Nancy fought back laughter. "You . . .you have been in love with *me*?"

He nodded slowly.

She closed her eyes, and joyful tears escaped.

"I'm so sorry, Nancy." He placed his hands on her cheeks and wiped at the tears. "I meant to help you and had hoped you would get over Henry eventually and grow to love me as much as I love you."

She pulled away and wiped her eyes. A smile crept up her face, and she shook her head. "Don't you see? At some point, my crush became love, and I never stopped loving you, Walt. I never thought you would feel the same for me, so I worked hard all these years to find others to love. I did love Henry until he refused to let me back into his life or acknowledge this child." She rubbed her belly. "But I'm ashamed to say, if during my engagement to Henry, you had told me you loved me since I was seventeen, I might have reconsidered. I rushed into the idea of marriage with him. Especially after what happened with Brian. I was looking for someone to show me I was worth loving."

Something clicked in her mind, and she bit back her smile. "You said you were still single because the timing had never been right with the woman who held your interest. I was that woman?"

"When did I say that?"

"It was the night Brian came over to try to convince me to date him. Remember, I spoke with you while you were working on the dining room table in the shop? I said I was surprised you were still single, and that's when you told me."

"Yes, you are that woman—the reason I was still single. You have a good memory."

She shrugged. "Even though I was still getting over Henry's rejection, the thought that there was someone you loved stuck with me because I felt a twinge of jealousy. That conversation is one reason I kept thinking you still loved Brenda."

He shook his head, placed a hand on her cheek, and leaned in. "It's only been you for a very long time."

She met him halfway, and their lips connected.

"I love you," he said against her lips before kissing her repeatedly. It nearly took her breath away.

"I love you too," she said as she gasped for air.

"Nancy." Walt leaned his forehead on hers. "When I said I wanted our marriage to be built on Christ, I meant it. I . . . I think we've been under spiritual attack. We both need to work on honesty, and I want to protect our marriage. Whatever happens with Davie, our marriage comes first, and before that, God."

"Yes," she whispered. It was what she desperately wanted.

He leaned back and looked into her eyes. "Two things need to happen. The first, I'm not excited about, but I need to meet with Brenda."

Nancy sucked in a breath. Even after their confessions, she still didn't like the idea.

"It needs to be today, so we can get this over with. And it shouldn't happen anywhere around work. I'd like for you to go with me so we can present a united front in this and she doesn't imagine there's something between her and myself that isn't there. I can call her and set up a time to go after Davie is in bed. He shouldn't be part of the conversation until we confirm if he's even my son."

"That's true."

"The second thing is"—he reached for her hand—"now that we've established how much we love each other, I'm moving back into our room."

Nancy sighed and couldn't hold back her smile. "Finally."

He pecked her on the lips. "Yes, finally. I'm sorry I've been torturing us. I thought I was doing the right thing."

"Maybe it was. It gave us a chance to get to know each other in a different way."

One side of his mouth curled up, and he wrapped an arm around her waist. "Well, no more of that." He closed his eyes and prayed over them, praising God for the way he had brought them together and was working out their story. He also prayed for the situation ahead with Brenda and Davie.

On the front porch of Brenda's duplex, Walt and Nancy stood hand in hand while Walt knocked. Nancy looked around at the cute home. A wreath hung on the door with red ribbon woven through it and a large red bow. A toy soldier the size of a small child guarded the door, looking like a prop straight out of *The Nutcracker Ballet.*

Footsteps echoed inside what Nancy imagined was a small entryway. The door eased open with the latch-chain still in place, and Brenda spoke. "Hey, Walt. Just a minute."

She slid off the latch and swung open the door. Her smile dropped when she saw Nancy. "Oh, I . . . thought it was just you, Walt."

"It wouldn't be appropriate for me to come into your home without her."

"Come on in. Just don't get too loud. Davie's room is upstairs, but the place isn't very soundproof." Brenda didn't comment on what Walt had said as she led them to her living room.

Nancy noted Brenda's makeup looked freshly applied even though it was eight thirty in the evening, and she was dressed for a night out with her low-cut burgundy dress.

The room was simply decorated, but the furniture was nice for a woman who'd recently had to move out on her own. An antique book-case, a coffee table, and a tan sofa looked new alongside a rocking chair and leather high-back chair. A small Christmas tree decorated with colorful balls and lights filled one corner.

"Have a seat." She waved towards the sofa. "What were you wanting to discuss?" Her eyes stayed on Walt.

Walt glanced at Nancy before turning back to Brenda. "You may have some idea. Yesterday, when Davie mentioned his birthday . . ."

Brenda's face paled, and her jaw ticked.

"I put two and two together, and I want to know if he's my son."

She gazed at the Christmas tree, then found his eyes. "I don't know," she said softly.

"You don't know?" Walt questioned.

Shaking her head, Brenda avoided his eyes.

"So either of us might be his father?"

"Yes."

"Your ex never questioned paternity?"

"No, I . . ." She looked between Nancy and Walt, and color rose in her cheeks. "He and I went out soon after you and I ended things—actually the same week."

"So you convinced a man you barely knew to marry you when you found out you were pregnant, even though it was possibly my child?"

"My dad found out about the pregnancy after I had been going out with Kenneth a few weeks. Dad didn't know it might be yours. He thought you and I had broken up several weeks earlier than we did. He made Kenneth an offer he couldn't turn down. If he would marry me, Dad promised to pay off his school and car loans, and the downpayment on a house for us. Dad even got him connected with the company he works with. It all happened so fast."

"Still, I would have thought you would have given me a chance to be a father to my son."

"I panicked. Dad threatened to make me abort my baby if I didn't marry Kenneth. I worried you wouldn't marry me after the way I treated you. If it was discovered I wasn't sure who the dad was, I imagined neither of you would marry me. I would have been back to my dad making me abort him."

Walt closed his eyes and took a deep breath. "I want to have a blood test and see if he's mine." He opened his eyes, and she nodded.

"I'm sorry. I did what I had to for my son," she whispered.

Walt rubbed a hand down his face. "And possibly mine. It sounds like Kenneth is an absentee dad, from the things you've told me. If I'm his father, I'd like a chance to be in his life."

A hint of a smile formed on Brenda's face.

"My marriage comes first, but I promise to consistently be there for him if he's mine."

"Of course."

"I'll call my doctor tomorrow morning and get the test sometime tomorrow, if they have an opening. I'd like for you to do the same with

Davie. You can take off the time needed to take him in for the test. I'm assuming he's out of school, since Christmas is Friday."

"He is. I'll let his sitter know. I'm sure she wouldn't mind bringing him by the office for me if it means she'll get some free time."

"Thanks. I'd like to find out the answer sooner rather than later. If you wouldn't mind, can I pray over this situation?

"Of course."

Walt prayed a short prayer. "We won't keep you. I'll see you in the morning." He stood and held out a hand for Nancy.

She grabbed his hand and followed him to the door. She'd felt like a spectator the whole time. What was there for her to say? It was a complicated situation.

Brenda stopped Walt with her hand on his arm. "Thank you for being willing to step up."

"I'm a Christian, and though I did things I shouldn't have when we dated, I'm trying to honor God by making them right now."

Brenda glanced at Nancy but said nothing. Nancy noticed her eyes were green. On the wall behind her hung a picture of Davie. He had blond hair that was lighter than his mom's, and brown eyes . . . much like Walt's.

Nancy reminded herself that God was bigger than this circumstance, and he could use even this for his glory.

Once in the car, Walt pulled Nancy's hand to his lips. "I'm so sorry to put you through this. I know God is the one who will get us through, but it helps knowing you're on my side. I promise I will do everything possible to keep our marriage first."

"I trust God to work in this, but I'll admit it worries me. We've had a rocky start."

He leaned across the front seat and placed a hand on her cheek before giving her a lingering kiss. "I love you, and you love me. God brought us together, despite us both being oblivious to the feelings we shared. We can trust him to keep us together."

She nodded but couldn't stop the tear that slipped down her cheek.

"Nancy," Walt rasped out her name as he wiped the tear and pulled her into a hug.

A few seconds later, he leaned back. "I would hold you longer and pray over you, but . . ." He glanced back at the house. "I don't think we should linger in Brenda's driveway. It might seem a little creepy."

His hand slid down her arm and squeezed hers before shifting the car into reverse.

As they drove down the road, Walt prayed with his eyes wide open. "God, please forgive me for creating this situation and not being sexually pure, even though I knew that was what you called me to. Please help us despite my unworthiness. Protect our marriage. Help us grow stronger together through this. Guide us in becoming the parents you have designed us to be to all our children. Give us the ability to keep this at your feet and not take it up and try to fix things on our own. In Jesus' name, Amen."

Nancy squeezed his hand. She recognized the difficulty of admitting his responsibility. As frustrated as she was with the situation, she remembered how hard it had been for her to confess what she had done. Walt's humility sparked a deeper appreciation for him. How had she won the love of such a man?

Upon entering their home, Nancy tugged Walt under the mistletoe and kissed him. They might have been wading into difficult waters, but she loved him with all of her heart. Seeing the man he was in difficulties only deepened those feelings.

As he held her, he rocked in time with an imagined tune. Eventually they slowed, and she leaned her head against his chest.

"You'll move into my room tonight?" Nancy questioned, feeling shy but hopeful.

His chuckle rumbled against her ear. "If you'll still have me."

She quickly pulled him upstairs.

Chapter Twenty-Seven

A mixture of contentment and worry swirled inside of Nancy as she worked at Rutledge's Monday morning. She was relieved to finally be on solid ground with Walt after all they had been through, but waiting for the blood test and its result loomed in the back of her mind. She didn't relish the changes a match would bring.

Walt had called the doctor's office as soon as they opened and scheduled the test during lunch. The nurse said it would take at least a week for the results, and possibly more with Christmas on Friday. Nancy attempted to shove it to the back of her mind so she could enjoy Christmas, but that was proving difficult.

Forcing herself to focus on the task at hand, she reread the sentence she had just gone over when a tap on her door drew her eyes up.

"Hi, Michael. Can I help you with something?"

"I was just about to ask you the same thing. I was passing by and noticed you still here. It's past the time you normally leave to meet your husband for lunch."

She glanced at her watch. "I guess it is." She'd accomplished far less than she'd hoped. "Now that you mention it, I am hungry." She was surprised her body had not protested earlier.

"I imagine your husband will be calling soon to find out where you are."

"We're not meeting for lunch today. He has an appointment." The words tasted bitter on her tongue, and she tried to keep her mind from lingering on where he was.

"In that case, why don't you join me? I'm about to head out."

"I hate to intrude on your lunch with your dad."

"I wouldn't consider that an intrusion, but as it stands, he won't be eating with me. He brought food so he can work through lunch today."

"If you're sure I won't be a bother, I'll join you."

He grinned. "Great. And of course you're not a bother."

Minutes later, they entered the diner across the street. It smelled of ham, scalloped potatoes, and baked apples, the special of the day, according to the sign.

Michael nodded at a waitress and led Nancy to a booth in the back. "We'll need a menu," he called out to the waitress.

Before they were settled in their seats, the waitress brought a menu for Nancy and took her drink order.

"She didn't ask what you wanted to drink."

"She knows. My dad and I are regulars." He leaned back and draped his arm across the booth. "He's been coming here since he started the firm. I have memories of sitting in a booster seat with him in this very booth."

Nancy chuckled at the image. "Well, I'm glad she wasn't just ignoring you."

"Sally?" He glanced across the room at the waitress. "She's known me so long. She'll have my sweet tea out here with yours."

Nancy surveyed the restaurant. It wasn't as polished and new looking as The Screaming Peach. Instead, everything was worn with age. Some of the wood laminate on the table was faded. Cracks marred the vinyl seat of the booth, and the vinyl tile floor was dull. Yet everything appeared clean. Her eyes flicked back to Michael.

His mouth quirked. "I know. You're thinking this doesn't look like the kind of place we would enjoy. But it's got character. Besides, they always save this back table for us so we can discuss cases in private. You can't get that kind of service just anywhere."

"I guess not." The picture on the wall next to her caught her eye. It was a pencil sketch of some of the buildings across the street, including the Rutledge and Rutledge office. She glanced around and saw similar sketches hanging above each table. "That's a fun touch. Is it a local artist?"

Michael nodded, and the waitress returned with both of their drinks, just as he'd said. On Michael's recommendation, Nancy ordered the beef tips.

"Something's bothering you," Michael stated after the waitress walked away.

Nancy looked up from her food, unsure how she wanted to answer. "What makes you say that?"

"You have that crease." He pointed between his eyebrows. "Right here. I've seen you get it sometimes. It's my job to read people, and I think something's bothering you. How can I help?"

"It's . . . well, there is something bothering me, but I'd rather not say. It's personal."

"Okay." He nodded. "I won't press, but I'm here if you need someone to talk to."

"Thanks. I know that's part of your job too—listening to people describe their problems so you can sift through their situation and provide legal counsel."

"Well, yes. But you're a friend, so it's a little different."

"Tell me about your children." She changed the subject. "You mentioned a preteen daughter and two younger boys."

He grinned, and a brow rose. "Yes, they're a handful. My daughter is twelve, going on twenty-one. She's been pushing us to our limits, and we dread the next few years if that doesn't change. I think we were too lenient on her when she was younger—especially with her being the only girl."

"Yikes. I'm taking mental notes for when we start our family."

His eyebrow lifted. "Hoping to start soon?"

Her face heated. She'd not thought that comment through. "Yes, we're hoping." She was also hoping this lawyer wouldn't see right through her. He held her gaze, and she almost admitted the truth. Instead, she looked down and took a bite of beef tips.

For the rest of lunch, she avoided unpleasant topics, though that narrowed the acceptable subjects. Talk about babies—no. Discuss spousal issues—double no. Christmas traditions seemed neutral, but she proceeded with caution.

When their plates were empty, she realized they'd been there almost an hour and a half. "I should get going. Sorry for chatting your ear off. I'm sure you have plenty to do."

"It's fine. I don't have an appointment. If I don't finish by five thirty, I'll head home and wrap things up after dinner. I . . ." He shook his head. "Have a good afternoon. You're coming in tomorrow?"

"I am. See you." She grabbed the ticket from the table.

"I'll get it." He stood and reached for it.

She guessed it would turn into an argument, so she pulled out enough cash from her wallet to cover her part and dropped it on the table.

He bit back a smile. "You're stubborn. You'd make a good lawyer."

"Thanks. I'll see you tomorrow morning. Don't dawdle too much —maybe you can give your wife a break with your daughter. Maybe even invite your daughter and the boys to play a board game or watch a Christmas show. You might have to offer treats to make it worth their while."

"That's actually a good idea. I'll ask Sally. I bet she still has plenty of goodies here in the bakery case. See you tomorrow, Nancy."

Footsteps echoing through the hallway alerted Nancy to Walt's arrival. She looked up to see her handsome husband enter the kitchen.

Years earlier, when she'd fantasized about marrying Walt, she'd never dreamed marriage to him would start in such an unusual way and fraught with so many difficulties. Their marriage was both harder than she'd imagined and more wonderful. Following their confessions the previous day, he had showered her with love and tenderness, making it clear how much he cherished her.

Nevertheless, she felt inadequate for the challenge of co-parenting a child with a woman he had once loved and who seemed to love him still.

"Hey." He pulled her into a kiss, then leaned back and ran his fingers across her forehead. "You've been worrying. I'm so sorry I've placed us in this situation." He kissed the furrow at the top of her nose. "God, give Nancy peace in the midst of this. Continue to deepen our relationship. Amen." He squeezed her tightly, then tugged at her hand. "Come sit with me."

Nancy resisted and pointed to the table. "Dinner is ready."

He smiled. "It smells wonderful. I can tell you've worked hard on it. Would you mind if I popped the platters back into the warm oven? I'd like to sit with my wife for a few minutes."

The look in his eyes could convince her of nearly anything. She nodded, and he placed the food in the oven, then led her the kitchen table. She squealed as she lost her balance when he pulled her into his lap. He wrapped his arms around her and nuzzled her neck.

"You smell like cinnamon. Yum." He peppered her neck with kisses.

"It's from the spice cake I made for dessert."

"Mmm. Thank you. I'm a lucky man to marry such a good cook."

"You're welcome. How was your day?"

"Fine." He kissed behind her ear.

"Does it bother you having Brenda as an assistant now that you've found out you may be co-parenting Davie?" The question had been plaguing her.

He squeezed her tighter. "Yeah. Let's not talk about Brenda or Davie." He leaned back and caressed her cheek. "There's nothing we can do until we have answers, and that won't be until after Christmas. Next year, everything will be different. Even if Davie isn't mine, we'll have another little one. I want to enjoy my wife while I have you all to myself. I know it's hard to ignore the thoughts running through our minds, but let's try."

Her heart leapt. "That's what I want too."

"The next few days will be all about us. When our thoughts stray to the what-ifs, we'll take every thought captive to obey Christ like Paul says to the Corinthians. After dinner, let's do our advent devotional and maybe some extra Bible study. Then we can spend the rest of the night snuggling." He wiggled his eyebrows before kissing her neck again.

Her face heated, but she managed to speak. "Sounds perfect."

Chapter Twenty-Eight

Only a few more minutes of work, then Nancy could go home and . . . be left with her thoughts. Over the past few days, she'd become a pro at pushing thoughts of being a stepmom out of her mind. Walt might be George Knightley, but she was far from Emma Woodhouse. Maybe instead of *Emma* being her favorite book, she should consider *Gone with the Wind*. She might give Scarlett O'Hara a run for her money with her "tomorrow is another day" attitude.

She closed her eyes, asking God for help before getting back to work.

"Knock, knock," Michael's voice called from her office doorway.

"Who's there?" Nancy tried not to laugh at her own joke as she looked up, but Michael had a knowing grin.

"It's that time again, and you're still here. Am I going to have to set a timer for you?"

"I finally got myself focused and lost track of time." She finished writing a sentence on a document and stood up to stretch.

"Join me for lunch again?"

Nancy looked down at the files on her desk. "Sure. Let me put these away."

"Are you up for the diner, or should we branch out?"

"I don't mind eating there again. They had a few other items I haven't tried that sound good."

"Great. I'll grab my coat."

Ten minutes later, Sally seated them in the back corner booth.

"I think I'm having déjà vu."

"All over again." He winked.

This time, Nancy knew just what she wanted, and when Sally came by for her drink order, she ordered the chicken potpie.

Once they were alone, Michael said, "I took your advice."

Nancy raised a brow. "You did?" She tried to recall what he meant.

"I sat with my family and watched a show. We even had hot chocolate and the pie I bought here yesterday."

"Did it make any difference?"

"The kids all responded well. Dot said she had a headache and walked out partway through *It's a Wonderful Life*, but three out of four isn't bad."

"I guess not." She felt bad for him.

"You look like you feel better today."

Nancy shrugged. "I'm getting better at not thinking about things I can't change."

"Sorry, I shouldn't have said anything."

"It's okay. I'll get through it. It's definitely increased my prayer life."

"I understand that." He reached down, placed his briefcase on the table, and popped it open. "I've got something for you."

"Oh, is there something you need me to do before I leave town?"

"No, nothing like that." He lifted several files and pulled out a present wrapped with gold paper. "Here. This is for you."

"Thank you." She took the rectangular gift from him. "I'm sorry to say I didn't get you anything."

He waved a hand. "It's not a big deal. You'll understand when you see it."

"Okay."

"Go ahead. I want to see your face when you open it."

She felt slightly uncomfortable with him giving her a gift but opened it anyway. As she tore at the corner, a wooden picture frame peeked through. Once it was entirely unwrapped, she found the frame held a sketch by the same artist who had pictures hanging over all of the diner's tables. Hers was similar to the one over the table with Rutledge and Rutledge included, but the angle was different, and the law office was to the left side of the sketch instead of the center. "Thank you. That's so thoughtful. I'll have to keep an eye out for more of this artist's work."

She examined the picture more closely, looking for the artist's name. M. Rutledge. She looked back at Michael, who was smirking. "It's you?"

He nodded.

"Wow, a lawyer and an artist. These are really good." She glanced around the diner at the other sketches again. "If you ever get disbarred, you have other options for income."

He raised his eyebrows in mock horror. "Me—disbarred? Perish the thought."

"Seriously, though, you're really good. When do you find time for drawing?"

"I keep a sketchbook with me. Sometimes when I'm stuck on a case, I stop and sketch. It helps my mind unwind. Often I figure out the best solutions when I'm sketching."

"I like that. Maybe baking is my thing. When I'm stressed or trying to figure something out, I bake. Yesterday I made a spice cake and cookies." Maybe she shouldn't have said that. She looked at Michael and shook her head.

He pretended to zip his lips.

"Thanks. Anyway, what's your family doing for Christmas?"

"I'm taking them down to Palm Beach, Florida, to meet up with my parents. Mom and Dad are already down there, staying at The Breakers Hotel. Dad and I will play some golf, the kids will enjoy the heated pool and beach, and the ladies get waited on hand and foot."

"Sounds nice."

"It's a long drive, but to enjoy some nice weather, it will be worth it. We've gone the last few years, and the kids like it so much, they don't even fuss in the car. They're too afraid they won't get to do it next year."

"I don't blame them. A trip down south would be so relaxing right now. It's a little cold for my taste here—even at fifty-five degrees today."

He chuckled. "Dad called this morning and said they expected a high of seventy-eight."

"Nice. That *is* worth the drive. I could lie on the beach in that kind of weather."

Their food arrived, and Nancy enjoyed the distraction from her other thoughts.

"Today, I can't hang around like yesterday," Nancy said after finishing her meal. "I've got a cookie swap with my Bible study ladies, and then I need to pack for our trip."

"You're going home? Didn't you say you and Walt are both from Greenville?"

"I did. He was my neighbor from the time I was three."

He raised a brow. "From friends to family? Or did you crush on the neighbor boy for years?"

"A little of both. I had a crush on him since I was little, but I was about nine when I realized there was more to romantic love than just saying you loved someone. He was seven years older, and I saw him kiss a girl."

Michael whistled and winked. "I bet that changed you forever."

"I'll say. I never dreamed he would pick me, but here we are. It will be our first time home since the wedding, and it seems strange to go back as a married couple to celebrate Christmas."

Sally stopped by the table to check on them, and Nancy asked for the ticket.

"I absolutely insist on getting it today. Consider it part of your Christmas present," Michael said as he grabbed the check.

"That's not right. You just gave me a really nice gift." She pulled out her wallet, but he threw a hand over hers.

"I'm not taking your money." He turned and called out to Sally, who was walking to the nearest table. "Put all of this on my tab, please."

"You got it, Michael." She walked back over and picked up the receipt. "It's good to have a new face around here, Nancy. Merry Christmas to you both."

"Thanks. Everyone has been welcoming so far."

"That's how it should be. And Michael . . ." Sally looked his way. "Safe travels, and get some sun for me."

"Will do." He reached for Nancy's coat and helped her put it on, then gave her shoulders a squeeze. "I'm hoping you'll be able to have a wonderful Christmas and keep your mind off of that thing you can't change. That's all I'll say about it. But after we get back Sunday night, I'm happy to lend an ear if you need to get it out."

"Thanks. I appreciate it."

"I'll walk you to your car since I'm heading that way."

After she left him, she thought about his offer to talk. She just might need that after Christmas if she didn't lose her mind before then. She didn't want to tell anyone Walt knew well or would have to see often about the situation in case Davie wasn't his—though it seemed highly probable he was.

In the meantime, the cookie swap, wrapping presents, packing, and making dinner would keep her distracted this afternoon. Once they arrived in Greenville tonight, catching up with her parents and sister would keep her mind occupied.

Chapter Twenty-Nine

Dinner was in the oven keeping warm, and Nancy had placed the last couple of items in her suitcase for their trip. She laid out her cosmetic bag and placed her toothbrush and toothpaste beside it to use just before they left.

"Hey. Here you are."

The baritone of Walt's voice startled her. "Hi."

She turned, and he wrapped her in a hug and kissed her.

He mumbled against her lips, "Change of plans."

Nancy looked up. "What do you mean?"

"I want to stay here tonight and leave in the morning. That way we can exchange our gifts and have our own mini Christmas before we join everyone else."

"But everyone is—"

Walt held up a hand. "I called both of our homes, and they think it's a great idea. Nothing important is going on before noon tomorrow. It's our first Christmas, and . . ." His gaze drifted beyond her. "Considering the circumstances, we need all the peace and alone time we can get. Like I said before, it's our last Christmas alone whether Davie is mine or not."

"True." She tensed.

"And I want my wife all to myself for a bit."

"Okay." Warmth started in her chest and ran down to her toes. All the tension melted away. He wanted her—all to himself. "I like the sound of that."

After helping Nancy wash the dinner dishes, Walt dragged her into the living room, where he had set up blankets and pillows before the fireplace, just like the first night of their honeymoon.

"When did you do this?"

"While you were pulling out the food for dinner. Since on our first night here, we didn't realize"—he tugged her hands to his lips and kissed them one at a time—"how much we were loved by one another, I thought we could recreate that night. Sort of a fresh start."

He helped her sit down on the blanket, and her heart leapt. She likely looked silly with her huge grin.

"You stay there just a minute, and I'll bring your gift in."

When he left the room, her eyes went to the gifts she'd wrapped for him under the tree.

"Close your eyes," Walt called from the hallway.

She placed a hand over her eyes and wondered at his request.

"Okay. Open them."

There sat a wooden rocking chair. "Walt, it's beautiful. When did you have time to make it?" She stood up and ran her hands over the turned back and the smooth armrests.

"I did most of it before we married. I had a lot of extra time then." He winked. "I did slip into the workshop a few times and work on the finish after the wedding."

"Oh, Walt, I can see myself rocking Julie in it."

He nodded and looked solemn.

"You're not going to contradict me anymore and say we're having a boy?" she questioned.

He shook his head. "A girl would be nice."

She wondered if he was thinking about already having a boy but didn't want to spoil the moment. Sitting down in it, she tested it. "This is perfect. Thank you. It will be a family heirloom."

His smile returned. "They have some cushions at the department store that fit. You can pick out the color you like."

"We should go together after Christmas." She stood up and gave him a hug. "I absolutely love it."

"I plan to make a bassinet for our room, too, but I'll wait to start on that until after we announce the pregnancy."

"Good idea." She pointed to his presents under the tree. "Your turn."

She had wrapped his presents in thick gold paper with red fabric bows that sparkled.

"Mine don't quite have the meaning that yours does. I didn't make them with my own hands."

He took the first gift from her. "Anything you bought me has meaning because it's from you. It could be a pack of gum and I would be happy."

When he opened the first box and saw the leather tool pouch, he grinned before unrolling it. "These are those chisel-turning tools I was talking to your dad about." He unrolled it and examined the set. "With these, I can make some beautiful designs on the bassinet. Thank you."

He leaned over and laid a hand on Nancy's cheek, and his thumb caressed her lips before he leaned in for a kiss. She melted into the kiss as she wrapped her arms around his neck.

A minute later, she pulled back. "You have one more."

She handed him a larger box, and he carefully removed the paper and unboxed it. His grin grew when he examined the portrait of the two of them on their wedding day. His eyes glistened.

"If I knew then what I know now." His voice came out husky.

"What, Mr. Moore?"

He carefully reached over and placed the framed portrait on the coffee table before turning and laying her down on the blanket. "I wouldn't have waited so long to move into our room." He kissed her on the chin. "I love you so much, Nancy. You are the woman of my dreams. I never thought I would win your heart."

She chuckled as he kissed down her neck. "That's how I felt about you. And here we are."

"Here we are." He pulled back and stared into her eyes. His look reflected the love she felt for him.

"Merry almost Christmas, my love." She reached up and tugged his mouth back down to hers.

"Later on, we'll conspire . . . as we dream by the fire . . ." Walt and Nancy sang a duet as trees passed them by on their way to Greenville.

"I always wondered why you didn't sing in the church choir," she told him when the song ended.

"It wasn't the cool thing to do when I was a teenager, and once I was older, I preferred to sit with the congregation so I could be near you."

"Really?"

"Yeah. Well, after I broke up with Brenda."

"I thought I was the luckiest girl in the world when you stood by me and sang. Even though my voice isn't the best, I think we harmonize nicely."

"I love your voice."

She scoffed.

"It may not be perfect, but I've always thought it sounded sweet. When you sing in church, I can tell you mean it." He reached over and squeezed her hand, sending tingles up her arm.

"Walt, how did we misread the cues for so long?"

"I blame it on me. After losing Dad, then the breakup with Brenda, I worried more about rejection than I should have." He shook his head and glanced at her before turning back to the road.

"Maybe, but I feel just as much to blame."

"Let's not cast blame. Let's enjoy the blessings God has given us today. Our family might be starting off as a strange hodgepodge of his, hers, and hopefully ours, but it's clear we're meant for one another."

"We are." Nancy watched Walt and giggled.

"What's so funny?"

"I'm trying to imagine you in my room at my parent's home—us in my room."

He smirked. "It will be strange. I've had glimpses of your room here and there when I've helped carry up a box or suitcase, but your parents always made it clear the bedrooms upstairs were off limits to me. Their rule gave it a mystique."

"Like I said, it will be strange having you in there."

"And I can't wait. Maybe I'll uncover some of your teenage secrets. Notes you wrote to your friends and that sort of thing."

"You'll see that I had a perfect view of that spot where you always parked your dad's truck. I'd hide behind the curtain and watch you."

"Oh yeah?"

"When I was younger, of course."

"Of course."

"Well . . . maybe some when I was older. I hung out there, hoping I would see you coming and going. When I first started watching you. I was only a kid. At nine, I caught you making out with some girl, and it both worried me and left me curious. It definitely opened my eyes to the nature of relationships between guys and girls."

"Making out?" He winced. "I'm sorry. That's too much for a nine-year-old." He reached over and patted her belly. "Do you hear that, Julie? That's too much for a nine-year-old."

"I guess I shouldn't say making out. But it was some pretty intense kissing. The kind I didn't know existed."

"Again, I'm sorry. Not only did I expose a young mind to something I shouldn't have, but I hate that you saw me that way with another woman. Obviously, that was before I became a Christian, since I didn't slip up in that area again until Brenda, and you were well beyond nine then."

"Mm-hmm. I don't like thinking of you with Brenda."

"Sorry. So, do you think my mom will have made her famous Yule Log?"

"I certainly hope so. I've been thinking about that chocolatey goodness the whole month of December."

"That's a long time."

"I'm blaming it on the pregnancy."

"Speaking of, you were squirming quite a bit last night. One time, you made groaning noises."

"Oops. I thought I did that in my dream. It's that hip pain I get periodically. Remember, the doctor said it was normal from the ligaments loosening."

"I do recall him saying that. Would it help if I massaged it before bed?"

"I don't know, but I won't say no to a massage."

"Then a massage you'll get."

"I just might want to get pregnant right away after Julie's born if you keep spoiling me."

"I would love to put another baby in you that is from the two of us. Not that Julie will be any less my child. But it would be cool to see what a baby with our genetics would look like."

"A baby from the two of us would be a blessing."

He lifted her hand and kissed it, eyes still focused on the road. "We'll do our part, and God can decide the rest."

⬥

Nancy hesitated at her parents' front door. "Should we knock?"

"After this." Walt leaned down and kissed her deeply.

"There you are!" Her mom popped the door open. "Well, I see you two finally admitted you're in love with each other."

Nancy furrowed her brow. "What do you mean finally?"

"It's been obvious forever that you two are in love. We've all just been waiting for you"—she gave Nancy a pointed look—"to catch up to that fact. And for you"—she turned to Walt—"to ask her out."

"Who is all?" he questioned.

"Oh . . . just everyone in our two families."

Blinking, Nancy looked back and forth between Walt and her mom.

Her mom leaned in and whispered, "And don't worry, your dad and I haven't told anyone about the other little surprise. But your dad will be overjoyed you two figured things out. You have figured things out, haven't you?"

"Oh, we've figured things out." Walt chuckled and pulled Nancy into a tight hug.

"Well, come on in and join Lucille, Yvonne, Grace, Kathy, and me in the kitchen."

"You two go on in, and I'll grab the bags and join you ladies in a minute." Walt kissed Nancy on the cheek before turning back to their car.

"What do you mean, it's been obvious for years? Why didn't you say anything?" Nancy pulled her mom into her father's study so the others wouldn't hear.

Her mom placed a hand on her shoulder. "There are some things a parent shouldn't do, and one of those things is push their child into a relationship with someone they wish they would marry. We knew you had a crush on Walt as a child and watched it grow into more when you were older. Then we saw him awaken to you after he broke up with that girl from college." She shook her head. "We knew we had to wait on God's timing if it was meant to be. When you started telling us about Henry . . ."

Nancy bit her lip as memories of Henry surfaced.

"Sorry, but when you told us about him, there was nothing to do but pray that God would guide you to whoever you were supposed to marry. We were sad to let our hope for you and Walt die, but it's clear God was working it out. Oh, honey, don't cry."

Touching her cheek, Nancy found tears streaming down. "No, it's okay. I'm happy. Not happy it's been such a hard start for us, but happy God brought us together in the end."

"I'm so glad too. Your father and I already loved Walt like he was our own. You two were made for each other, and God has been writing your story all along." Her mom gave her a hug. "So tell me how you're feeling?"

"Everything is going fine. The nausea is finally subsiding. Other than that, it's just the normal things. I'm a bit swollen around the middle and have to be more careful with what I wear."

"I'm glad you're feeling better." She stood back and eyed her daughter. "Now . . . we need to get to the kitchen. Everyone will be wondering what happened to us."

"Lead the way, Mom."

A chorus of "Nancy!" echoed in the kitchen when they entered, and she made her way around the room to hug everyone.

"You'd think I've been gone for months rather than three weeks," Nancy said.

"You're a different person now, Mrs. Moore." Lucille chuckled.

"Come sit down and eat these cookies Kathy and I made." Yvonne pointed to a plate of decorated sugar cookies.

"They're beautiful. I'll take that stocking-shaped one." Nancy joined them. "Yvonne, you've got your mom's excellent baking skills," she commented.

Yvonne looked at Lucille proudly. "She taught me everything I know."

Walt entered the room, sat next to Nancy, and kissed her cheek. All the ladies swooned.

"I'm glad you two finally ended up together." Kathy grinned at the two of them.

Nancy looked at Walt and thought about what her mom said. "Me too."

Chapter Thirty

Monday morning, Nancy heard Walt in the shower and hurried downstairs to make him breakfast. Christmas with their family had been special, but she was glad to be back at their home and have him all to herself. By the time he entered the kitchen, fried eggs were ready and the bacon was finishing up.

"What's all this? You work today, so I planned on cooking and leaving some for you like usual," Walt said as he surveyed the food.

"This gives me extra time with you."

He pulled her away from the stove, wrapped his arms around her, and grinned. "You're not tired of me?"

She shook her head and tried to smile.

"What's wrong?" He tucked her hair behind her ear and caressed her cheek.

"I don't want our time to end." She wanted to add, *Or share you with Davie and indirectly, Brenda.* Now that they were home, the pressure of the wait for the paternity test returned.

"I promise I'll hurry home after work." He tenderly kissed her, nearly melting her worries away. "Better yet, join me for lunch."

"Okay." She kissed him and turned to plate the food, pushing the disturbing thoughts away.

Walt poured the milk and prayed over their food. Sitting side by side on the bench, they recounted the events of their first Christmas together.

"I don't ever want to forget any detail of our first Christmas. I'm afraid this next year will go so quickly that our first few months together will be forgotten."

"You could write it down."

Nancy grinned. "I like that idea. I'll put the memories in my journal."

"Will I ever get to read your journal?"

"Maybe one day." She thought of the events of her life over the past few months. There was enough drama to write a novel.

"Nancy, there's a call for you on line two." Theresa's voice came through the intercom. "It's your husband."

"Thank you." Nancy's mind raced with questions and worry as she picked up the receiver and switched to line two. "Walt. Are you okay?"

"Yes, sorry to scare you. I'm calling to ask you about our lunch today."

"If you need to cancel, I'll understand."

"No, I don't need to cancel, but . . . well, Brenda said her sitter is bringing Davie by so she can take him to lunch while the sitter runs some errands. It seems like a good time to join them and take the opportunity to get to know him better. I know we're still waiting on the results, but next week, he'll be back in school. This is a low-key way to spend time with him before making it official."

"You want to go with Brenda and Davie to lunch?" She didn't like the idea of the two of them eating together.

"Yes, with you, of course."

"Oh . . . I thought you meant without me."

"No, I wouldn't do that. It wouldn't be right for me to go out alone with a single woman. I don't consider Davie a good chaperone. It would also give people the wrong impression and put temptation in our paths.

I wouldn't go out alone with a married woman either, for that matter. I will always guard and protect our marriage."

"Oh." Nancy thought of her lunches with Michael. She'd not considered how others might view them.

"So that's okay with you?"

"Um. I guess so."

"I've not told her yes. If you don't want to today, we can try another day this week."

"No, today is fine." Better to get it over with.

"Okay. Thanks. Sorry to bother you at work, but I didn't want to blindside you with it when you arrived."

"I appreciate it. I'll see you then. Love you."

"I love you, too, Nancy."

She hung up before he could say anything else. That was not the conversation she'd expected when she answered the phone. Was this how it was always going to be if he was Davie's father? Brenda and Davie wedged into their life, eating away at the time they should have together. They were newlyweds who'd just realized their love was reciprocated. They'd not had a chance to enjoy one another.

"Ugh!" Nancy slammed her hands down on the paper in front of her.

"What did that paper ever do to you?" Michael walked by just as she let out her frustration, and leaned into her office.

"Sorry, I didn't mean to say that out loud."

"Okay, but something is obviously wrong." He sat in one of her guest chairs. "I told you I'm happy to lend an ear if you need to talk through something."

"Thanks, I . . ." Could she tell him about what she was going through? Or maybe she could tell him part of it? "I'm figuring out some family issues with my husband." Surely that was vague enough.

"Oh, the old in-law issues. I've dealt with those for years. I try to avoid them whenever possible."

"Not exactly that. His mom is great and his dad passed away a long time ago. It's . . . other family."

"Well, again, if possible, I'd say avoid, avoid, avoid."

Nancy chuckled at the thought of Michael avoiding his in-laws. "Can't a good lawyer convince them to see things his way?"

"A good lawyer knows how to keep the peace in his own home and when a case is a lost cause."

"Well, I'm glad that works for you." Time to change the subject. "Looks like you got some sun on your trip. Good weather?"

"Beautiful. It's Florida." He shrugged. "We had afternoon showers, but nothing to ruin a game of golf, and lots of sun the rest of the time. Dad and I put in plenty of hours on the course. I even got the kids to try it once. Dot and Mom used the time to go to the spa."

"That sounds like the best gift you could have given them—time to have fun and relax."

"Everyone was pretty happy when they came back." He looked over her shoulder. "I see you put my sketch in a prime spot."

She looked back at the frame sitting on the credenza, then turned to Michael. "It looks good there, doesn't it? I still can't believe you're the artist. I love your work."

He chuckled. "I'm happy to sketch any building you'd like—just don't ask me to sketch a person. I can never get the facial features right."

"Art was never my thing—buildings or people. I am in awe of someone like you who can draw so well."

"Hey now, don't be hard on yourself. Baking was never my thing, but it sounds like something you enjoy, and I bet you're great at it. If you ever need a taste tester, I'm happy to help. It sounds like you might be doing some baking soon."

"Yes, don't remind me."

"Sorry." He raised his hands in surrender. "I'll let you get back to accosting the papers." He started to turn away, then stopped. "By the way, do you want to join Dad and me for lunch?"

"Thanks, but I have lunch plans."

He nodded. "Good deal. If your plans change, there's room at our table."

"I'll keep that in mind."

He grinned. "And, Nancy, I'm happy to talk anytime you need someone to lend an ear. See you later."

"Thanks. Bye."

She watched him walk away, and her mind drifted to her upcoming lunch. Pressing her hands to her face, she closed her eyes and tried to release the negative thoughts battling through her mind and heart and give them over to God. Those thoughts seemed determined to destroy every last remnant of joy.

⤸⤷⤸⤷

Nancy stared at the cafeteria tray of food before her while Davie chattered away on the other side of the table across from Walt. Anyone could see he was enamored with Walt. It was a good thing—if Walt turned out to be his father.

She glanced up at Davie's big brown eyes. Yep. They still looked similar to Walt's, though she didn't see other similar features. She wanted so badly for it not to be true, but she needed to adjust her mindset to the idea just in case. Asking Walt to give up a newly discovered son would be wrong.

Her eyes drifted from Davie to Brenda, who looked content as she smiled softly, looking between Walt and her son. When Brenda looked up and caught her watching, Nancy forced a smile, then took a bite of broccoli casserole. Thankfully, their time was limited since Brenda and Walt had a meeting after lunch. Though it still bothered her that the two of them worked so closely, and she planned to talk to Walt about that once they had the results of the blood test.

When lunch finally ended, she silently breathed a sigh of relief. Would these types of things get easier? At Walt's office, she gave him a quick kiss goodbye, then hurried away. If she stayed any longer, she was afraid she might say something she'd regret.

As she drove home, she decided to tell Fanny the situation. If she didn't tell someone, she thought she might explode. She didn't want to tell her mom, and none of her friends knew about her pregnancy, much less this new situation. With Fanny's past, it seemed Fanny would understand some of Nancy's difficulties.

She put her car in park, walked directly to Fanny's front porch, and knocked. There were no noises inside. She knocked again and rang the doorbell. Nothing.

"I saw Miss Fanny leave about an hour ago."

Nancy turned and saw an older neighbor from a few doors down walking his dog.

"Thanks." Slowly she trudged to her own home and didn't stop until she got to the window seat of the living room.

She looked out at the yard. Was it her imagination or did the sky grow darker? Leaning back on the pillow, she let her mind drift over the day. It started so well—breakfast with Walt, her chat with Michael, and then . . . lunch. How often would they do things like that if Davie was Walt's? Would dealing with Brenda and Davie make her resent Walt?

She felt like she would burst with anxiety and worry over the future if she held it all in. Maybe she should call Michael after all. Checking her watch, there was still plenty of time to talk before he left for the day. He said he'd be there any time she needed to talk.

Sitting up, she thought about how she'd start the conversation. It didn't matter—she knew he would be patient and understanding. She stood up and nearly tripped over something.

Leaning down, she found her Bible. Strange. She didn't recall it being there when she sat down. She picked it up and saw the list of scriptures Fanny had given her when she had a bad day. Psalm 40 was the first one listed. She turned to it and began reading.

To the choirmaster. A Psalm of David. I waited patiently for the Lord; he inclined to me and heard my cry. He drew me up from the desolate pit, out of the miry bog, and set my feet upon a rock, making my steps secure. He put a new song in my mouth, a song of praise to our God. Many will see and fear, and put their trust in the Lord.

"God, help me praise you like this," she whispered, then continued to read, feeling more hopeful with each verse. "Yes, God, I want to trust in you."

As she finished out the chapter, she glanced over at the previous chapter. The first few words caught her eye. "I will guard my ways that I might not sin . . ." She recalled Walt's words on the phone earlier—*I will always guard and protect our marriage.* He'd mentioned protecting them from temptation. It hit her that she'd been leaning into her friendship with Michael in ways that could harm her marriage.

"God, forgive me. Help me protect my marriage. Help me trust you and lean on you for strength."

She had no business calling Michael about her marital problems, and she determined to be more careful around him. Yet a battle continued to rage within her—the push and pull of her desire to get out of taking on Davie as a stepson versus what she knew was right.

"God, help me lay this situation with Davie down. Help me give it over to you."

She sat in silence, letting God do a work inside her while watching the rain as it pelted down in a sudden storm.

"Keep me from resenting Walt for his past, and help me to appreciate that he is a man of honor."

Peace settled over her and smoothed out her sadness and worry about the future.

"As hard as this is, I give it all to you, and if Davie belongs to Walt, I will love him and accept him."

The rain stopped just as quickly as it began, and light broke through the clouds. A tear slipped out, and Nancy smiled. Time and again over the past few months, God had provided help and healing when she thought she couldn't go on. "Thank you, God."

Chapter Thirty-One

"Knock, knock."

Nancy looked up from her work to see Michael leaning against the doorframe.

"Hey, Michael."

He pulled away and walked to the front of her desk. "You look happier today. Did you get some things worked out?"

"Not with the family, but I had a little talk with God."

"Yeah? How did that go?"

"He straightened me out."

Michael smiled. "Good deal. I was ready to set some people straight for you if necessary. Perhaps hand them a letter with so much legalese, they'd do whatever you wanted." He winked.

"I might take you up on that, but for now, I'm good." If Walt was Davie's father, they would need to set some legal boundaries, and knowing two good lawyers who dealt with family law would come in handy.

"Just let me know. Are you up for lunch today? They have the Wednesday specials at the diner."

She recalled Michael's dad had a lunch appointment. "No, thank you. I have plans." Her plan was to go home and eat.

"Your company will be missed. Maybe next time."

"Thanks. See you later, Michael."

As he waved and turned away, she congratulated herself for following Walt's example and taking a step to protect their marriage.

Nancy stood back and surveyed their Christmas tree one last time, then snapped a picture. Years of memories hung from it. She grinned as she recalled decorating it with Walt. Even though she'd not known how much he loved her at the time, she still cherished that day. It had been filled with sweet moments together. She closed her eyes and remembered the way he looked at her when he held her. How had she missed the love in his eyes? Those dreamy eyes.

She opened up one of the ornament boxes Walt had brought back down from the attic and began carefully wrapping the ornaments. Walt had promised to take her out for dinner, so she had plenty of time to put everything away and maybe even take a quick nap. The little one was taking more and more of her energy.

"I missed you, my love."

"Mmm." Nancy pulled the throw around her neck. This was too nice of a dream to wake up. In her dream, Walt greeted her and kissed her on the cheek while she rested at the beach. It felt so real.

"I don't think you'll want to miss our dinner reservation at Breisch's." His voice spoke softly.

Dinner reservations at Breisch's? That was a Columbia restaurant, not a beach restaurant. And why was she using a throw on the beach? She opened her eyes and smiled up at Walt. "You're real."

"Yes, I'm real." He leaned down and kissed her tenderly.

When he pulled back and pressed his forehead to hers, she said, "I'm so glad. That was better than any dream kiss."

"Let's try again to make sure." He leaned down and pulled her into another dreamy kiss. It started slower, but soon he wrapped his arms around her and his kiss became intense and urgent. He moved from her lips to peppering her face and neck.

"Maybe we should move our dinner back," she said breathlessly.

He didn't respond, but his kisses stopped. He continued to hold her while breathing heavily.

"Walt, are you okay?"

"I love you so much. I can't believe I ended up with you after all these years." His arms tightened around her.

"You're worrying me."

He finally leaned back, and his eyes were moist with unshed tears. "It's over. We're free." He smiled, but she could tell he was holding back.

"What do you mean?"

"The test . . ." His voice was strained, and he shook his head. "It came back negative. I'm not Davie's dad."

Her hand flew to her chest as if it could keep her heart from exploding. "Walt . . ." She could hardly process her emotions, and she launched herself back into his arms and wrapped hers around him. "Walt, that's wonderful."

She began to shake and sob. Soon he did too. Once their crying subsided, he looked into her eyes, and they shared a laugh.

"I must look like a mess." She wiped her eyes, and mascara smudged her fingers.

"You're my beautiful mess."

"Come on then." She stood up and grabbed his hand. "You're coming with me to the bathroom while I fix my makeup. I'm not letting you out of my sight."

"I'll gladly follow you anywhere, beautiful."

"Thanks for taking me out tonight." Nancy dipped her spoon in the French onion soup and gently broke off a piece of the cheese-covered bread at the top. "Your news deserves more celebration than this. I almost feel like we need another honeymoon. It's as if this past month we were just playing at marriage, and it's finally real."

He grinned wolfishly. "Don't worry, we'll take a second honeymoon. Maybe somewhere warm this February or March, well before your due date."

"Sounds nice." She imagined sitting on a beach in south Florida, watching a shirtless Walt lie next to her in the sun.

"But we can *pretend* we're on our honeymoon now." He wiggled his eyebrows, and heat rose to her cheeks. "We have a long weekend."

"Does your news mean we won't be taking Brenda and Davie out to eat again this weekend?"

He smirked and raised a brow. "Change of subject? Yes, it does mean that. I'll call her when we get home. Hopefully she did as I asked and hasn't told Davie. I'd wanted to wait for this very reason."

She let out a breath. "Good. I wasn't looking forward to it."

He nodded slowly. "I'd thought I might try and stay in his life and be a sort of surrogate father since his is so absent."

Nancy frowned and shook her head as tension rose in her chest. That was the last thing she wanted. He might as well be Davie's biological dad if he was still going to be involved in Brenda's life outside of work.

"Hang on. I see the worry on your face." He raised a hand. "I was going to add that I have already decided against it. I realized my past relationship with Brenda makes that a bad idea. I'll explain that to her if she tries to get me involved further."

"Good. I finally worked through things with God, and if you were his father, I would have made it work. But now that you're free from Brenda, you need to stay free. I don't like the idea of you being around her any more than you have to. From what I can tell, she still has feelings for you and would happily use your relationship with her son to regain your affection for her."

He reached across the table and ran a hand down her face. "There's little chance of that, but I hear you. I won't put myself in a compromising situation with her. Like I said before, I want to protect our marriage."

"Thank you."

"Now . . ." A gleam filled his eyes. "We have more happy news we can focus on as we figure out when to share about *our* little one over the next month."

Her heart fluttered . . . or maybe that was Julie moving. She placed a hand on her stomach. "I think I just felt her move."

Walt pulled his chair to her side of the table and subtly reached under the white linen tablecloth to lay a hand on her belly. "Do you think she'll move again?"

Nancy shrugged and smiled up at him. "Maybe we should get our meals to go." She looked around the dining room. "I think I'd prefer a quiet evening eating in front of the fire with just you."

Walt winked and waved the waiter down. "Your wish is my command."

Seven months later

Joy
In the pain, there is joy.
In the heartache, there is joy.
In the good times, there is joy.
In you, Lord, there is joy.

A glimpse of you, Jesus, is all it takes to turn away a
    cloudy day.

Footsteps drew Nancy's eyes up to her husband as he approached her in the window seat. She moved to stand, and he held up a hand.

"I'll come to you. You look comfortable there." He leaned down to kiss her, then sat at her feet. "What are you reading and smiling about?"

"Margaret Corbyn's book of poetry. This poem is called 'Joy' and is about how Jesus is our joy in good times and difficult ones."

He nodded. "That will bring a smile to your face."

"And so does the arrival of my husband."

"Good to know. How did Julie do today?"

"She was a perfect little princess, except when I had to change her poopy diaper. Thankfully, she didn't do it at The Screaming Peach Café while I was meeting with Marie for prayer. She's napping in the study."

Walt rubbed her calves while she spoke, and she relaxed into the pillows. "Good. Marie from your Bible study?"

"Yes. Mmm. That feels nice. Also, did you know that Megan is a variation on Margaret?"

Walt chuckled and shook his head.

"That's what Marie told me when I mentioned that if we have a second daughter, I'd love to name her after Margaret Corbyn, but I've never been fond of the name Margaret. It seems a little old-fashioned. What do you think about Megan for a name if we have a girl?"

"I think our little Julie is barely a month old, so it will be a while, but *if* we have another little girl someday, Megan is a beautiful name."

"Can't you just see two little girls playing and growing up together?"

"I can. I'll be happy with whatever God blesses us with."

Julie's cry from the study had them both moving to stand.

"You stay put, dear. I'll bring her to you."

"Thanks."

When he returned and she got into a better position to nurse Julie, Walt laid her in Nancy's arms and turned away.

"Wait. I wanted to tell you about the other person I saw today."

He raised a brow. "Who was that?"

"Brenda stopped by the café while I was there. She was on her lunch break. She said she loves the new bank location, and she's even started dating a guy who is a customer at that branch."

Walt nodded with a gleam in his eye.

"You never said, but did you have something to do with her new job?"

He bit his lip. "I did. A couple of weeks after the news that Davie wasn't mine, a job opening came up at the other location. It was a lateral move, but I mapped out the distance from her home and Davie's school and saw that the other location was a few minutes closer to her school. I spoke with the regional manager and explained that my past with her was becoming a problem, but she was a good assistant. They asked her to interview for the job, and I might have dropped the hint that the location would help her get to Davie faster if he needed her during the day."

"You sly thing. You're even better than Mr. Knightley."

"From your book *Emma*?"

She nodded. "He looked after her in many ways, but he was so slow to ask her to marry him. In the end, he still almost didn't because he didn't feel assured of her regard. But you jumped straight into marriage with me and took on a baby too. And you're still conquering our obstacles."

He shook his head. "That last obstacle was of my own making. And you're forgetting that I nearly waited too long and lost you, not unlike your Mr. Knightley. But you should know, I would go through fire for you. Or should I say, 'If I loved you less, I might be able to talk about it more.'"

"You've been reading *Emma*."

He winked.

Nancy finished nursing Julie and passed her to Walt, who laid her over his shoulder and patted her back.

Reaching up and running a finger across Walt's chin, Nancy said, "I'll tell you another way you're much better than George Knightley."

"What's that?" He peeked at her over Julie's head.

"You never made me feel bad about my mistakes. Rather than point them all out like Mr. Knightley constantly did to Emma, you gently guided me back to God so I could realign my thinking with His. You're a good husband, and I am so thankful God saved us in marriage for one another."

Chapter 32 - Epilogue

M egan - Present Day

Journal of Nancy Wilson Moore
June 25, 1985

Julie,

I'm writing this entry specifically for you. This journal will be yours when I'm gone. I offered it to you today, but you said you didn't want to read it. My precious daughter, you amaze me. I've been waiting so long to tell you about your biological father. Walt and I had originally planned to wait until you were sixteen, but you are so mature that fourteen seemed appropriate.

Last night, after your birthday celebrations, I told you your biological father is in England and explained the circumstances of your conception. I also gave you the necklace that is your heritage. You handled the news better than I could have imagined. When your father and I promised to help you find him, you said you wanted the night to think and pray about it.

At breakfast this morning, you told us you decided not to find him.

You said Walt is your father and you don't want or need another one. You also said that the only thing that concerned you was his salvation and you would trust God with that and pray God would put people in his life to point him to the Lord.

Such wisdom from a fourteen-year-old! I will be praying for your father's salvation as well. I'll admit I have not prayed for it as faithfully as I should have. A small amount of resentment remains because he never claimed you. But after you handled the news so graciously, my lack of consistency there is glaringly obvious.

P.S. In the midst of our discussions, you said you liked the name Megan that I had always hoped to name your sister if you had one. You said if you had a daughter, you would name her Megan if your husband agreed. Ha! We'll see what God has planned for the future. I feel confident God will do great things through you and look forward to seeing what he has planned.

Megan looked up from the journal and laid it on the sofa beside her. Her grandfather paced around her living room.

"Grandfather, maybe I shouldn't have read this final entry to you. I'd forgotten what my grandmother said about you."

Henry stopped mid-stride. "It's okay, Megan. I'm only surprised she didn't say worse things about me. She had no idea that my father had my butler under his thumb to make sure I never heard about any calls, telegrams, letters, or visits. She's not at fault."

"But it makes me sad that she thought those things about you. It makes me sad she lost that chance with you."

"It's as it should be, and I've given it over to God. I'm too old to hold onto the what-ifs. And just think—you are the answer to your mother and grandmother's prayers. They prayed God would put people in my life to share the gospel . . . and here came you. I won't have that many years left until I see Nancy again, and our reunion will be a sweet one in heaven. I don't know how it will work, but the truth will be known."

"Grandfather! Don't say things like that. I want you to stay here a while longer. I'm just getting used to having you around."

"And I love being here for you. But I'm on God's time, and at eighty-three, it's true that I'm far closer to the grave than the cradle. What's that verse? Ah, yes. Philippians 1:21 says, 'For to me to live is Christ, and to die is gain.'"

"I can't argue with that. Did you catch the part about Grandmother wanting to name a second daughter Megan and my mom agreeing to use the name? And she did. It's so strange learning about this after all these years. Do you know the most interesting thing—actually, it's an interesting God thing."

"What's that?"

"In other parts of Grandmother's journal, she mentions reading Margaret Corbyn's books and how much they meant to her in her Christian walk. In fact, she found out Megan is a form of Margaret and decided to name a daughter Megan if she had another girl."

Henry ran his fingers through his white hair and chuckled. "That is a God thing—the very woman whose memory you are going to be honoring tonight at the annual Margaret Corbyn New Year's Eve Regency Ball for Alzheimer's."

Megan nodded, and tingles ran up her spine as she thought through all that God had done to bring her grandmother's story full circle.

"And before I forget, did the armed guard bring your necklace?"

She smiled and tugged down the neck of her shirt to reveal the red pendant. "My heritage." Lifting it from her neck, she held it towards her grandfather.

He touched the pendant and smiled. "I do wish I had seen it on your grandmother, but it looks beautiful on you." Moisture filled his eyes.

"Oh, Grandfather. I didn't mean to make you cry." She wrapped her arms around him.

"I'll be fine. Don't you worry." He looked at his watch. "I imagine you'll want to get ready for the ball, so I won't keep you, my dear." Leaning down, he kissed her on the head. "Tell that husband of yours hello. And enjoy your evening with Kate and Corbyn at the ball. I'm sure you'll be the most beautiful woman there."

"Especially in the lovely Regency gown you bought me."

Henry winked. "I'm making up for lost time. It brings me joy."

The End

What to read next: If you enjoyed this book, make sure you're all caught up on the series. Have you read the prequel-***Not Quite Miss Austen*** (book 4) with Margaret's love story from her younger days? Be sure to check KimGriffin.org for the latest in the series and **sign up for her newsletter to get a free novella:** *Not Quite Mr. Tilney.*

Excerpts from chapter 1 of Not Quite Miss Austen

July 1955 London, England

Sipping tea in the reception room of a Belgravia, London, estate was not at all the way Margaret Elliot expected her interview with Corbyn Publishing to begin. Not that she minded. It was Darjeeling tea, and after so many years of rationing during the war, it felt like an extravagance.

Margaret took in the elegance of the room. It was formal with its chandelier, intricate trim and molding, and mahogany furnishings, but Mrs. Corbyn's friendly manner set her at ease.

Something inside fluttered at the thought of seeing one of her stories bound into a book. "I'm optimistic—"

Before she finished her statement, the tall paneled wood door at the other end of the room swung open, and in the doorway stood the most handsome man Margaret had ever seen. Margaret tensed. He was tall, with blonde hair much lighter than hers, and he looked about her brother's age. She pondered that briefly, but it was his frown that unsettled her.

Psalm 139:13-16 ESV - For you formed my inward parts; you knitted me together in my mother's womb. 14 I praise you, for I am fearfully and wonderfully made. Wonderful are your works; my soul knows it very well. 15 My frame was not hidden from you, when I was being made in secret, intricately woven in the depths of the earth. 16 Your eyes saw my unformed substance; in your book were written, every one of them, the days that were formed for me, when as yet there was none of them.

Thank you, God, for life—both now and eternally through Christ. I was adopted as a newborn the year that this story begins. I've never met my biological mother, but have often wondered if she was tempted to have an illegal abortion. Whatever her decision process, I am thankful she chose life for me. Many have not had that chance. My brother and sister are twins and were born soon after Roe-vs-Wade. Their mom planned to abort them before my parents were put in contact with her. She didn't even know she was having twins until she delivered them. Ultrasounds were not common at the time.

The sanctity of life is personal for me—yet I know there is forgiveness in Christ even for this. If you've been part of an abortion decision, please be sure to check out the resources I've provided in the next section.

I am also thankful to my mom and dad, my real ones—the ones who adopted me and raised me—for their encouragement through the years that I could accomplish whatever God put before me. My mom was in the late stages of Alzheimer's when I began writing and had passed by the time I published my first book, but I know she would have been cheering me on. My dad has certainly done his share in her stead, and I am blessed beyond measure to call them Mom and Dad.

The sanctity of marriage is another topic explored in *Not Quite Mr. Knightley.* I am thankful to have found a man who fights to stay faithful to me through daily choices to protect our marriage. At the time of this writing, we've been married for almost 33 years! He has been a steady encourager for me in my many endeavors through the years and now in my writing journey.

Special thanks to Dani and Dulci for Beta reading and their wise words, and to Heather for her amazing editing skills and guidance.

Thank you also to my great ARC team! You ladies are amazing!

And to you, dear reader, thank you for purchasing this book. I hope it has drawn you to God and into His word. God's love is the only perfect love and in His word, you will find His love for you from the beginning to the end.

The topics of abortion, avoiding abortion, and healing after an abortion decision are weighty ones that are often taboo to discuss in the Christian community. But the Christian community has the power to bring hope and healing to those who have been affected by an abortion, by their own choice or otherwise.

At the time of writing, approximately 1 in 3.5 women have had an abortion. The statistic does not change for those inside the church. That means even if you have never had an abortion, there are likely people in your life who have—perhaps even people who are close to you but too scared to speak up.

Below I have listed 2 resources that you should be familiar with either for yourself, or to help others: Care Net and Deeper Still.

I have been on the board of my local Deeper Still chapter for several years and am excited about the healing I have seen in men and women through this fairly new ministry. Once people are set free from the bondage of their sin, they become some of the best spokespeople for life.

You can support ministries like these through prayer, finances/donations, and or serving. I highly recommend familiarizing yourself with your local Crisis Pregnancy Center and nearest chapter of Deeper Still.

1. If you would like to connect to a Pro-life Crisis Pregnancy Center in North America, **Care Net** is a good resource. Find a Crisis Pregnancy near you on their website through the Pregnancy Centers tab. Many other resources are available on their website.

 care-net.org

2. Another resource for women who have had abortions and men who have been part of an abortion decision is **Deeper Still**. This ministry provides weekend retreats free of charge to people who struggle to forgive themselves or to believe they can be forgiven for past abortions. The retreats are scripturally sound, Christ centered, and highly effective at bringing deep healing that allows participants to find wholeness and freedom to fulfill their God-given purpose. Find chapters throughout the U.S.A. on their website. This growing ministry has also been hosting retreats in other countries. If you are outside of the U.S.A., contact the ministry to find out what options may be available to you.

 deeperstill.org
 Info@DeeperStill.org

Extras

For a behind-the-scenes glimpse into my story, check out the Extras page on my website. It's only accessible through this link (or with the QR code):
https://www.kimgriffin.org/home/books/extras-nqmk

Don't forget to get your free novella: *Not Quite Mr. Tilney* with newsletter subscription at KimGriffin.org

About the Author

Kim Griffin is a former interior designer and homeschool mom who has been leading Bible studies for over 35 years and working in Women's Ministry for over 25. Several years ago, God led her to begin writing words of hope. She writes Christian women's fiction with clean romance and devotionals/Bible studies. Her desire is that her books will draw readers closer to the God who sees all of their imperfections and loves them still.

If you enjoyed this book, please consider leaving a review on Goodreads and Amazon! As an independent author this helps Kim get the word out about her books.

You can learn more about Kim and her books and sign up for her newsletter at her website:

kimgriffin.org

Scan the QR code to see my other books or visit KimGriffin.org

Scan this QR code to join my newsletter and receive a free novella: Not Quite Mr. Tilney, a free Gospel of John simple self-paced study guide, and a link to my Fruit of the Spirit Bible Study. You'll also receive updates on my writing, book and author suggestions, discounts on books, freebies, and more!